THE RINGMASTER

DC Sam Shephard is stationed in Dunedin CIB, a newbie at the bottom of the pecking order. When a university student is found battered to death and floating in the Leith, she is pushed to one side by her boss and given grunt work. Despite this, it is Sam who discovers that there has been a string of unsolved murders on the South Island, and that each has occurred while a travelling circus was in town — the same circus that is presently in Dunedin. Angry at being marginalised, Sam decides to work alone, ignoring the attempts of her friends to help her, and keeping her lines of enquiries secret. But her headstrong attitude, and the fact that she is human and makes mistakes, put her and those she loves in very real danger . . .

Books by Vanda Symon
Published by Ulverscroft:

OVERKILL

VANDA SYMON

THE
RINGMASTER

Complete and Unabridged

AURORA
Leicester

First published in Great Britain in 2019 by
Orenda Books
First published in New Zealand in 2008 by
Penguin Books (NZ)

First Aurora Edition
published 2019
by arrangement with
Orenda Books

A catalogue record for this book is available
from the British Library.

ISBN 978–1–78782–145–3

Published by
F. A. Thorpe (Publishing)
Anstey, Leicestershire

Set by Words & Graphics Ltd.
Anstey, Leicestershire
Printed and bound in Great Britain by
T. J. International Ltd., Padstow, Cornwall

This book is printed on acid-free paper

Prologue

'Rosie, wait.' He lengthened his stride to catch up with her. She turned and he couldn't help but enjoy the immense smile that lit up her face as she realised who'd called after her.

'Hey, this is a pleasant surprise. I thought you were working late tonight.' She started to lean in to kiss him, but checked herself and put her hands in her pockets instead, a blush spreading across her cheeks.

She was such a pretty young thing, he thought; pretty and clever — a winning combination. They turned and continued walking together along Dundas Street, past the bottle-strewn fronts of the down-at-heel terraced houses inhabited by university students.

'You know I don't like you walking along that track by yourself when it's getting dark,' he said. 'I thought I'd come and keep you company. I'd never forgive myself if something bad happened to you.' It was early evening and the gloomy weather made the light lower than usual for this time of year.

She laughed, so melodic. 'You worry too much. Nothing's going to happen. Dunedin's as safe as. Everyone takes this shortcut from uni to the Valley. Besides, walking through the bush helps me unwind — it's so beautiful and serene.'

She had a point — the track was very picturesque. They turned into Gore Place and

1

passed through the large iron gates into the enchanted realm of the Botanic Garden. The track meandered between the Water of Leith and the curve of the hill before it crossed over on to the flat expanse of the lower park with its lawns, flowerbeds and the impressive Winter Gardens. The route passed through lush native bush and on a fine day it made for a lovely stroll. The deserted playground by the gates was testament to the hour and to how drizzly the day had been.

'I don't worry too much,' he said, pretending to be piqued.

'Oh, you'll trip over that lip if you're not careful,' she said, playing the game. 'By the way, I like the new coat and hat. Didn't even recognise you at first. You're not getting hip on me, are you?' Again the melodic laugh.

'If you can't beat them, join them, as they say. Maybe being around you youngsters all day is rubbing off on me.' He made an attempt at a twirl and grinned at the girl's yelp of delight. He stopped and turned to face her, taking a big breath as he chose his next words.

'Look, Rosie, there is something I need to talk to you about. Something important.' He saw a flicker of a frown cross her face and realised she thought it was bad news. 'No, no. Nothing bad. It's good news.'

She leaned forward, expectant. 'You mean you're finally . . . '

The crunch of approaching footsteps on the gravel path made her pause. They both stepped back slightly from each other, and he turned and looked up the path. He heard her say hello to the passer-by and then watched the back of the young man as he carried on towards the gardens.

'Do you know him?' he asked, when he thought the student was out of earshot.

'No, just being friendly. It's a big campus and despite what you may think, I don't actually know everyone,' she said. 'Why, are you jealous?'

He gave her a 'yeah right' look and motioned with his head that they should keep on walking. They were now under the canopy of the trees, making their way along the path by what little light filtered through the dense foliage. 'See how dark it gets in here,' he said. 'I really don't like you walking this way now the days are getting shorter. You don't know what weirdos could be here, lying in wait for a lovely creature like you.'

'It's very flattering that you worry so much, but I feel quite safe. If it'll make you feel better, I'll start walking along the road when it gets too dark. They shut the gates earlier in winter, so I won't have any choice soon.'

They came to a massive pine tree, its branches thin and octopus-like, reaching out into the bush. A small path disappeared through the undergrowth beside it.

'Come down here, where we won't be disturbed. I really need to talk to you.' He grabbed her by the hand and led her down the trail; she had to skip to keep up with him.

The gravel ended and they walked a hundred metres along a mown grass verge bordering the Leith until they came to a small clearing at the river's edge. He looked around to make sure they didn't have any unwanted spectators; he could see no one. His pulse began to beat faster; his face felt hot. He took her hands in his, wishing they weren't both wearing gloves to ward off the chill; wishing he could feel her soft skin.

'Look, you know I love you, and that you're the woman for me. I haven't been able to be with you as much as I'd like. And I realise you've been very patient about it. My . . . commitments have got in the way. But I'd like that to change.'

Her face lit up with that beautiful smile. 'Oh, my God. You're going to leave her, aren't you? You're finally going to leave her.' She looked into his eyes, searching his face for a response. He simply nodded, and with that she threw her arms around his neck and he used the momentum to swing her off her feet. Landing on solid earth again, she planted a kiss on his mouth. Her lips felt cold, but incredibly soft.

He didn't want to pull away, but he did, and laughed. 'Wait, wait, there's more.' He stepped back, creating a space between them. 'I want to give you something — a sign of my commitment, I suppose; a promise that you're the woman I want to spend the rest of my life with. Close your eyes and hold out your hands.'

The sight of her — gorgeous, flushed with excitement, jiggling up and down — brought a lump to his throat and filled him with a moment of apprehension about what he was going to do. But no, he had come this far, had planned and worked so hard for this. He took a deep breath and reached into his pocket.

It only took a second to slip the already looped

cable tie around her outstretched wrists and then to pull it tight.

In the time it took for her eyes to flash open and her to start saying, 'What . . . what are you doing? I don't . . . ' he had pulled the duct tape out of his pocket and ripped it open. He slapped it across her mouth and around the back of her head. By now, terror had registered in her eyes and she ducked down and turned, trying to escape and run. But he anticipated this, tripping her and making her fall elbows first to the ground. She tried to wriggle forward, but was hindered by a large rock in her path. He stepped over her squirming form, straddling her shoulders. Her damned backpack made the job more difficult, but he managed to grab her by the head and, despite her resistance, slam her hard over and over into the rock. There was a cracking noise and then silence. She went limp in his hands and he dropped her on to the grass.

Hands on knees and panting heavily, he had to hold his breath so he could listen and look around to ensure there had been no witness to his work. But all was silence and gloom.

He dragged her over to the Water of Leith and slid her in, holding her face down in case the cold of the water revived her.

It didn't.

He waited a few minutes to make sure, but there was no more movement from his beautiful Rosie. He hadn't tried it this way before, but it had worked a treat. In fact, it had been easier than he'd thought.

He was getting good at this.

1

'What a bloody circus.'

Just when I thought I'd seen it all, here it was — a new page in the album of the ridiculous. The lion roared, despite the efforts of its keeper to calm it. The lion was in a cage. So was the animal-rights activist with the megaphone. He was busy announcing to all who would listen — not that anyone had a choice — exactly what he thought of the plight of the four-legged performers. The caged activist's support crew, including someone in a gorilla suit, cheered and waved their placards with every expletive, provoking further roars from the lion. The immense and dangerously grumpy man being restrained by his colleagues had to be Terry Bennett, owner of the Darling Brothers' Circus. I wasn't sure who was the more menacing: the man or the lion.

The presence of television cameras and a sizable rent-a-crowd sure as hell didn't help matters.

Fabulous.

'What the hell is all this?' Smithy said, as we wove our way through the hordes that had gathered to gawk at the entertainment sited at the southern end of the Kensington Oval. On any normal day, the expansive, lush green fields that were the Oval were home to cricket matches or football — awash with swarms of little kids

7

and their overanxious parents yelling overambitious instructions from the sideline. Not today.

The circus was set up at the pub end and had that unmistakable carnival look, with strings of coloured lighting, enormous inflatable clowns, brightly painted animal trailers and the double-peaked, damned impressive big top that dominated the scene. Smithy looked less than excited by it all. 'I thought the call-out was because of some students breaking into the lion cage. No one mentioned protesters.'

'Looks like they're an added bonus,' I replied. Nice bonus. Normally we wouldn't be sent out for a ruckus like this, but due to the Highlanders playing a Super Rugby game at the stadium, most of the regular officers had been called in for crowd control, so they'd had to dip into the CIB pool for this one. After a look around the motley mob here, I thought I'd rather be dealing with drunks at the rugby.

'Well,' Smithy said. 'What do we tackle first?'

'Ugh, I hate protesters,' I said, my face screwing into a grimace. 'Why don't you go check the idiot in the cage, see if you can persuade him to make a graceful exit? Get rid of his cheerleaders too; mass evictions always were your speciality. I'll talk to Mr Bennett.'

Smithy was built like the proverbial brick shithouse. He had an impressive set of cauliflower ears, courtesy of being front-row forward for his rugby team, and they complemented his don't-mess-with-me face. People seemed to take his presence rather seriously, unlike mine. A barely five-foot-tall waif of a thing

8

didn't tend to have the same deterrent effect, even if she was armed with a mouth and wasn't afraid to use it.

Smithy headed towards the vocal section and I turned towards Bennett. He was standing alongside the big top; a man-mountain sur-rounded by an interesting array of humanity. They only partially buffered the waves of anger radiating from him. Oh, how I longed for the rugby.

I sucked it up and went over to say hello.

'Mr Bennett?' I asked. He nodded. 'I'm Detective Constable Shephard. You reported someone had tried to break into one of the animal cages?'

The flesh barrier parted in response to a grunted instruction and Terry Bennett shuffled forward until he towered above me.

'First the fucking students, and now this bloody mob. How the hell am I supposed to run a show when all I get is idiot pranksters and bloody Nazi activists.' His voice carried the gravel of a seasoned smoker. 'And now the friggin' TV is here, so if I go and belt one of the bastards, I'll be the one getting crucified on the news.' His breath confirmed my suspicion. 'And where the hell are the rest of the police? What do you think the two of you can do by yourselves?'

I ignored the vote of confidence.

'We'll deal with the protesters; we'll move them back out of the way. But first, I want to know about the lion-cage break-in. Is it true that you're holding a couple of students? Can I see them, please?'

His face went a deeper shade of crimson.

'Yes, we had the little shits, but when we tried to detain them, they said they'd have us for assault and kidnap charges. So we had to let them go — couldn't even give them a good boot up the arse.'

If they'd been tampering with animal cages, they probably deserved a boot, or a psychiatric assessment, at least. 'I'd hazard a guess they were law students,' I said. 'Are you able to give me a good description of them?'

'We can do better than that,' said a man with some rather interesting facial piercings and an Eastern European accent. 'We have pictures.' He held up a digital camera.

Someone had had a brainwave. The advantages of modern technology. 'That will certainly make life easier. I'll have to take the memory card with me, but we'll return it as soon as we've copied the files.'

I felt a tap on my shoulder and turned to see Smithy's face; it was scrunched up into a perplexed expression.

'Detective Smith — Terry Bennett,' I said, and they both gave a cursory 'Gidday', or mumble to that effect, before Smithy gestured back towards the crowd.

'We've got a little problem with the guy in the cage.'

'What kind of a problem?' I asked.

'An immovable one. Not only has he padlocked himself in, but he's also driven pegs down and secured the cage from the inside. I can't shift it.'

'Oh, bloody marvellous,' Terry Bennett boomed. 'Now he's stuck there for God knows how long. I've got a show tonight. How the hell do I get the crowds in with that git stuck there, yelling at everyone?'

'We could get a crane in and pull him up,' Smithy suggested.

It was an idea, but one that would provide the perfect fodder for the television crews waiting for just such a spectacle. I could imagine it headlining the evening news, with plenty of choice sound bites coming from the bloke dangling in mid-air. No, there had to be a better way.

'Well,' I said as I looked up at the big top. 'There's no show without the star.' I turned back to the circus guys. 'Do you have any tarpaulins or a marquee that would fit over that cage?'

Terry Bennett's face broke into a grin — probably for the first time that day. Yep, definitely a smoker and in need of some serious dental work.

'I'm sure we can find something for the job,' he said, and he and two of his cohorts disappeared around the back of the enormous tent.

'Let's go deal with the rest of the protesters,' I said to Smithy, setting off towards the action. I thought it very quaint how he liked to let me take control, even though we both knew damned well who called the shots.

The protesters group seemed to number around twenty, but the spectators had grown to more than fifty and had inched their way closer to the action. I went for the spectators first. It was moments like these I wished I had my police blues on again, instead of the civvies — black trousers and white shirt — that had become my substitute. People knew how to behave around a uniform.

'Police,' I yelled, trying to be heard above the general chatter and hoping like hell they could see me. 'Okay, everyone, I'm going to have to ask you all to move back to the roadside. Come on, move back please, people. Clear the space here, thank you.'

Smithy worked the group over to the right of me, and I was relieved when they immediately obliged. It was easier than herding sheep. The only exception was the camera crew who steadfastly refused to budge. Surprise.

I lowered my voice and spoke directly to the reporter, who I recognised from the six o'clock news. 'Come on guys, move back please. There's not going to be anything interesting or newsworthy here. Let us get on with our jobs. If you move by the trees over there, you'll be out of our way and you'll still be able to see if you want to.'

'Can you make a comment on the actions of the protesters, and how you will remove them?' the reporter asked, pointing a fluffy microphone in my direction. It brought back memories. At least I wasn't wearing my pyjamas this time.

'I'm sorry. You know I can't comment right now. But thank you for cooperating and moving back.' Politeness recorded on camera won the day, and they edged towards the tree line.

12

Next were the protesters. I didn't think they would be as amenable.

'Okay, the show is over. I'm going to have to ask you to move away now.'

'Sod off, pigs. We've got just as much right to be here as you have,' yelled the man in the cage via his megaphone. I was only a metre from him, so the amplification was hardly necessary. The charming name-calling must have embarrassed some of the others, as a well-dressed lady with greying hair quickly stepped up and addressed us while gesturing at Cage Guy to stop.

'I'm sorry, officers,' she said with impeccable enunciation, 'but this is a public place, so we are perfectly entitled to exercise our right to protest. This circus exploits animals for its financial gain. It doesn't care for them humanely or to any recognised standards. It's unethical and we — '

'I'm sorry, ma'am,' I interrupted, 'but as this circus has a council permit to occupy this public space for the purposes of its show, it is temporarily deemed by law to be a private place and therefore you are trespassing and can be asked to leave. If you choose not to leave quietly, you can be charged with trespass, and then you can explain your purpose to a judge.' This news was greeted with much muttering and many confused looks from the protesters. Then several of them spotted the small tent, fully erected and being carried along by four of the circus men.

'What on earth . . . ' murmured the woman.

'Look, come on, now. It's time to move along, please. I don't want to have to start taking your names.' Most of them moved back ten metres or so, but several, including the woman and gorilla man, stayed to see what was happening with the tent.

It didn't take long for Cage Guy to figure out what was about to happen. He yelled at the top of his lungs, this time without the megaphone: 'You can't put me in that. That's wrongful imprisonment.' I wondered if he was in the same law class as the university students.

'Come on, guys,' I said to the circus men, as I gestured to them to straighten up, so they could position the tent gently over the cage, It was a perfect fit, with about a foot clearance each side. Nice and claustrophobic. Cage Man screamed the whole time the tent was being lowered. Great, now we had a talking marquee.

His 'You can't do this to me' scream was echoed by the 'You can't do that to him' cries from the protesters. One or two tried to shove me aside and stop the tent's progress, but slunk back when I yelled, 'That's assault of a police officer,' and Smithy struck a pose that would have intimidated Mike Tyson.

'This is illegal detainment. You haven't arrested me. I'll have you for wrongful imprisonment,' came the voice from inside the tent. It had developed a distinct whine.

I yelled loud enough to make myself heard by all concerned: 'Well, sir. The tent is not locked. It is merely there to shelter you. We were concerned about your safety and comfort on such a sunny day.' The sunshine certainly was in abundance; the temperature, however, did not match it. A bank of cloud rolling in from the south indicated the Dunedin weather was going to be its usual schizophrenic self. But that was by the by. I paused for effect before continuing. 'You are not being detained,' I said. 'In fact, you are free to leave at any time you wish.'

Several expletives erupted from within the tent, but I could tell from the tone of his voice that Cage Man realised he'd been outmanoeuvred. The circus crew were pissing themselves, and it was all I could do not to snigger. The remaining protesters gave up and had the grace to smile as they retreated further still.

'Nice one, Sam,' Smithy said, a big grin plastered across his face. 'I didn't know about the permit and trespass thing.'

'Neither did I,' I whispered. 'But it sounded good at the time.'

2

This was not how I'd envisaged spending my Saturday morning. Dunedin had abandoned yesterday's sunshine in favour of a mantle of mist and drizzle that hung around like some sullen teenager. A fair amount had attached itself to me. The gloomy atmosphere made the vision before me all the more miserable.

She was discovered by a resident from the units on the far side of the Leith, who'd come over to the river's edge to call her cat in for breakfast. Instead of kitty, the old dear had been shocked to see a body in the water near the other bank. She'd been so shaken, she'd needed medical treatment; the ambulance was still in attendance.

So here I was, on a riverbank, plagued by a sense of déjà vu — the body of a young woman face down in the water before me, like a piece of flotsam. This time there was no doubt as to foul play. Her hands, floating in front of her, were bound by a clear plastic tie, The silver tape covering her mouth extended around the back of her head like some warped, glitzy headband from which her long dark hair fanned out across the water.

I had to push aside my instinct to wade in and drag her out. After my initial, futile check for signs of life, my role was to stand guard and wait for the forensic experts and scene-of-crime officers, or SOCOs as we called them. It was not the role of a small-bit trainee detective to examine anything; any interference on my part would certainly not be appreciated — my boss had made that patently clear. In fact, I wouldn't normally be allowed to be the first so near a crime scene, but someone had to keep watch and today that someone was me.

I filled the time by making a visual sweep of the scene from my appointed position, but I dared not move for fear of disturbing any potential evidence. I barely dared breathe.

I stood in a small, grassed clearing with the river before me and at my back a steep hillside clad with native bush — flaxes, kowhai and ngaio. The clearing was at the end of a narrow path that ran down from the main walkway, which itself ran around the base of the hill, following the Water of Leith from the Botanic Garden to Gore Place, before leading out on to Dundas Street. I shuddered. The Botanic Garden was one of my havens in Dunedin. Twenty-eight undulating hectares of picturesque solitude only minutes from home. Two days ago, I'd jogged along the walkway; it was a regular on my running circuits, and in all the months I'd been here, I hadn't realised this path existed. I'd noticed the big, spidery tree at its entrance, where Smithy now stood guard with a bit more shelter than I had, but I'd never registered the path itself. The main walkway was high above and behind me, well obscured by the dense bush and trees. The clearing and the water would be invisible from up there, although voices would probably carry.

In front of me the Leith gently wended its way over rocks and past the banks. It was fairly shallow at this point and was open, unlike in other parts of the garden, where it was confined by the steep concrete walls of the flood-control channels. It would have been a pretty spot if it weren't for the body. A large boulder jutted out into the water, preventing her from drifting away with the current, helped by what I imagined was a stack of wet books in her backpack: a badge of studenthood that now only served to weigh her down. With the modern student, though, the backpack was just as likely to hold a laptop.

Another nearby boulder had traces of blood and tissue on it, which pretty much confirmed this as the site of the murder, as did the skid or drag marks in the grass. The blood traces were another reason why I felt so wet and miserable. The drizzle had threatened to wash the remaining blood away, so in desperation I'd covered it with my jacket rather than risk losing valuable evidence. I figured potential contamination from one easily identifiable person was preferable to nature erasing any clues. I still hoped they wouldn't rap me over the knuckles for it, though.

It was a risky site to stage a murder. Whereas this side of the river was well obscured, several flats and houses backed on to the other bank — including Mrs Franklin's, the old lady who I could now see being stretchered off to the ambulance. So the killer or killers must have felt certain they wouldn't have an audience when they murdered this young woman. And the only real chance of that happening would have been under cover of darkness. But how would you get someone down here in the dark without physically dragging them? There was no visible evidence of that. The only place the grass was disturbed was near the bloodied rock. I shuddered again.

They must have coerced her somehow. Either that, or they knew her, and she came down here with them willingly, perhaps for a smoke, a chat or a snog. The murder had to be premeditated, though, that much I was sure of. Most people didn't walk around-with long plastic cable ties and duct tape in their pockets. Well, the people I knew didn't.

However the killer managed to get her down here, the end result was dumped before me. God, what a waste. Even in this condition, I could tell she was pretty. Sometime soon her parents and loved ones would receive the call that would wrench their world apart. I bit my lip to try and force back the tears that sprang into my eyes. Sometimes, I really did wonder if I was cut out for this job.

Man, I wanted to be out of here. I wasn't exactly comfortable around dead people — especially young, violently killed, female dead people: they were too similar to what happened in Mataura. But that wasn't the only reason I wanted to leave: all of this cold, damp air and running water had left me desperate for the loo. I jiggled from foot to foot in an attempt to find a

19

position that was almost comfortable.
Failed.
I badly needed to be relieved.

3

Warmth and dry clothes were what I was looking for after the bone-numbing chill caused by standing in the rain and having to look at that bedraggled body. I had planned a quick dash home to change before going back to work, but it didn't quite pan out that way. First I'd had to park half a mile away from home, at Roslyn Village, as some dick-head had their car parked outside our gate and left it marooned there for the last two weeks, selfish bastard. Then, when I headed back to work and when I got to my usual parking area down behind the old railway station, someone else had nabbed my spot and the rest of the place was chocka, courtesy of the Saturday morning farmers' market. It had taken me two drives around the block and another ten flaming minutes before I finally found a place to park, somewhere near Christchurch. By the time I'd walked to the police station I was wet and cold again, so what with that and the morning's events, I was about ready to rip the throat out of the next person to annoy me.

'Grumpy alert: be nice,' I said to Smithy as he sat down next to me at the back of the briefing room.

'You didn't need to warn me — you're radiating nasty vibes. Why do you think no one else is sitting here?'

He had a point.

'I thought you'd gone home to get dry,' he said. My fingers twitched for his jugular.

The room was filling up with police and CIB. Many had been on duty at the rugby the previous night and had been called in from home for the murder enquiry. The Otago Highlanders had done the unthinkable and won the match, which resulted in a fair amount of carousing by the fans, so it had been a busy night and there were several hung-over bodies warming the cells downstairs. There was an awful lot of yawning and eye-rubbing going on upstairs, too. It was only eleven o'clock in the morning and, considering the victim had been discovered at a quarter past eight, the police behemoth had proved it could move pretty quickly when it needed to.

Some initial murder-scene photographs had been stuck with magnets to the whiteboard at the front of the room. I was too far back to distinguish any detail, but I didn't need photos — the vision was burned into my brain. At this moment, the SOCOs were down at the Leith, doing their thing, and the forensic experts from Environmental Science & Research were on their way from Christchurch. Courtesy of her student ID card, we knew the identity of our young victim, so it was game on.

This was the first murder investigation here since I'd been accepted for detective training and quit the bright lights of Mataura for the great metropolis of Dunedin. This said something about the serious-crime rate in the city, as I'd already been here for half a year.

22

I was one of those in-between creatures — not a detective, nor a constable; a hybrid adrift in this esteemed institution. I had just come out of my six-month trial and was officially a detective constable. This had all happened rather more quickly than expected — people could wait years before becoming a trainee detective — but the powers that be had smiled upon me and here I was. Others were not so thrilled about my promotion through the ranks. So right now I was wondering what sort of a role I'd get in this investigation — not only because I was a newbie, but also because the officer in charge of the investigation was Detective Inspector Greg Johns. I hadn't exactly endeared myself to him during my Mataura days. It was probably when I told him he could go rot in hell that did it. Or was it when I informed him he was a hack with a paper degree who couldn't solve a mystery if the answer was tattooed across his forehead? I'd also insulted his favourite poncy briefcase. That was most likely the clincher. The fact I'd solved the murder of Gaby Knowes didn't seem to make a jot of difference to him. I always got the crap jobs.

The Saturday-morning buzz simmered down as DI Johns took centre stage for the day's briefing. His body language told me he was entirely comfortable with — no, make that relishing his role as the focus of attention. Some people were just like that.

'Right people, let's get things under way.' The DI clapped his hands like we were a bunch of errant schoolchildren. 'This meeting is going to be short. We're not going to waste time in here. I want everyone out there, on the streets. The officers in charge are on the board. Everyone else: Detective Sergeant Gibbs will give you your brief and tell you where you'll be assigned.' The DI moved over to the board with the photos. 'The victim is Rose-Marie Bateman. She's twenty-three; a student at the university. Her body was discovered in the Water of Leith, near the walkway from Gore Place to the Botanic Garden, at eight-fifteen this morning by a resident in the area. SOCOs are at the site now and ESR on the way.' Bang. Bang. Bang. A bullet-point presentation. He wasn't one for superfluous detail.

'The investigation will be called Operation Sparrow.'

I cringed. One thing that irked me was the police's little habit of naming operations after birds. I supposed it made it easier than having to talk about the investigation into the murder of so-and-so — but birds? And 'Sparrow'? Sparrows were boring — drab, brown, puny things. Rose-Marie was young and pretty. Surely they could have come up with something a little more appropriate?

'The body is still in situ and we won't be able to confirm anything until a post-mortem is carried out, but indications are the murder took place last night. The victim's hands were restrained with a plastic cable tie and her mouth was taped. She suffered blunt-force trauma to the head, most likely from being banged against a rock, but she probably died by drowning. Her clothing was intact and there doesn't appear to have been any sexual assault.'

I studied the faces around me. Put like that, in shopping-list fashion, it didn't seem to make much impression on them. But I had seen it. I had seen her in the cold, waxen flesh, murdered and discarded, bedraggled and pitiful. The chill settled back into my bones, and I couldn't stop a shudder. The only face that mirrored my own distaste was Smithy's. He'd borne witness too. He felt my stare and gave me a gentle thump on the leg. It induced a small smile. I returned my attention to the DI.

'As the attack happened so close to the university, we will start our investigations there. She appears to have been walking home from the university to her flat in Opoho Road. There doesn't seem to have been much of a struggle, so it is likely she knew her attacker. She'll have had hundreds of classmates and university associates for us to work through. Of course, we'll be looking at her boyfriend, flatmates and friends too. Her family are from out of town — Napier. So altogether there are a hell of a lot of people to talk to and eliminate. Also, the Botanic Garden is a busy place. Someone must have seen something. We need to talk to every person who walked through there last night. Let's get busy, people.'

The room jumped into movement. Voices buzzed, papers rustled, people got busy, as ordered. Everyone else seemed to know their place, whereas I felt a bit like a spare nut rattling around loose in the engine. When I was in

Mataura, I was it: sole-charge police officer. So I got to talk to everyone — do the interviews, analyse the information. I was the thin blue line. I only hoped I'd get a chance here.

How would I handle this investigation? If I was calling the shots I'd start with the boyfriend, then work my way through the flatmates. As stereotypical as it seemed, statistics told it was, as often as not, the boyfriend. Maybe they had problems, couldn't talk through them, so he decided to take other measures. Then there were the flatmates. They could've fallen out over burnt dinners or the electricity bill. Perhaps she'd borrowed someone's hairdryer and accidentally blown it up; eaten someone else's yoghurt. Stranger things had happened.

We were at the back of the room and Alan Gibbs, one of the senior officers, only now worked his way along the row. He handed me a piece of paper, and said, 'For you. From the boss.'

'Thanks,' I said, as he moved on to talk to someone else. Please let it be something front-line. Please. I unfolded the page.

'Oh crap,' I murmured to myself. It was a bit too loud, though, as Smithy leaned over to look at the note.

'Lucky you,' he said, with a grin.

'Well, I wouldn't get too cocky if I were you,' I said. 'You know who you always end up with — me.'

'Not this time, sunshine, I'm with suspects. Looks like you're flying solo today. You must have really pissed that man off.'

'Don't I know it?'

There would have to be hundreds of places in Dunedin you could buy a plastic tie, and it was my job to find where the one used in the murder was purchased. That's assuming it was even bought in Dunedin. A mass-produced, bog-standard, come-in-a-pack-of-a-hundred, non-identifiable, indistinguishable plastic bloody tie. Normally, ESR did this kind of leg work, not CIB. They had all the flash databases and extensive files to compare things, from brands of carpets to tyres. This was their territory. It wasn't a very subtle backhand. To add further insult to injury, I was directly answerable to the DI.

No intermediary, no buffer.

Bloody marvellous.

4

The man standing behind the counter looked at me like I was wearing a Crunchy the Clown outfit or had something nasty stuck to my face. Having made five similar requests at five similar stores, it was a look I'd become familiar with and was well and truly over.

'You want to know if we can identify everyone who has bought plastic cable ties in the last week?' He was a little more forthright than the others and laughed openly. 'What do you think we do all day?'

Eat donuts, I thought, from the look of him.

'No, of course not. Don't be silly. We know you can't identify each individual.' I tried to diffuse the situation. Difficult, when I was sick of it and felt I was pushing shit uphill with a rake. 'But you are computerised, so you'd be able to let us know the dates of sales and how they were paid for.'

'Huh.' He grunted. 'To a point. I could look up the pre-packs, but the individual ties go under miscellaneous.'

'What about how they were paid for? Does the computer record debit- or credit-card details for each sale?'

He gave me that look again. I was tempted to wipe it off his face.

'This is Dunedin, love, not a US TV show, where you can waltz in and, hey presto, every little detail is nicely recorded for you. So, no, mine doesn't. The systems are separate.' The last four words he said real slow.

My fists clenched tighter. Condescension and a 'love'. I cursed the fact Smithy was off doing the interesting stuff while I was flying solo with the plebs. I took a deep breath and counted to ten in my head, in order not to lose the shred of control I had left. I reminded myself that, for the privilege of wearing that bright-yellow shirt to work each day, he was probably paid bugger all. There was some justice in the world.

I'd already checked out the stock on the shelves before approaching Mr Attitude, and found some very long ties that matched the one used in the murder. The tie used to bind Rose-Marie Bateman's hands was still attached to her, so all I had for comparison was a measurement and a grisly photo. One small satisfaction was that the discovery of possible candidates meant I had the pleasure of relieving the man of some of his stock.

'I'll need to take some samples of those ties for the investigation.'

'Well, I hope you're going to pay for them.'

Bloody hell. Here we were, working on the murder of a young woman, and he was worried about a few cents for some crappy bits of plastic. It must have shown on my face as he dropped his eyes and had the decency to look abashed.

'I'll give you a requisition form, so you need not worry about losing any money. We would hate to inconvenience you in any way.'

'Okay, that's fine,' he mumbled.

His discomfort gave me a small stab of pleasure. I turned and looked towards the area where the plastic ties were shelved. There was a surveillance camera nearby that possibly covered that section. I turned back to the manager.

'Your security cameras. Are they constantly recording?'

'Yes.'

'What about that one there.' I pointed to the front corner. 'How far back would the footage go? Would it be a week or more?'

He assumed that sheepish look again. 'No, it wouldn't go back quite that long.'

'What, only a few days?'

'Well, no.'

'What then?'

'We record over the same file each day.'

I was about to ask why the hell they bothered with it, then? But what was the point? Life was too short. It was almost four o'clock; he'd be counting down the seconds until closing and yesterday's recording was probably overwritten.

'Can I get you to at least print out the sales of cable ties going back a week, then?'

'Yeah, I can do that, but not straight away. It takes a while. These things aren't instant, you know.'

'That would be appreciated,' I said, forcing myself to be polite. 'Can I pick them up in the morning?'

'Yeah, fine.'

5

'Well that was a colossal waste of a day,' I said, plonking my butt on to a chair at the kitchen table. One of the joys of being adopted into this household was the insistence, when timetables and schedules allowed, of family dinners together, with civilised conversation over good food and, more often than not, wine. The reason I'd been adopted was Maggie, my former Mataura flatmate and current fellow boarder who, fortunately for us both, had very amenable relatives. Her Aunty Jude was shaking up, cocktail-style, what I assume was some kind of dressing for the salad. Her concoctions were always delectable, and she had a vast collection of cookbooks on hand if she ever lacked inspiration. My nose was being wooed by the aroma of roasted chicken with a hint of what I thought was smoked paprika, and my stomach gurgled in anticipation. Uncle Phil was busy consulting the oracle that was the wine fridge — yes, this household could boast its very own, purpose-built, wine fridge. God, I loved Maggie's family. Although, if I was going to be picky, their commitment to culinary delights didn't extend to a dedicated chocolate fridge.

'I thought you guys would have been flat out on the job today,' Maggie said as she placed the salt and pepper grinders in the centre of the table. 'I heard there were nasty things going on around the gardens.'

'Nasty isn't the half of it. Urghhh,' I shuddered. 'It brought back all the wrong kind of memories. What is it with me and having to deal with dead young women in rivers?'

'Well, you do seem to get more than your fair share. Any more and you'd call it a speciality,' she said as she slid on to the neighbouring seat. Maggie had been my flatmate back in our Mataura days and like me had decided to upgrade to first class and Dunedin after our lives in the little town went up in smoke. Once we'd gotten back to a more stable financial situation we'd probably look for a flat again, but for now we were both enjoying mates' rates at her aunt's.

'I can think of better specialities. Not that I got to specialise in anything today other than running around after the minor stuff, while everyone else got the good jobs. If this had been Mataura, I would have been the one interviewing the poor girl's boyfriend or flatmates, or anyone for that matter. God, I'd have even settled for talking to her postman, not getting the crap jobs, as usual.' My voice sounded whiny, Not good. I promised myself to watch that.

'Well you are the junior, so to speak, so you're at the bottom of the pecking order. What do you expect? You should be glad you're not sweeping floors and making the coffee,' she said, with a cheeky grin.

'I do make the coffee.'

'Oops.' She gave me a conciliatory pat on the arm.

'Ah, but you're probably right,' I said, this

time without the whine. Maggie had far too level a head on her sometimes. If I'd been inclined to believe in reincarnation, she would have been one of those wise old women in another life — the ones with flowing robes, manes of black hair streaked with white and deeply lined faces oozing serenity. Maggs was the modern version; she had the serenity vibe, but was a stylish young thing who could throw the most unlikely garments together and look effortlessly cool. She was also the only person I'd ever met who could make a brown and yellow zip-front tracksuit top look good. Cow. My style, if you could call it that, was more frenetic conservative.

'You know I can't help but think I get lumbered with the crud because DI Johns has got his little grudge. Sometimes I wonder if I'd have been better off sticking with being constable of a shithole little town, oops, sorry about the language.' I looked up at Aunty Jude. 'At least in Mataura I made a difference rather than getting delusions of grandeur in the city. Here I feel like, well, anonymous.'

Maggie laughed. The sound echoed from two other locations in the room. 'For a start, you're anything but anonymous, and secondly, I believe you did rather insult the man, so he's perfectly entitled to hold a grudge. And, most importantly, I seem to recall some of the locals in that, quote, 'shithole little town' you're so fondly reminiscing about blew up your house and tried to have you killed — and me, for that matter. Got the scars to prove it. In fact, you should come with a public health warning.'

'Surely you're not having doubts about your career, Sam?' Uncle Phil said, as he poured a very welcome drop into the wine glass in front of me. With his foppish hairstyle, almost boyish good looks, high-necked jumper and moleskin trousers, he was the epitome of British country living meets delusional colonial. Despite the airs, like the rest of us, his family were Kiwis from way, way back.

'No.' Maggie raised her now-filled glass in a toast. 'Sam is having trouble adjusting to the fact she's no longer the centre of attention.'

'Oh, that's sad. Haven't they promoted you to commander yet?' Phil asked. Finely honed sarcasm ran in the family.

'Thanks, thanks for that. Just gang up on the guest, see if I care. Whatever happened to pandering to my needs, massaging my ego?'

'Sorry, Sam,' Aunty Jude chipped in. 'You're not a guest, you're family now. Abuse comes with the territory; that and chores. You're on dishes duty, by the way.'

'I thought you'd be on my side. What is this? Pick-on-Sam Day?'

'That's what it said in my diary, what about yours, Unc?' Maggie asked.

Uncle Phil made a ridiculous parody of checking his invisible calendar. 'Yes, you're right, here it is under Saturday the twelfth, national Pick-on-Sam-Shephard Day.'

'Well, there you go. There's nothing like coming home from a hard day at work, dealing with dead people, and dumb-nuts, and then getting bullied in your own home.' I took a

34

dramatic swig of my wine.

'Bravo, bravo, dinner and a show,' said Aunty Jude, giving me polite applause.

'Thank you, thank you, now pass me the bottle.'

'Must have been a bad day.' Maggs got the understatement-of-the-day award. 'So it was a university student, is that what they're saying?' she asked, bringing the conversation back to more serious matters.

'It looks that way.'

'What was her name? I hope she wasn't one of mine.' Phil lectured in Social and Preventive Medicine at the Medical School. It seemed almost everyone in town had some connection to the university. It swelled the local population with nigh on twenty thousand young, exuberant, and, it seemed, often drunk students every year. It was one of those love-hate relationships between the city and the students. The city loved them for the vibrancy, knowledge, culture and income they brought with them, but they hated them for some of the yahooism, excessive rubbish, broken glass and the occasional sofa-burning.

'Her name hasn't been released yet, probably later on tonight now the next of kin have been notified.' That had to be one of the hardest jobs in the force. I'd had to do it on occasion and it never got any easier with experience. That was one aspect of the Mataura job I didn't miss. There was no such thing as a gentle way to shatter someone's world.

'I do hope she's no one you know, or me for

that matter,' Maggie said. 'Everyone seems to know everyone else at the uni — or know someone who knows them. Degrees of separation and all.'

'Ha ha, very funny,' I said. Maggie looked confused. 'Degrees,' I said.

She grinned at her own cleverness. 'Oh yeah, I am funny, and I don't even have to try.'

'Well when you've finished congratulating yourself on your wondrous humour, bearing in mind that as she was a student, along with half the population of Dunedin, it seems, we have an awful lot of people at the uni to talk to. You never know, I might end up questioning you, and you too, Uncle Phil.'

Maggie, with great flair, and intake of breath threw her hands up to her cheeks.

'Oohh, the prospect of being interrogated by you makes me very, very nervous. I'll have to go work out my alibi.' Aunty Jude placed a platter of delicious-looking chicken and roasted cubed potatoes in the middle of the table, to go with the café-trendy salad already waiting. 'But that might have to wait until after dinner.'

6

Sunday morning and work was a madhouse. Under normal circumstances the detectives here would be involved in a range of activities from cheering the kids on at sports, to absorbing the Sunday paper, to snoring. A murder had upped the ante. A considerable amount had been done in the twenty-four hours since Rose-Marie Bateman's body had been discovered, all of this while I was swanning around on my pointless, poxy pursuit at the whim of DI Johns.

Police and CIB had been out canvassing the streets, door-knocking around Rose-Marie's flat, and the houses and flats that backed on to where she was found. They had set up stands at the Gore Place entrance and at the Botanic Garden, hoping to jog the memory of any passers-by. The story was big news on radio, but, as the *Otago Daily Times* didn't do a Sunday paper, we'd have to wait until tomorrow's issue to put out a public plea for information. It was all go, and it seemed to be going without me.

My only saving grace was that Smithy had been put with the Officer in Charge of Suspects and snuck me in on proceedings as much as he could. It was courtesy of his goodwill that I was here at the university, sitting in the Pharmacy Department, listening to him interview the students and staff Rose-Marie knew. The university had always intrigued me, with its mix of stunning Gothic bluestone buildings such as its iconic registry clock tower, contrasting with some sixties' monstrosities that defied all rules of aesthetics, and several modern cutting-edge glass-and-metal numbers. This building, alas, fell into the monstrosity category and was over by the hospital and Medical School, rather than the central campus. It was so ugly, with its flat, concrete utilitarian walls and inset iron windows in cack-green it was just as well it was tucked back off the street. Probably more fascinating to me was the thought of all that intellectual might going on in the university's hallowed halls. If you looked past the well-publicised drunken shenanigans of a few students, it was incredible to think of the young people passing through the halls and buildings, striving for higher and greater things. Of course, the fact that none of them seemed to have mastered the art of crossing a road would surely knock back the tally of graduates at the end of the year. That, and the few who insisted on skateboarding down the busiest and/or steepest streets in the city. They were head injuries waiting to happen. In a way, that was another form of Darwinian selection. Those who were dumb enough to do that wouldn't live to propagate the species. See, I didn't need a flash paper degree or diploma to prove I had a clue. Still, that didn't stop me feeling a pang whenever I set foot on campus, wondering if perhaps Maggie had the right idea, after all. Maybe some study could be useful. But no, I'd dedicated myself to being a detective, and I loved this job. I lived and breathed for this job.

Which made it rankle even more when the arseholes tried to spoil it for me.

There was an air of pomposity about the professor we were interviewing. In fact, I felt it hard not to laugh at the stereotype of an academic he embodied. Framing a surprisingly youthful face, he had grey streaked hair that looked about four weeks overdue a cut. I'd guess him to be early forties, but according to his birth date, he would be celebrating the big five-oh later this year. Perhaps some of his research pertained to the elixir of youth. That, or working with young people all day was rubbing off. His glasses didn't help with his airs. The way he peered over the top of them suggested they were for reading, not looking, so why the hell he didn't just remove them was beyond me. His clothing suggested that he hadn't had time to shop since the mid-seventies, and he'd lost weight since then. He couldn't have been married — no woman would let him out of the house in that state. But then, he had a certain Conneryesque appeal, hi fact, if you spruced him up, he'd be really quite dishy.

'So Professor Simpson, if you were supervising Miss Bateman for her doctorate, how often would you work with her?' Smithy asked.

'We met regularly to talk about her research.'

'Every day?'

'Oh, no. The majority of her day-to-day lab work was with Dr Penny Hawkins and Dr Jeffrey Collins, so they would have seen her all the time. I met with Rosie once a week or so to discuss any issues and get an update.'

'So, you didn't do any of the lab work with her?'

'No, not the practical work. That's for the graduates and junior staff.' It was stated simply and without any perceived snobbery, but I noted Smithy's eyebrows rose as he jotted that down.

'And she got on well with her colleagues?'

'I imagine so, she was a lovely girl. Fun, polite, very conscientious. I'm sure everyone enjoyed working with her.'

'But you don't know for sure. You didn't hear any murmurs of discontent, nothing on the department rumour mill? I'm sure the university must be a hotbed of gossip, everyone talking about everyone else.'

'Well, I don't like to give too much credence to that kind of thing.'

'But?'

'I think there may have been a few petty jealousies.'

'What kind of jealousies are we talking about here? Relationships? Boyfriends?'

'No, nothing like that. Anyway, Penny is married, and I think Rosie had a boyfriend. No, professional. I believe there may have been a little tension between them over their research workload. Academics can be a little particular about protecting their patch.'

I gave some consideration to whether a woman would be strong enough to smash a head against a rock in the way that Rose-Marie's had been. I supposed it was possible, but I couldn't imagine women sorting out their differences quite that directly. I'd have thought supposedly intelligent women would never get to that point in the first place, and if they felt the need to take action, it would be a damned sight more subtle — a bit of sabotage, maybe, or muck-racking, something with a bitchiness factor about it. But murder over stepping on toes or a few research hours? It seemed a bit of a stretch. Mind you, there were plenty of murderesses rotting in prison to prove me wrong. I would be very interested to hear Penny Hawkins' slant on the situation.

Smithy must have been thinking along similar lines. 'We'll be talking to Dr Hawkins later in the day,' he said.

'For heaven's sake, don't tell her I mentioned anything.' Simpson looked very uncomfortable with the idea of being identified as the nark.

'You don't need to worry. I do know how to conduct an interview, Professor.'

I turned to stare. Smithy's frostiness surprised me, but seemed lost on the prof. Although Smithy was the one asking the questions, I blurted one out to allay any possible awkwardness over the comment. 'So what exactly was she researching?'

This time it was the professor turning to look at me. It was as though he had only just registered my presence. He gave me a searching look and a smile which left me feeling warm and thinking again of that earlier incarnation of James Bond. 'She was researching drug-delivery systems, specifically looking at a new way of administering insulin.'

'Sounds interesting.' Smithy's fine brand of

sarcasm again. I had to turn away and pretend to look at some equipment to hide my smile.

'It was very important research which looked like it would have very useful commercial applications and potentially save lives. Unfortunately, I can't go into it further, as it's commercially sensitive.'

Like a couple of detectives were going to spill the beans. Smithy took the reins again. 'What were you doing on Friday evening?'

The prof looked a little taken aback at the directness. 'I would have been here, in my office. I think I was going over another doctorate student's thesis. I worked to about six, then met up with some friends at the Staff Club for a few drinks. That's what we do every Friday night. After that I went home.'

'And do you have anyone who'd be able to corroborate that?'

The prof's eye's narrowed, but to his credit, he maintained an air of calm.

'There were a few people on this floor when I was working. I'm certain one of them would have seen me. There must have been, I guess, twenty people or so at the Club, and my wife, once I got home.' So there was a Mrs Professor, and she dressed him funny. 'Do you want everyone's names?'

While Smithy quietly took down the list of names being passed on with a long-suffering tone, I looked around me. The office was a contrast to the man. Although filled with books, folders and papers, it was orderly and everything seemed to be in its place. No scruffiness around the edges here. There was an impressive number of framed degrees and certificates on the walls which no doubt intimidated the fresh-faced undergraduates who found their way here. There were some from Europe, as well as Australia.

My curiosity was interrupted by my cellphone. I took a look at the caller display and felt a knot form in the pit of my stomach. 'Excuse me,' I said as I retreated to the corridor. 'Shephard,' I said, trying to sound officious, yet cheerful.

'Johns. Where are you?'

'I'm at the university.'

'What are you doing there?'

'We're interviewing Professor Simpson and then some — '

'Who said you could do that?'

'Smithy invited me along to help interview the victim's associates.' I wondered if Smithy would get it in the neck later.

'Get yourself back here now. I need you to do another job.'

'Can I finish the interviews fir — '

'No. Now.' He ended the call as abruptly as he'd spoken, and I had to take a few deep breaths to compose myself and resist the urge to fling the phone down the hall.

Arsehole.

7

Fan-bloody-tastic. Here I was, back at the circus, which normally wouldn't be such an onerous task — they were supposed to be fun, after all. But today the necessity pissed me off. The oh-so-important thing that DI Johns pulled me off the university interviews for was to return the digital camera card to the circus folk and tidy up their complaint. Whoop-de-do. At the morning's briefing, the DI had gone on at how much pressure we were under to solve this case and quickly, in light of the string of unsolved murders in the lower South Island recently. Government and the media were putting the acid on about the rate of solving or lack of solving in these cases. God knows the police didn't need any more bad press after the recent taint of sex scandals and corruption. If he was so concerned, why the hell was I here and not doing something useful? My cynical little self knew the answer to that one.

Some calming down was in order before I faced the walking abrasion that was Terry Bennett. I didn't want to fly off the handle at him because I was pissed off with the boss. Fortunately for me, the equivalent of Valium on four legs was corralled just around the corner. 'Hello Cassie,' I said quietly to the forlorn-looking elephant.

I climbed up the metal steps to the booking

trailer. A middle-aged, twinset-clad, bespectacled lady greeted me from behind the security grille window. A less circus-like woman I could hardly imagine. 'Detective Constable Shephard. I'm here to see Mr Bennett.'

'I'll text him to let him know you're here; won't be a minute.' She may have looked all steamed pudding and knitting, but her voice had a gravelly steel to it.

The circus was a damned sight more peaceful than the last time I visited. The absence of protesters had a lot to do with that. The only visible activity in the midday light was someone walking purposefully towards one of the trailer homes. Judging by the general desertion, it must have been lunchtime for the troops. And in spite of myself, I found I was impressed at the size and number of their mobile living quarters. There was an orderly line-up of eight along this perimeter of the circus town and more around the corner. There were all the typical trappings of family life with bikes and trikes discarded in front of doors, as casually as you'd expect to see littering the driveways of suburbia. One nearby trailer even had one of those big half-shell plastic things with a bit of sand in the bottom and a colourful collection of plastic buckets and spades. And clothes airers were laden with all manner of washing, making the most of the return of the sunshine and a pleasant sea breeze while it lasted. I smiled at the normality of it all. Not even the glamour of the circus could escape the drudge of doing the laundry.

The door opened on the deluxe trailer at the

front of the queue and the sizable form of Terry Bennett appeared. The whole thing listed to the right as he walked out on to the step. 'Don't they give you a lunch break?' he called out.

Judging by the dusting of crumbs on his chest and belly, he'd just consumed his.

'No time for anything as unimportant as food,' I answered. 'Things to do, places to go, people to see. You know how it is.'

'I hope you're here to tell me you've caught the little shits that had a go at my lion and have them safely locked away. They'll be a damned sight better off with you guys than if I ever got my hands on the bastards.'

I didn't doubt it for a second.

'I wish I could tell you that, but no, not yet. We've taken the photo files of them off your camera card, so we'll be able to pick them out at the university easily enough.' If they were regular troublemakers, the Proctor would know them by sight. Otherwise, I didn't mention the reality that there was probably no way in hell the university would let us have access to the students' identification photographs for a misdemeanour as minor as hassling a big cat. It came into the pushing-steaming-smelly-stuff-uphill-with-a-rake category.

I handed the camera card over to him. He didn't look all that grateful.

'If I'd known it was going to take you guys this long, I would have gone down and found them myself. God Almighty, we end up having protesters here accusing us of being cruel to animals, then they ignore the stupid buggers who tried to kill one of them by feeding it a can of Coke. Some people live in bloody fantasyland.'

'How is the lion?' I asked. 'Did they do it any harm?' I imagined the poor beast had enough hassles in its highly restricted life without being stressed out by drunken students.

'Yeah, he's fine. Fortunately, he's got more sense than those stupid buggers, and left the can alone. Lucky for them.' The implied threat didn't need elaboration.

'Well, let's hope the rest of your stay here is uneventful and you can get on with the business of putting on a show. No more visitations other than the paying kind.'

8

If this was modern policing at its best, it was a farce. My sense of peeve at being shuffled from one pointless task to another had been heightened by the fact I'd had to wait for almost an hour just to get near a bloody computer. DI Johns, in yet another transparent effort at keeping me from anything useful, had put me on to the riveting job of checking through the open murder enquiries nationwide, to see if there were any connections. Okay, maybe it had a small degree of usefulness to it, but bloody hell, an hour to get to a computer? Even the local kindergartens had a better computer-to-kids ratio than we had here. I bet the Minister of Police didn't have to share with four others.

I also knew that at this moment, while I was swanning around on the dross, Smithy was interviewing Dr Penny Hawkins and I would very much have liked to sit in on that one. The whole idea of a female killer was somehow thrilling, in a sick kind of a way. The likelihood was zilch, but you never knew. Smithy would have to give me a full report later — he wouldn't be allowed home until he did.

My search did throw up one interesting fact, however. Usually, Auckland was grand crime central which, considering a third of the country's population lived up there, was to be expected. That, and the fact it was a claustrophobic, jarring and manic sort of a place where the entire population seemed to be obsessed with getting into their cars at exactly the same time and then spending the next few hours in impatient gridlock. I didn't do cities. Dunedin with its hundred and twenty thousand was at the upper limit of my tolerances. The best thing about Auckland was the departure lounge at the airport, and even that was pretty crummy. But for once, it wasn't leading the points on murder cases; the South Island had that dubious honour, which surprised me. There were only two recent unsolveds in Auckland, another in Hamilton, and a couple of cases they were near enough making arrests for to tick them off. The rest of the cases, four in all, were in the South Island. One was in Christchurch, which didn't really surprise me as Christchurch had just nudged Auckland for the highest crime rate per capita. The others were in smaller towns, Timaru, Ashburton, and Oamaru. None of them even remotely resembled the case of Rose-Marie Bateman, other than the fact that someone was prematurely and unnecessarily dead. They were a mix of male and female victims, varying ages, weapons and causes of death. In fact, a couple of them were most likely accidental. I could quite safely say DI Johns had succeeded, yet again, in wasting my day. Hooray.

9

The figure on the screen seemed diminished by the room. His entire body transmitted his grief, the story amplified by the raw emotion on his face. This was not the face of a killer. This was the face of utter disbelief. Rose-Marie Bateman was not murdered by her boyfriend, of that I was certain.

The interview room was spartan — it was not designed with comfort in mind. Quite the contrary. On one side of the table came the barrage of questions from Detective Reihana; on the other side, weathering the brunt, was James Collingwood, aged twenty-three and about to break down into tears again. I reached forward and hit the rewind button as I didn't catch the question the first time.

'Did you and Miss Bateman have a sexual relationship?'

The young man's shoulders shook as he tried to keep the sobs at bay. 'Yes, well, no, not exactly,' he said, through rasping breaths. 'Rosie and I are Christians. We don't believe in sex before marriage, so we didn't have intercourse as such, but we messed around a bit.'

'What exactly do you mean by messed around a bit?' the detective asked.

'You know, kissing, fondling, that kind of stuff?'

Not only was the poor boy trying not to cry,

his squirming and the ruddiness of his cheeks told me he was hugely embarrassed by this line of questioning.

'Did the fondling extend to oral sex?'

Shock darted across his face, which reddened even more.

'God, no, we never went that far. No, she wouldn't let me. Rosie was a good girl, such a good, good girl.' At this point James broke down completely and Detective Reihana reached towards my screen to pause the recording.

I was sitting in the very room where the interview had taken place twenty-four hours earlier, but on my own clock, not the station's. DI Johns might have been able to keep me off the front line as far as questioning was concerned, but he couldn't stop me from watching the recorded interviews on my own time, especially if he didn't know. I was buggered if I was going to be left out of the loop, The station was now tomb-like as it was late Sunday afternoon and everyone else with a life had gone home. It was the perfect opportunity to get up to speed on the murder investigation.

So far what I'd learned from James was that he didn't do it. Yes, they all say that, but in this instance, I believed him. He had last seen Rose-Marie on the Friday; they had lunch together on the University Union lawn with several other friends. They had first met at a church students' youth group and had been seeing each other for well over a year, and they didn't flat together. I found it hard to believe that a hot-blooded young couple could be dating

51

that long and never have jumped in the sack. My hormones were a damned sight more demanding than that and the abstinence would have driven me insane. I guess they were, as he said, very good little Christians. A bit better than a few others I knew who used the title, but who were busy shagging each other's brains out at any opportunity. Each to their own.

A few zigzaggy black lines danced across the screen as the interview resumed. The timer indicated that it took James ten minutes to compose himself.

'How often did you see Miss Bateman?'

A very juicy sniff made one eye twitch. 'Normally, I'd see her most days on campus and perhaps two or three nights a week; we'd study together at our flats or at the library, and then we'd hook up at youth group on Sunday nights.'

'Normally?' the detective asked. 'Had that pattern changed recently?'

'A bit. This year we were both doing more study. Rosie and I are both doing doctorates, so getting together has been a bit more difficult. We're in different departments, so I guess I only got to see her for lunch a few times a week and not so much in the evenings. She had a lot of lab work to do.'

'What sort of lab work?'

'She was doing work in the Pharmacy Department with medications, dosage forms for insulin, that kind of thing.'

'You don't do those kinds of things?'

'No, I'm in Computer Sciences. Our building is on the other side of the campus.' He didn't look like what I'd consider a computer geek. His short-cropped dark hair had a very up-to-date cut and his clothing had a hip kind of style. None of that could deflect from the pain written across his face.

'So how often did you talk, then?'

'You mean on the phone?'

'Yes.'

I was pleased the detective's voice was firm and patient. He must have realised James Collingwood was no suspect. He seemed a bit of a sap, a good-looking one, but a sap all the same, truth be told.

'Not that often, actually. A couple of times a week. We messaged or texted all the time though.'

What a strange age it was when you did your romancing via text message. I supposed it helped with the abstinence if you didn't actually get within arms' length of each other. What you can't touch you can't get into trouble with. They can't have been hopelessly in love. If they were, they would have seen each other every day come hell or high water. Little things like clashing timetables and pressing deadlines would not have kept me from my Mr Right, if there was such a creature. Rampant ardour was a hard beast to restrain. I decided they'd had an odd kind of a relationship.

'When you did talk, did Miss Bateman mention she was having difficulties with anyone? Her flatmates or anyone at the university?'

He shook his head slowly.

'Her flatmates are cool. I thought she was

53

really lucky with them. There was one who kept leaving her heater on thermostat all day when she wasn't even home, which pissed them all off cos they divided up their power bill equally, but I think they'd sorted that out. They're a great bunch of girls and they were good friends.'

'What about at university? Did she say there were any issues?'

'No, not that I can think of. She didn't really talk much about her studies.'

'Why was that? Was she avoiding talk about her studies? Was she struggling with them?'

Too many questions at once, I thought, don't bamboozle the guy.

'No, I don't think she avoided it, although she did mention some of the things they were doing could be commercially sensitive. She'd never repeat anything said in confidence, she was careful like that . . . ' He trailed off like he was thinking about other things.

'And her work?' Reihana prompted. 'Was she coping with everything?'

James snapped his head up again and nodded repeatedly. 'She was really bright, right at the top of her class. Study was never a problem. It all came easy for her. She had a pretty big workload, but it never fazed her. She was happy to put in the long hours. We never talked that much about our studies,' he said again. 'It's just we talked about other stuff.'

'What kind of other stuff?'

'You know, friends, family, what was happening around the place. The usual things.'

'So you had no reason to think she was

concerned about her safety?'

The shoulder quaking and thick voice started up again. 'No, she was just her usual happy self.'

The interview ended shortly after and offered nothing in the way of helpful information other than eliminating one person from the list of likelies. The impression that young man gave was he wouldn't hurt a fly and was far too well-mannered. I clicked on the next file, one of Rose-Marie's flatmates. It might give a better picture of the young woman to hear from those who had to live with her day in and day out. So far, she'd been described as an angelic, intelligent young woman who held very old-fashioned views on loyalty, love and propriety. She sounded too good to be true. Perhaps they might offer a different perspective. Nothing like the grind of daily life to show what someone was really made of.

10

Rosie Bateman for Pope. That is the poster her flatmates had apparently stuck on her bedroom door for a good-natured joke. They'd even Photoshopped her picture and added a papal mitre and staff. According to the flatmate interviews, her worst vice was gingernut finger biscuits or pineapple lumps — it was too close to call. Her strongest beverage was Red Bull and her worst habit was leaving strands of hair in the shower, clogging the drain. The last claim was made by a flatmate with waist-length black hair, so was most likely unreliable. Her taste in music, always at a considerate volume, was retro — Steely Dan, Cat Stevens. She was rostered to cook on Tuesday nights and always cooked spaghetti bolognese. She saw her boyfriend occasionally; he never stayed the night and she always came home to sleep. The overall consensus was she was a good girl, a statement that was becoming a familiar mantra when talking about Rose-Marie. She was a fun, intelligent young woman, dedicated to her studies and very involved in her church.

Just as her boyfriend said, Rose-Marie seemed to have struck it lucky with her flatmates. As far as I could tell, they all got on well, and they seemed to have an almost family-like camaraderie. I could relate to the benefits of a good flatmate — Maggie and I had flatted together for years, in different places, and I would have to say she was a calming influence on me. I couldn't quite say what benefits Maggie got from the relationship, but she continued to put up with me, so I couldn't be too bad.

I thought about Rose-Marie's involvement with the church. It would be interesting to talk with her priest, or youth pastor, to see if she'd mentioned any concerns. If she couldn't confide in them, who could she confide in? I jotted the thoughts down in my notebook — I'd put it to Smithy in the morning.

Smithy had finally got to go home to his family around three. It didn't leave the poor man much time to play with the kids, so I hadn't quizzed him for too long. One of the consolations of singledom was not having to keep tabs on the work hours.

According to Smithy the interview with Dr Hawkins wasn't that interesting. The main impression he got was that politics was alive and well in academic circles. The pursuit of higher learning didn't exempt the university from the curse of the large institution — in-house posturing and turf guarding. Hawkins and Rose-Marie got on fine: there may have been one or two disagreements on small matters, but according to Hawkins, they were all her own doing because, as she put it, Rose-Marie had a brilliant mind, and she found it hard to compete. Smithy had been quite disarmed by her honesty. Most people in a murder investigation wouldn't admit, up front, to any form of jealousy, lest it incriminated them. This woman had no such qualms and admitted she'd have loved to have half of the natural ability of this girl. She insinuated that she wasn't the only one in this situation, and that Prof Simpson had felt more than a little threatened by his student's skills. A further trip to the university would clearly be in order in the morning, and hopefully, I'd be able to sneak in on the ride.

For the moment, I was done in. I leaned back in the chair and stretched my arms up and back behind me, loosening up the accumulated shoulder tension of the day.

A run, a hot shower, Sunday-night roast with a nice glass of red — you had to love families with old-fashioned traditions. Then a DVD and early to bed with the weekend crossword puzzles. That was the soother I needed. It had been a hell of a few days.

11

It was only nine o'clock in the morning and already the gloss had been knocked off my day. DI I'm-God-with-a-grudge Johns had taken his usual dose of perverted delight in sending me off on another dregs job, and this one surpassed all others with respect to the ugh factor.

Just for a change, I was at the circus. By now, any joy my brain had previously associated with The Greatest Show on Earth had been displaced by dread. Somehow, I didn't think this visit was going to go down too well with the surly Terry Bennett. Madame Time Warp behind the ticket-office security grille window didn't look that pleased to see me here again, and I was certain what I was about to ask Bennett would put him in a right shitty liver. I seemed to have become the unofficial circus liaison, yippee, and DI Johns appeared to derive a great deal of pleasure from sending me back here again. I only wished he'd sent Smithy or some other company with me. Terry Bennett was one of the few people in this world who had the knack of making me all too aware of my vertical shortcomings.

I passed some of the time fidgeting, while looking at the cheerful circus posters that adorned the ticket-office walls. They did get around. Before Dunedin, Darling Bros Circus had been to six other towns or cities in the South

Island, with more to perform in yet. I bet they were all glad to get home at the end of a tour, wherever home was. There were a fair few foreigners among the travelling company, judging by the array of accents and Babelish languages. There was no question of where Mr Bennett originated from though, as his harsh, eardrum-grating accent was all Kiwi.

'To what do we owe the pleasure of a visit this time?' I hadn't heard his approach and the magnitude of his voice made me jump. He certainly knew how to project.

'Mr Bennett, yes, here again. You'll be giving me a job here soon.' I laughed, a thin, nervy giggle.

He gave me a kind of up-and-down look. 'Well, you're small,' he said. 'The acrobats need someone to throw.'

I didn't know whether to say thanks, or not. There was no point in procrastinating my task, so I swallowed hard and pitched straight in. 'I need to ask you a few questions about some motorbikes.'

'Motorbikes? What motorbikes?'

'I don't know if you've been following the news, but three specialised miniature motorbikes were stolen from a Dunedin property earlier in the week, and we have had a witness come forward claiming to have seen one of them over the back of the circus.' I indicated towards the rear of their set-up. I'd already been down there for a nosey and had found no trace of the bikes. I would have been tempted to leave it at that if I'd thought I could get away with it, but was

60

obliged to follow-up verbally with the mercurial Mr B. I braced myself.

'And did this person happen to mention what the hell business they had skulking around the back of my circus?' The reaction and its volume were as anticipated.

'They said they were passing through.'

'They were trespassing or casing us out, and don't think I don't know exactly where this line of conversation is going. You people are all the same. Where the hell do you all get off treating us like we're criminals? The circus comes to the town, so they must all be ratbags or thieves, every one of them.' Okay, more than anticipated. I had to work hard not to openly stare at the array of death symbolism and straight-out expletives tattooed all over his arms as he mentioned the word 'criminal'. Hard to figure out where that kind of impression might come from.

'You come with me.' He grabbed me by the arm and I wondered if I should be alarmed at being dragged off towards the middle of the compound. He stopped abruptly before I could make a decision on whether to panic or not.

'See that container there.' He pointed at a large white shipping container on the back of an equally sizable black truck and trailer. 'There is over half a million dollars' worth of equipment kept in there. He pulled me around the corner to the big top. 'Do you have any idea how much that thing is worth?' He stabbed at the air with his forefinger.

I shook my head, quite certain he was about to educate me.

'Four hundred thousand dollars, four-hundred K. The lighting and sound systems alone are worth over two hundred grand. What about the animals?' He pointed over to what I considered the cramped and unappealing cages of three lions and several morose-looking monkeys. 'I paid out a small fortune for those, they're worth a bomb. The elephant alone is worth . . . well, she's irreplaceable.' He turned me around so I was facing him. 'So why the fuck do you think anyone at this circus would bother to steal some piddling crappy little motorbikes? Tell me that will you? Why do you think we would need to do that?'

I could have done with an umbrella and he could have done with a breath mint. 'Look, I don't mean to cause you any offence,' I said. God knew he took offence like an Olympic hurdler. 'But someone has reported this and it is our duty to follow it up. I am certain none of your people would have had anything to do with the thefts, but I would still appreciate it if you'd quietly keep an eye or an ear out just in case.'

'I'll do no such thing, young lady.' He moved slightly closer in a deliberate attempt to intimidate me. I was eye-level with his sizeable chest and already well aware of how imposing he could be. His move only served to piss me off, so I stood my ground and maintained firm eye contact as he continued on his rant. 'I can tell you right here and now none of my crew would steal anything, not only because they are decent people, but because they all know they would have to deal with me first.' It didn't take much imagination to work out how they'd be handled. 'So you can take your little enquiry and stick it, as far as I'm concerned.'

Count to ten; you're the bigger person, Shep, I coached myself, don't make it worse. I seemed to have been doing a lot of maths lately. When I was certain my dander was under control, I spoke with deliberate calm. 'There's no reason to be rude.' I couldn't resist some admonishment, delivered with what I hoped was a soothing kind of voice. 'If it were your equipment that had been stolen, you'd expect us to make a complete and thorough investigation, as is our duty. It's the same for this person.'

He reciprocated with what I guessed was his version of control. 'Yeah, well I'm sick to bloody death of everyone treating us like scumbags. You can go back and tell your superiors they're looking up the wrong tree here. They should be looking at the sod that was poking around my property, not at us. He was the one up to no damned good.'

'Yes, I know that, and of course we'll be looking into his behaviour too. Do you want to make a formal complaint about trespass?' I thought maybe if I turned it around his temper might fully defuse.

'Bah.' He threw his hands up into the air. 'Like it would make any difference. You'd be amazed how people think they can walk through our compound at any time of day or night. Wander where they like, like it's all one big sideshow attraction. They wouldn't take kindly to complete strangers wandering through their backyards, looking at their laundry, hassling their pets.'

I wouldn't have thought of a bloody great elephant and several wild animals as pets, but I could see it would get a little tiresome. Meanwhile, something I'd seen earlier was playing on my mind a bit, so I took the opportunity to change the subject completely. 'I think that's all I need to ask about the bikes. Like I said, please let me know if you hear of anything. While I'm here, my niece is a huge circus fan. Her folks are bringing her along tomorrow night. Do you have any spare copies of your circus poster she could have for her bedroom wall? I think she'd love that.'

Actually, it wasn't for my niece at all, and her mum probably wouldn't let her have posters on the wall anyway — they might make pinholes. No, there was something about the towns on the itinerary that was bugging me.

'Yeah, sure, we've got hundreds of the things. You can have a couple. It's the kids that keep the circus going, isn't it? We can put up with all the crap because in the end, its the kids who love it and have a good time.' I didn't peg him as the sentimental type, so was quite sure it wasn't all about the kids — publicity speak if I ever heard it. Cynical, I suppose. But judging by how flash the trailer unit was that he lived in, he could put up with the crap because he made a damned good bob out of it. It was all about business. That's how he could keep lions caged up all day and monkeys imprisoned, miniature ponies and dogs in less than ideal conditions and as for that

64

poor bloody elephant . . . I was brought up on a farm where animal welfare was paramount. My impression of this place was that welfare was secondary to profits.

The circus had lost its appeal. I'd get out of here, head back to the station, write up the report on this wild goose-chase and then sit and try to figure out why the posters were bugging me so much.

12

There was quite the hubbub going on at the station as the other CIB members worked hard on what I considered the good stuff, interviewing Rose-Marie's friends, family, university associates, while I toiled away, as usual, on the dross. Maybe I'd get lucky one day and DI Johns and his grudge would get transferred out of here, but I wouldn't hold my breath. Wankers never walked. God only knew what it would take to impress the DI and get into his good books, and even he probably couldn't manage it. Whoever would have thought I'd have wistful thoughts back to my sole-charge Mataura days and the simplicity of policing there? This was supposed to be my dream, detective training, the big D, advancing my career, today the CIB, tomorrow, the world. No one mentioned some of the bloody great obstacles in the way. Reality bit.

Once at the little scrap of timber and veneer in the corner that was my desk, I rolled out the circus posters and had a good look. It wasn't the impressive pictures of roaring lions and ridiculously costumed monkeys that held my interest, but the towns that had hosted the greatest show on earth. Kaikoura, Christchurch, Ashburton, Timaru, Oamaru, Dunedin. They were working their way down the east coast, then returning up via the West. After their stay in Dunners they'd plunge further south to Balclutha and Inver-cargill, then up to Queenstown and Wanaka and the Central Lakes, then over the Alps to Greymouth, Westport, and Nelson before heading back to the North Island. Some of those alpine passes would be interesting to negotiate with their collection of vehicles. I wondered if elephants got car-sick? Wouldn't want that clean-up job.

'Yo, Shephard, you back from the circus already? Oh, and I see you got yourself a souvenir.' Smithy dumped a wad of paper on the desk next to mine and came over for a look. One day I'd work up the courage and tell him that words like 'yo' didn't work coming from the mouth of a middle-aged, slightly plump, white guy. He pointed to the pictures. 'I like the hats on the monkeys, very stylish. You should get yourself one of those.'

'As soon as you go get yourself one of those clown suits.' Judging by the less grumpy than usual look on his face, it looked like he'd been on to more interesting jobs than me this morning. 'Who'd you get to interview?' I asked.

'Been back down at the university. Professor Simpson was lecturing this morning, so I couldn't follow up on the little inconsistencies of accounts between him and Dr Hawkins and Dr Collins. That whole thing sounds so much like tit for tat. I've come to the conclusion the university is just a more articulate version of a primary-school playground, except the school kids are better behaved.' Academics weren't Smithy's thing; he seemed to have an innate distrust of anyone who used their brain for a living, which was amusing really, when you considered detective work was precisely that, and that Smithy possessed a damned good one. 'We were working our way through Rosie's colleagues and the students she tutored. Nothing surprising so far, other than the usual 'she was so nice, she worked hard' etcetera, etcetera. Tell you what though. They all look so damned young. It made me feel geriatric.'

'You are. They probably think you're their parents' vintage, and they wouldn't be too far off the mark.' Smithy had a lovely wife, Veronica, and two young kids. He was a bit of an older dad, having not found his true love until his forties.

'Yeah, thanks for that, like I needed reminding.' He gave me a pretend clip around the ear. 'Anyway, how did you get on with the charming Mr Bennett?'

'Exactly as you'd expect. I got nowhere. He was a bit miffed by the insinuation they could be a pack of criminals. He just couldn't see how anyone would get that impression.'

'I think that man's policy is to take offence at everything. He's so damned overreactive. No wonder the media love following him around, he's perfect camera fodder.'

'You got that right. He's a consummate performer with a well-rehearsed line for any occasion. He's a bit like my old dog — any attention's good attention for him.' I was pleased Smithy read Terry Bennett the same way I did.

'I see you've got a couple of those posters; can

I grab one for the kids? Katie would love that in her room,' he said, hovering over my desk like a blowfly.

'Course you can.' I slid the top one off and passed it over.

'What's the story with those?'

'They're not for my bedroom wall, if that's what you were meaning. I think I've outgrown the need for posters. No, there was something bugging me about them. I'm sure I'll figure it out if I stare at them long enough.'

'You stare away, then. I'm off to meet the Mrs for lunch, I'll catch you later.' He rolled up the poster and headed off with it towards the door.

'Say hi from me.'

'Sure thing. Have fun.'

I sat down and stared at the poster in the hope something would jump out and take me by the jugular. I didn't know what, exactly, but I knew my instincts well enough to trust that if something was bugging me, it was worth looking at.

I didn't have to stare too long before the bug flew into view. Both of the computers in the room were free for a change, so I hopped on to one and logged in. I typed in the names of the towns the circus had visited and confirmed what had been banging around in the back of my mind. I'd been looking at these place names yesterday, when I was wasting time on my pointless task du jour from DI Johns. Perhaps the task hadn't been so pointless, after all. Most of the places were there. But it was the dates that made me utter a very rude word.

Christchurch, unsolved murder.

Ashburton, unexplained death.

Timaru, unexplained death.

Oamaru, unsolved murder.

And of course, Dunedin, very recent unsolved murder. Any thoughts of coincidence evaporated when I compared the dates of the murders to the itinerary of the circus. They were in town every single time.

Shit.

I hoped Smithy hadn't handed that poster over yet. He might not want a killer's schedule hanging on his little girl's bedroom wall.

13

'One moment please, constable.'

DI Johns continued his conversation with Detective Wallace while I tried not to visibly seethe at being addressed as 'constable'. Did he do these things on purpose? I passed the time concentrating on the array of printers and copiers that congregated in the hallway outside his office and breathing out my anger. No communal office for the bigwig — he got his own space, which was a good thing really, as it kept him out of our faces. I had occasional fantasies about having my own office, my own dedicated work computer. Oh well, I knew what to do about it. Work hard, move up the ranks and climb up the food chain. Trouble was there was a bloody great shark at the top that appeared to have an appetite for Sam. My hands felt slippery against the shiny surface of the rolled-up poster I gripped.

'Alright,' he said to Wallace, 'if you can get back to me with that by the end of the day, thanks.' The detective gave me a wink as he headed out and the DI picked up the phone. 'I've got one important phone call to make, then I'll be right with you.'

I figured, to him, I was down there somewhere near plankton. No, make that something lower, a single-cell organism, a foram, I thought as he made a high-priority appointment for a haircut.

One could live in hope my status would elevate after what I was about to show him.

'So, constable, what can I do for you?' For the sake of my career, I let that one slide too.

I passed him the poster and enjoyed the puzzled look on his face.

'I went to the Darling Brothers Circus earlier this morning to follow up on the stolen motorbike report and while I was there noticed this.'

He unrolled it and stated the obvious. 'It's a poster.' With those few words the edge had crept into his voice, along with a sizeable dollop of sarcasm.

'Yes, but what caught my attention was the itinerary of the circus. Have a look at the towns they've been to so far.' He put the poster down on his desk and anchored it with a stapler at the top and his hand at the bottom. I moved around and tapped on the word Christchurch. 'I came back here and checked it out on the network and was stunned to find the dates match perfectly.'

He interrupted before I could explain further.

'Match what? Look, I'm a very busy man and I don't like having my time wasted. Is there a point to this?'

'Yes,' I said with deliberate calm, 'a very important point.' I indicated to each town and date on the itinerary as I went. Christchurch, first of March, young woman murdered, unsolved. Ashburton, sixteenth of March, man killed in what was thought to be a hunting accident, never resolved. Timaru, twenty-fourth of March, unexplained death, town bum, never resolved. Oamaru, sixth of April, young man murdered, unsolved. Dunedin, two days ago, young woman murdered. It all corresponds. The circus was in town at the time of every death. It can't be coincidence.'

I was certain I saw the twitch and tussle in his face as he realised I was on to something and there was no way, try as he might, he could refute it. 'Good God,' he said. 'If you're right,' which of course I was, 'someone in that circus has been having a killing spree down the island. Okay, we're going to have to call people in and formulate a plan of attack here. I'm going to need to talk to the area commander and these other towns, check out any patterns. He grabbed up the poster, strode out the door and left me standing there. No thank you, no well done, no nothing.

Bugger that.

I took off after him.

14

My lungs and legs were screaming at me to ease off, but I was damned if I was going to relent. The lush bush, earthy scents and birdsong of the green belt and Queens Drive had not quelled my mood in the slightest, so I'd continued to run down towards town, then headed back up the hill by assailing Stuart Street as hard out as I could go.

Unbelievable. It was me who had noticed the pattern in the itinerary of the circus, me who had followed it up and checked against other unsolved cases to confirm the pattern, and me who had presented the information to the DI. So why the hell was it me who had been left behind at the station when the hotshots went down to investigate?

Despite the protest from my lungs and legs, I upped the pace even more.

I'd provided the first significant break in the murder of Rose-Marie Bateman, and possibly unearthed something huge and sinister, and once again I'd been left in the dust, sidelined, discarded like some spent wad of chewing gum. Then, to top it all off, when I finally got home, that shit-heap of a car was still marooned outside the gate, and I had to park two blocks away from my own bloody house. I reached the Highgate Bridge and stopped, bending over, hands on knees, trying to suck in enough oxygen to satisfy my body's screaming need. The urge to vomit was another of its unsubtle ways of telling me to stop, but I was too pissed off to listen. Not even the panoramic view across this harbour city could evoke a flicker of appreciation today.

'Ah, fuck it.'

I stood upright and forcibly propelled myself forward. I wasn't through with this yet.

15

Your car has been parked here for over two weeks and is restricting our access to our gate. Can you please shift it to another position if the car is not in regular use? That would be greatly appreciated.
Thank you.
340 Highgate.

That was pretty polite. I'd considered putting *Shift your shit-heap right now or I'll tow its arse* but didn't think it would go down that well. My handwriting was a bit dodgy, and it had taken a lot of concentration to control the adrenaline tremor. It wasn't helped by my still-sweaty hand slipping on the pen. But it was first things first — I hadn't showered and changed yet as I'd wanted to do this little task while I was in the right mood. I lifted the windscreen wiper up and popped the note underneath. There was a clean line in the dusty windshield where the wiper blade had been resting. Yet another indicator of how long the car had been stuck here — that, and an ever-growing colony of spiders and their architecture in the wing mirror. I had clapped eyes on the owner once. With a heap like that I'd have thought it belonged to a scruffy no-hoper, but the guy was actually quite tidy looking. It probably never occurred to him that leaving his car there could be a major pain to anyone else

— inconsiderate bastard.

That done, I was finally beginning to feel on a more even keel, at least dealing with the car was something I had a chance of remedying. The work situation was a different prospect entirely. I bounded up the front steps and headed inside to freshen up.

It was amazing how great food, fine wine and sparkling dinner conversation could lift a mood. Unfortunately, one of the topics du jour related to work. Uncle Phil had a turn talking with the detectives today, along with most of his unit, which shared the same building as the Pharmacy Department and Rose-Marie's sixth-floor lab. Social and Preventive Medicine was on the ground floor and he'd recognised her face from the photos as he'd seen her waiting for the lifts and recalled saying hi on occasion. He said she was very polite and seemed to work long hours. A view shared by everyone, it would seem. He hadn't been able to enlighten the detectives much more than that. He'd have been saved the bother if the interview had been this afternoon. Things were off in a new direction now.

There was the usual crap on offer on the television, more than thirty channels to choose from and nothing to watch. We didn't do reality TV. I failed to see the fascination in watching wannabe celebrities eating things that were bound to give you a dose of the shits or nightmares for the rest of your life. Besides, that sort of programme made me feel so embarrassed on their behalf I wanted to hide behind the sofa cushions. So by unanimous vote, we opted for a

DVD. Maggie and I had been given the task of choosing, so here we were, privileged to be in Uncle Phil's study, sorting through the crammed shelves that housed his rather extensive DVD collection.

'What about some vintage James Bond?' Maggie asked as she leaned over and pulled out what looked like the entire set in a boxed collection. 'Here we go, Sean Connery when he was young and hot.'

'Or we could have Sean Connery when he was old and hot, Phil's got *Rising Sun* here.'

'Oh, yes, Wesley Snipes, yummy.'

Uncle Phil's DVD collection was indeed impressive. As well as a penchant for James Bond, *The Saint* and *The Avengers*, it looked like he had the full collection of *CSI*, *Criminal Intent*, *Law and Order* as well as the British series *Waking the Dead*, *Silent Witness* and others. Despite knowing those type of pro-grammes never reflected the reality of policing, they entertained, so I would have to raid those at a later date. Well, the British ones anyway.

I rarely went into Uncle Phil's den and was always amazed by the sheer volume of things. Both he and Aunty Jude liked stuff. There were books on everything from architecture, to history, as well as his medical-related texts. Some looked pretty old and I'd bet a few were fairly valuable. He also had framed antique maps and a number of scale models. And he could afford what looked to be the latest in computer technology. He had dual LCD screens for his rather stonking-looking tower, a separate external hard drive and a few other bits of hardware, a laser printer and an inkjet. He also had a lightweight laptop for work and for around the house, which he could hook into the internet and the printers via their wireless network. It was a comprehensive set-up.

'No wonder he disappears in here for hours on end,' I said as I bent over to look at a limited-edition model Denny Hulme McLaren. 'Give me a big pile of food and I could spend weeks in here. This has got to be every bloke's idea of heaven, not to mention mine. Books, DVDs, music, computer, flash telly — I bet there's a drinks cabinet here somewhere too. All it needs is a pool table and a sign on the door: 'Girls keep out.''

'Oestrogen exclusion zone. Perhaps I could get him a sign made up for his birthday. He'd like that.' Maggie was working her way along the row of DVD spines.

'I'm sure your aunt would just love it. Mind you, I noticed she didn't volunteer to come in and choose.'

'I'm amazed we were allowed in. He's usually so precious about his man cave. I've got it, something Tarantino, how about *Pulp Fiction?*'

'Perfect, just what I need to wind down after a hard day solving murders. Blood, guts, drugs, guns, needles and funky dancing. Funny and gory. Hand it over, let's get out of here.'

16

I dragged my apprehensive body into the building to face another day, wondering what triviality I'd get to waste it on. Sifting animal poo for evidence? Fingerprinting the circus tent? Fetching the coffee? My only cheer-up, as it were, had been the fact that the note I'd popped under the rustang's windscreen wiper was gone this morning, so I might at least have a hope of a place to put my car when I got home. Wishful thinking.

I couldn't face trudging up the stairs, so cheated and took the elevator, which always felt a guilty sin. I had barely made it into the door of our room when I was accosted by Smithy looking positively gleeful — a big ask with his craggy face.

'What the hell are you so cheerful for?' I asked. 'And grown men shouldn't jiggle up and down like that, it makes it look like you need to go to the loo.'

'Sam, Sam, Sam,' he said, his beaming phizgog bobbing up and down in front of mine in synch with each repetition. 'You are going to love this, you are going to love this so much.'

'Not half as much as you do, by the look of it. So are you going to share the cause of your excitement, or are you going to leave me in suspense?' I tried to walk around him so I could chuck my bag under my desk.

'Suspense,' he said as he blocked my path.

'Do you like being hurt?' He can't have been tuned in to my mood, or else he would have gotten the hell out of my way.

'It depends who's doing the hurting, but no. DI Johns wants to see you, and when you get out, let's see if you're doing the jig too.'

I frowned at him, puzzled, shoved my bag into his hands and, with a what-have-I-got-to-lose wave, headed down to the DI's office. It must be something good to get Smithy that animated. He hadn't even been that excited when his wife had a massive box of choccies and a dozen Mars Bar muffins delivered to his desk for his birthday.

Having circumvented the array of printers and shredders outside in the hallway, I took a deep breath, knocked at the DI's door and walked in.

The DI had an odd look on his face. It hung between expressions, like he wasn't quite sure whether to be amused or pissed off. 'Constable Shephard, take a seat.'

I walked to the proffered chair and sat down. 'You wanted to talk to me?'

'Yes.' He cleared his throat. 'A rather interesting situation has come up concerning Mr Bennett, the circus owner.'

'Have you already established him as the murderer?' I asked. That was quick. Surely, the only way that could have happened would be with a confession, but to be frank, he didn't look the type to own up to dropping a fart let alone a murder or two.

'No, we didn't get very far with Mr Bennett at all and . . . ' he paused, as though he didn't want to finish the sentence. 'He refused to talk to us.' The DI had his hands clasped together, resting on the desk. His knuckles were rather white. 'It would appear that Mr Bennett has developed a particular liking for you. He has made it very clear he will only deal with the police if you are present.'

'Oh,' I said. Apart from my initial surprise, I had to swallow hard to force down the laugh that was trying to escape my innards. No wonder Smithy was so flaming excited. That was a huge Up Yours to the powers that be. Despite my best endeavours, my face cracked into a smile, which the DI noted with first a frown, and then a smile of his own. Perhaps he had a sense of humour, after all.

'Does that mean I'll get to be with the front-line team down at the circus?' I was starting to feel a bit fidgety myself.

'Well, yes.' The DI seemed reluctant to confirm my hopes. 'It seems to be the only way we'll get any cooperation out of Mr Bennett, but there will be strict conditions. You are only a trainee, so you will not be the main interviewer. You will be there as an observer. I don't want to hear of any interference from you.'

I was perfectly happy with that. Hell, hierarchical disapproval or not, I was relieved to be involved at the coalface in any way. No more drudge jobs, trifling trivialities and wild-goose chases. Thank you, Terry Bennett. Of course, I didn't trust the man as far as I could kick him. There was some other motive in play here. I was sure it wasn't a sudden wish for my company and feminine charms. I seemed to recall our last conversation was a bit tense. Then again, it could have been because of my feminine charm. Odds were, he saw me as a soft touch, a naive little thing he could manipulate and arouse sympathy in for the poor, picked-on circus people. Well, he was in for a bit of a surprise. Mind you, it could be quite useful to play along with his silly game for a while.

'When do we start?' I asked. If I'd had any sense, I'd have hidden my excitement, but a little of it was spilling out the sides.

'We leave in thirty minutes, after the morning briefing. And remember what I said. The detectives call the shots. Not a squeak from you.'

The urge to skip back to the office was pretty intense but I resisted it. Or at least for most of the way until I rounded the door and saw Smithy sitting on my desk, grinning like a demented monkey. My step just seemed to rise of its own accord until I reached him, danced a little jig and gave him a high five.

17

I wasn't sure what alarmed me more; standing next to the cage of a very restless lion, or Terry Bennett's reptilian smile when he clapped his eyes on me. Mind you, if I were in his position, I'd be feeling pretty pleased with myself too. My presence was a small but significant victory for him over the police. The knowledge wasn't lost on my associates either, judging by the amount of posturing going on. I found it all rather amusing, but had to check myself and remember we were here for a very serious reason. A young woman, Rose-Marie Bateman had been killed, and it was looking suspiciously like those involved had been busy leaving a trail of death in their wake.

Bennett seemed very keen to move us indoors and out of view, as we were directed into a large gazebo-like tent in front of the big top — I guessed it was a shelter area for spectators in the event of rain. Not that it would be an issue today; it was a stunner. I didn't really understand why we were here at the circus at all. I thought it would be easier for all concerned if these conversations took place at the station, but it wasn't my call.

DI Johns was in charge of the case, and knowing what he was like, and with an inkling of what Terry Bennett was like, these two would be like flint on steel. If we were lucky, the presence of Smithy and a couple of other detectives would serve as a damper. Then again, the fireworks could be entertaining.

I was surprised Bennett had chosen not to have a lawyer present. Perhaps he thought he was big enough and ugly enough to handle any offensive. Of course, it could have come down to being too tight to pay legal fees.

He shot the opening salvo. 'Right, can you run these utter crap allegations past me again?' Hands on hips, chest thrust out like it was waiting to have a medal pinned on it, he went on, 'I couldn't believe my bloody ears. Do you want to tell me exactly what you think someone from my circus has done and what the hell you expect me to do about it?'

The DI did the honours on behalf of the police. 'As I said last night, there is circumstantial evidence to suggest that a series of murders have occurred in towns where your circus has been visiting, so — '

'Oh, I get it. Because the circus is in town and we're a pack of bloody ratbags, thieves and criminals, it must be one of us killing people off. Is that how it goes? We get the blame for effing everything because we're a pack of murdering gypsy bastards?'

Déjà vu. I seem to have heard this argument very recently, verbatim. It was probably one he practised in front of the mirror for just the right occasion — like pulling out the race or religion card to make people back off. Didn't think it would work for him here though.

'As I said, the evidence is circumstantial, but

the coincidence of murders occurring at the same time you were in each town cannot be ignored. It is our duty to investigate this further and your full cooperation is expected.' It was, in an odd way, gratifying to see that the DI's tone of voice had the same effect on others that it had on me. I could see the pink spreading its way up Bennett's neck and into his gargoyle face.

'You expect me to cooperate fully when all I've had since I got into this stinking hole of a town has been harassment from you arseholes and hassles from the idiots who live here. I think you lot even sided up with the bloody protesters and enjoyed them having a go. You probably set the whole thing up.' This statement came complete with gesticulations, and as his hands waved in the vicinity of my face, I could feel my blood pressure ratchet up. Considering it was me who'd had to deal with the protesters — and pretty damned well, I thought — and me who had apparently harassed him, I didn't appreciate being referred to as an arsehole. He steamed on, oblivious. 'I think you like giving us all this bad publicity, making us look like a bunch of crooks, giving us a bad name. You've got it in for us, you have. You pigs, you're all the bloody same. So you can take yourself and your heavy-handed crew here and fuck off as far as I am concerned.'

The mercury shot through the top of my barometer. 'Mr Bennett,' I said, my voice rather strident. 'Firstly, I don't like being referred to as an arsehole. Secondly, there is absolutely no call for being so rude.' I hadn't planned on opening my mouth, but it had done so, all of its own accord. My index finger rose to twitch right in front of his eyeballs and I took a step closer. 'Bad manners and name-calling aren't going to get you anywhere, so you can kindly start to behave yourself. You're not a child, for Christ's sake.'

My God, I sounded like a bloody school-teacher. My mother would have been proud. My associates stood with their mouths open, gawping, but I didn't care. Why the hell should I put up with that kind of crap? 'You invited me to be here, Mr Bennett, you did. So don't you dare turn around and insult me. If you took one moment to think about it, and used your brain, you should be glad we've come down to see you and not dragged you and your motley crew off to the police station. Then there'd be plenty of bad publicity to worry about. So for God's sake grow up and cut it out.' I glared up at him, hands on hips, making it perfectly clear I expected an apology. It was eventually extended.

'Sorry,' he mumbled. 'It's just we get the same old shit everywhere we go and I get sick to death of it.' Well, accusation wasn't the only shit following them around this time. There seemed to be a few bodies too. It wasn't him who was getting sick to death. He seemed to have ignored that.

'Ahem.' The DI grabbed my attention before I got started again. 'The detective constable is right.' I must have made an impression; he finally got my rank right. 'At this stage we are making initial enquiries, not finger-pointing or accusing. The sooner we get cooperation, the sooner we can have the matter cleared up and you can get on with your business. If we don't get it, you'll give us no option but to close down your operation until we have finished with our investigations.'

'You can't do that. We have shows booked out every night. It would cost us a fortune to cancel. You'd ruin us.'

'Well, if you and your employees assist fully in our investigation, we should be able to avoid it. It's up to you.'

It's amazing what an incentive the almighty dollar and the bottom line can be. It prompted Bennett very quickly to oblige, however begrudgingly. 'What do you want me to do?' he asked in a voice laden with resentment.

It didn't go unnoticed by the DI. 'This is a very serious situation, Mr Bennett. For a start, we will need a full itinerary of where the circus has been and when. Days and times travelled. The times of your shows and a roster of who performed in each and when people had free time. We are going to need to speak to every member of the circus, performers and hands, and we'll need to see the passports of all your overseas acts. It would be helpful if you could encourage them to be accommodating, and then we can be done as soon as possible.'

'Christ, you don't ask for much; that's going to take for ever. We've got fifty-nine people here, and we've got to have rehearsals, as well as do the shows. How long is all this going to take?'

'It will take as long as we need it to. As you said, we have a lot of people to talk to, so if you work with us, we can get on with it and interview everyone down here. If we get any grief from anyone, then we'll take the whole show down to the station. Do you understand me?'

'Perfectly.' His chest had caved somewhat, and shoulders slumped. DI Johns' posture had puffed up as Terry Bennett's had deflated.

'Do your overseas acts speak English? Do you have interpreters?'

'They all have at least one whose English is good.'

'We're also going to need fingerprint and DNA samples from everyone.'

'Bloody hell. Do you want a pound of flesh too?' Mr Bennett did sarcasm with polished expertise.

DI Johns shot him a look that would have withered a concrete fencepost. 'You have the right to have a lawyer present for all of the interviews. Can you nominate one, or would you like me to provide a list of local lawyers in Dunedin?'

'I'm not paying money to any blood-sucking lawyer. No one here has done anything wrong. I can assure you, you're wasting your time, and ruining us in the process. No, no lawyers. I'll sit in with each of my people — make sure you lot don't talk them into a corner.' It was so comforting to see the regard with which he held the police.

'I'm afraid you can't do that. You are a potential suspect yourself, so you will not be able to be present at the interviews with your crew.'

'Oh, fucking hell, you bastard.' Terry Bennett

89

spat the insult out. 'You think I killed all those people, do you?'

I waited for the explosion from DI Johns but was disappointed. The DI showed great restraint and didn't take umbrage at the querying of his parentage. 'No,' he said with exaggerated calm, 'it is a conflict of interest to have you present at the interviews, so to protect everyone's right to proper counsel and a fair interview, you cannot be present, and I'd recommend very strongly they have a lawyer. Especially if some of them do not speak good English. You wouldn't want any of your people to unwittingly incriminate themselves because they didn't understand the questions, would you?'

'Well, no.'

'And in the event that one of them, or some of them were brought to trial, we have to ensure that procedures have been properly followed.'

'In the event one or some of them were brought to trial because they'd killed anyone, they'd have to deal with me first.' Although Terry Bennett tried to deliver this line with great bravado, I could see the bluster had been sucked out of him and the full realisation of what was about to happen and its ramifications were sinking in. Besides the huge disruption to his operation and, no doubt, a fair amount of public scrutiny, he had to face the possibility that one or more of his company were responsible for murder. He'd take that pretty personally. Also, once word got out the police were investigating the circus, I imagined gate sales would diminish somewhat. This must have occurred to him too.

'Okay, so if we cooperate fully with this, will you guys keep the fact Darling Brothers is under suspicion a secret from the press? If it gets out, we'll be crucified. No one will bring their kids along to see the show if they think we could be involved in this. You're still supposed to be innocent until proven guilty in this country, so it's your duty to protect our rights too, you know.'

I looked at the DI to see what his reaction would be. I'd have thought he'd get some sick satisfaction from destroying a man like Bennett.

'I can't make any guarantees. Word has a way of sneaking out on these things. But I do think it is in the public's and the police's best interests for this to be as discreet as possible. Your set-up here is very open and visible, so we don't want any scenes if we can avoid it. I'll see what we can do.'

Perhaps I'd underestimated the DI. But he did have a very good point. We'd already had to deal with hot-headed animal-rights activists and adolescent stupidity. The last thing we needed now was a mob making judgements and meting out their own form of justice.

18

My eyes homed in on the bridge of the man's nose. His face was adorned with a vast array of piercings that looked like a bad case of metallic acne. But it was the dumbbell through the bridge of his nose that drew my sick fascination. Sick being the operative word. My stomach gave a lurch whenever he twitched his nose, which unfortunately for me was with the frequency of a rat sniffing out lunch. Every time my eyes went to engage his, they skewed off target and found themselves back on his nose. It was fortunate, then, that I wasn't conducting the interview and therefore wasn't the focus of his attention, otherwise I would have come across as unforgivably rude. Somehow, I didn't rate this guy as a suspect. It was difficult to imagine someone so identifiable committing the crimes, unless he was very careful and wore a balaclava to hide his appearance. If it came to it, we'd have a hell of a time trying to find comparable people for a line-up. Any witness would pick this guy out in an instant.

I would have loved to have been the one asking the questions, but as usual, I was riding shotgun and had been given the brief to be a warm body in the room. A warm body with a good memory and a pen and pad to record the interview. Being secretary was a girl's job, after all. It was no surprise as to who took great delight in informing me of my role. Although DI Johns had to suffer the indignity of Terry Bennett's insistence on my presence, he still found a way to remind me of my station in life. One small consolation was I didn't have to type the interviews up, but I tried to keep my scrawl as legible as possible for the lovely bevy of typists at the station. You couldn't pay me to do their job. It felt like a bit of a joke though. In this age of electronic wizardry and digital everything, why the hell were we still taking notes with something as archaic as a pen and paper? Modern policing at its budget-restricted best.

The interviews had been set up in a couple of the residential trailers and this one was incredibly plush and comfortable. It also had Tardis-like qualities. From the outside, it looked the size of two police cells max, but inside, it felt almost palatial. Wood-panelled cupboards adorned one wall, with a space for an enormous LCD television. Even a circus caravan could manage better technology than we did, it seemed. At one end, was a kitchen larger and with more bench space than my old one and a damned sight more modern. Running away with the circus might not be such a hardship after all, I thought. I poked my head through the door to look at the sleeping quarters and they were just as roomy. It must have been a family living here as there were a number of children's toys scattered about. In the background I could hear a washing machine in the last throes of the spin cycle. It all had an unexpected level of luxury, although I imagined wet days with children cramped in here would soon take the gloss off.

Despite my fascination for the interviewee's facial decorations I had to suppress a yawn. Bennett's insistence on my presence had proven to be a backhanded gift. This was the fifth person through this morning and I was already struggling to keep up the concentration levels. I recalled Terry Bennett's comment that they had fifty-odd staff and cringed. It was going to be a long few days. I fervently hoped we'd be able to eliminate the majority very quickly, just to keep me sane. A bit selfish, I know, especially as I'd been whinging mightily about being left out all the time. DI Johns was getting the last laugh. It was beginning to feel more like a punishment to be here than not.

Roll on lunchtime.

19

Twenty-four down, God knows how many to go. My hand was cramped into a permanent claw. Oh, how I wished we could just record the damned things. After a day of hard-out questioning, we were none the wiser, although we did have three confessions to possession of pot, one illegal overstayer and, unusually, one confession to unlawful connection with an animal. Ugh. The animal-rights lobby would have a field day if that one got out.

The interviews weren't proceeding as quickly as we'd have liked. Many were drawn out by the language barrier and the need for interpreters. Over half of the company were overseas acts from places such as Mongolia and South America. It was vital that people understood fully what they were being questioned about, or else misinformation would confuse the case and their lawyers could jump on it as a technical out. I suspected it was a degree of confusion that had led to the rather distasteful confession involving the miniature pony.

There had been concern voiced among the CIB that the killer or killers would bolt now the police were investigating, but for the moment all circus members were present and accounted for. Fear of what Mr Bennett would do to them probably helped there. I supposed if they did do a runner, at least we'd know who we were looking for.

It was also a case of so far so good as far as publicity was concerned. The police presence here had not attracted any media attention as yet. The protests and student pranks from Friday provided a valid excuse for our presence. In an ironic way, Mr Bennett should have felt grateful towards them. Yeah, right.

Cassie the elephant was in her usual spot beside the big top, in full view of the public. That position would have been carefully chosen to act as a kid magnet — aw, Mummy, look at the elephant, can we go see her? Can we go and see the circus, Mum? Come on, can we go? Whining children were a wonderful sales and marketing tool, and Terry Bennett's product placement made the most of their pulling power.

'Hello, old girl. Hi Cassie,' I called out. Her body didn't budge, but her eyes moved to find me. I didn't know if it was the standard look for elephants, but to me she looked melancholy and horribly bored. Her only company were the miniature ponies corralled next door. The ankle strap and chain would have contributed. She was roped off to keep the public at a respectful distance, and there was an additional electric fence a metre within the rope one. I guessed it wouldn't look good to zap kids who got a bit too close. I'd been told Cassie was generally amenable, but occasionally prone to grumpiness. Who wouldn't be in her situation? I was a farm girl, and in New Zealand we were accustomed to having our animals roaming about freely in huge lush, green paddocks, grazing at will. We were proud of our wide-open spaces and free-range approach to animal welfare, so to see such a large, magnificent creature such as Cassie chained up rankled. Surely, someone could at least have cleaned up the poo. And to see the lions and monkeys claustrophobically caged made me straight-out angry. I could understand why the activists lobbied to free them. Mind you, freedom wasn't always everything it was cracked up to be. Every time I walked through the halls of the Otago Museum I ventured up into the Animal Attic. I'd wander its Victorian-style displays of taxidermy heaven, and stop for a look at Sonia and Sultan, escapees from Circus Carlos during its notorious visit to Lawrence way back in the seventies. The lions' bid for emancipation had stuffed them, literally. Thinking about these magnificent creatures brought to mind visions of African savannahs and herds of wild animals freely roaming the plains. The stark contrast of Cassie's confinement was pitiful. If elephant body language was anything like human body language, she was as miserable as hell. How on earth could you cheer up an elephant? I made a point of doing my bit by coming for a chat whenever possible.

'I'm off, back to the station now. You take care and I'll see you tomorrow.' I'd try and have a word with her handler in the morning, see if I could give her a pat or a rub down. She was a tad bigger than Dotty, my old horse back home, and hopefully not as prone to farting, but I was sure I'd manage. Her handler was on the interview list first thing, which would give me a chance for a chat. I didn't think Mr Bennett would mind. He'd think it meant I was warming to them all and was on his side. Not bloody likely.

20

'Gidday, sunshine. How's your day been?' Maggie wandered into my room. Well, it was my room in name only. In reality, it was still the domain of its previous occupant, the talented Caitlin, as evidenced by the array of skiing posters and paraphernalia adorning every available space on the walls. There was also a significant display of trophies, medals and silverware on the bookshelf, testament to the high level of achievement the Kershaw girls had attained in their chosen sport. Caitlin's twin, also a world-class skier, had a similar overachiever look happening in her room. On the plus side, Caitlin and Lisette had achieved the ultimate of earning sports scholarships to the University of Colorado, so not only did their parents avoid having to pay a small ransom for their tertiary education and ongoing sports costs, they no longer had to be the long-suffering, but supportive taxi service to every freezing-cold, ice-ridden and accessible-only-by-goat-track ski field in the country. I didn't do skiing. As far as I was concerned, snow was just a damned nuisance that, when I was home on the farm, always came at just the right time to kill off the lambs and cut off the electricity. If pressed, I'd consent to building a snowman, but I failed to see the fascination.

It wasn't all skiing, skiing, skiing for the girls

though. This room had a corner shrine devoted to Brad Pitt. Apparently, even teenage sporta-holics had hormones.

'Well, my day started off well, deteriorated by noon and degraded into the truly tedious by mid-afternoon,' I eventually replied with a half-suppressed yawn.

'It was one better than mine then, which skipped the starting off well bit and jumped directly to tedium.' Maggie plonked herself down on the bed.

'After all that time looking forward to being a student, the reality bites, huh?'

'No, no, I'm loving it, actually. It's just this morning's lab seemed a little dull for a gal who's spent her working life playing with microscopes, animal body parts and cool electronic equipment. Their idea of a lab and mine are a little bit different. I'm sure it will improve as we get further into the course.'

Maggie had ditched the bright lights of the meat-processing plant at Mataura for a change in direction and further education at the University of Otago. She was indulging her fascination for human behaviour and studying psychology. I had no idea what she meant to do with it when she'd finished, but for now, she'd escaped her former trapped-in-rural-purgatory life for the big smoke — Dunedin, or Dunners as she affectionately referred to the place. I must admit to having been tempted by some of the courses on offer myself, but the extra papers I had to do for detective training kept me more than busy enough.

'You studying tonight?' I asked, as I pulled some clothes out of the wardrobe.

'I should be, but I could easily be tempted by a better offer.'

'That's displaying a complete lack of dedication, you know.'

'Maybe, but I can blame it on you. You shouldn't tempt me with distractions when you know I'm so easily led. You're being irresponsible. Great friend you've turned out to be.'

'Think of it as saving your sanity. A mental health break. Anyway, there's a do for one of the work guys, a fortieth birthday at the Trough and Porker, and I don't feel like flying solo. You should come along and meet some more of the gang. You never know, you might score yourself a date.'

'Oh yeah, 'cos I want to date a copper.' They say sarcasm is the lowest form of wit. Maggie had a first-class Honours in it. 'I happen to know what it's like living with the police. I had your fine example, remember. There's no way in hell I'd ever date a policeman. God, no.' The statement was accompanied by a shudder.

'We're not all that bad.'

'Right, none of you are overbearing, work-obsessed, pathologically suspicious individuals who can't switch off from the job? If policemen aren't that bad, why don't you date one?'

I threw Maggie the look. 'You know the golden rule: you don't screw the crew. Besides, most of them are already taken.'

'By the love-blind who haven't learned yet?'

'That's the one. They say there's only one job

worse than being a copper, and that's being attached to a copper.'

'I'm sure their kids are thrilled too, especially when mum or dad turns up to break up the underage booze fest party they weren't supposed to be at.' Maggie gestured towards the wardrobe door. 'So what are you going to wear?'

'I take that as a yes, you're coming?'

She smiled. 'Yes, I'll sacrifice my precious study time to spare you the horror of feeling alone and abandoned by your friends.'

'So very big of you. I can tell it will be a major imposition. It's a casual night, so jeans, jumper, nothing flash.'

'You're not out to impress, then?'

'Nah, got to give the other girls a chance sometimes.'

21

'You're a rat-fink, two-faced cow.'

My outburst made Maggie laugh all the more. So to further demonstrate my disapproval, I gave her a thump on the arm, which resulted in her having to grab the nearest tabletop to stop from falling over in hysterics. 'Don't think I don't know what you did up there,' I said, waving my finger in front of her nose. 'It's okay for you with your little-Miss-Leading-Lady-diva-la-de-da perfect singing voice.' It must have been the alcohol, because I couldn't think of any other way Maggie could have enticed me up on to that stage let alone sing karaoke with her. And that was the point — it was supposed to have been *with* her, but I saw how far the bitch kept the microphone away from her mouth, so all the poor sods listening got was my voice coming over loud and unfortunately clear. It was also rather unfortunate that a large number of the audience were my work colleagues, who were by now in no doubt as to my singing inabilities. My reputation did have one fighting chance — Sergeant Frater was now onstage butchering 'Unchained Melody.' Surely that would displace my efforts in their collective memories.

'Ah, God, you were funny, I can't believe you fell for that again.' Maggie had finally managed to exert enough control over herself to be able to speak, but her words came interspersed with gasps of air. Even I had to smile at the reference to 'again'. 'Gotcha. Man, you're gullible. That, or it was the beer singing, and if it was the Speights, it was flat.'

'Oh, ha-de-bloody-ha. I suppose you think you're clever. It's all your fault. You shouldn't have given me that second one. You know what I'm like. One glass and I'm happy, two glasses and I'm anybody's.'

'For God's sake, get this girl another drink.' Unless Maggie's voice had suddenly broken and cranked down to baritone, this wasn't hers. I swung around to see if my memory banks served me correctly. It did indeed belong to the face I suspected.

'Paul, hi. What are you doing here?' I tugged down on the bottom of my top which had ridden up a bit. 'You didn't see my . . . ' I gestured towards the stage. 'Did you?'

'Haven't expanded your repertoire any, I see. Still doing 'The Midnight Special'.'

Oh shit, he had seen me. And I didn't need a mirror to know there was a rather full-on flush rising up my face. Paul Frost was a detective from Gore and I'd had a fair amount to do with him in my Mataura days — with work, that was, not in any romantic sense. Paul was your consummate ladies' man. He looked a more rugged and, dare I say, sexier version of Ben Affleck, and he knew it. All his female work colleagues seemed to fall for his charms and had made fools of themselves vying for his attentions, but not me. He'd tried it on a couple of times, but didn't seem to get the hint. I wasn't interested. I didn't do egos.

'Maggie, lovely to see you as always. I gather you're still leading your friend astray. Can't believe she fell for that trick again, you must love being around someone so gullible.'

'Easy target, keeps me amused,' Maggie said, her face as pink as mine felt. She'd never admit it, but she was a sucker for his spell too. 'Anyway, I'll leave you two alone to catch up, I'm sure you've got lots to talk about.' She raised her eyebrows at me as she spoke, with one of those knowing expressions on her face, then the traitorous cow disappeared into the crowd.

'Can I get you another drink?' Paul asked, indicating towards the bar.

I wasn't one to turn down a free beverage. 'God, yes. Please. I think I deserve one after my public humiliation.'

'After that performance, I think the whole bar deserves one.'

I thumped him one on the arm, for being so bloody rude.

'Ow, hey now, be nice. I'm the one shouting the drink, remember,' he said, rubbing his arm with great exaggeration. 'Before you assaulted me, I was going to tell you how good it was to see you, and that you looked particularly lovely tonight, but I think I've changed my mind now. I'd forgotten about your violent streak.'

'Keep up the rude comments and I'll show you just how violent.' Lovely, my arse.

'Promises, promises,' he said. 'Now you're just teasing me.'

Trust Paul to twist things around.

'Don't flatter yourself, sunshine,' I shot back. I'd forgotten how annoying he could be, I thought, as I watched him head to the bar to get our drinks. Fortunately there wasn't much of a wait.

'So what tears you away from the den of iniquity that is Gore to the big-city lights of Dunedin?' I asked. I'd hardly call the Trough and Porker big city lights, but it would do in a crunch.

'Court case,' he said, as he passed me my beer and moved towards a table. I popped my drink on the top of the leaner while I clambered up onto the barstool, never an elegant process.

'Anything exciting?'

'Well that depends if you find fraud exciting or not. I suspect not. It doesn't do a hell of a lot for me.'

'Corporate stuff?'

'If you could call any business in Gore big enough to be corporate. Yeah, it's the usual; greedy buggers who think everyone else is too thick to notice the ledgers aren't quite what they should be or that the money is haemorrhaging out of the place.'

'Don't you just love it when the arrogant take a tumble?' He didn't notice the barb.

'Yes, but we've got to prove it in court, and all its associated rigmarole. So here I am.' He took a sip from his beer, and then fixed me in the eye with one of his intense looks. I sometimes wondered if he practised them in the mirror, as he seemed fully aware of the effect his set of crystalline blue eyes had on the fairer sex.

'You're looking well, Dunedin seems to be suiting you.'

My hand drifted up and brushed away an errant lock of hair. 'Thanks. It's the fresh sea air, as opposed to the charming rendering aroma from the Mataura meat works. Slight improvement, don't you think?' I certainly didn't miss that element of rural life. 'Speaking of Mataura, do you think they miss me?'

He threw back his head with a ha-ha. 'Oh, you're referred to often, but I'm not sure I could say it's in entirely complimentary terms.'

No surprise there. I didn't endear myself when I managed to expose a major conspiracy that saw a few community leaders enjoying the pleasure of Her Majesty's hospitality for the next few years. It wasn't them so much I was thinking about though. 'How's Lockie getting on nowadays?'

Paul flicked his look on to low beam and sat back. It was probably bad form to ask him about my ex, but I had to know. 'About as good as can be expected. Did you know he was moving on?'

'No.' Though I was hardly surprised. His wife had been murdered and he had a young daughter to think of. I'd be getting out too. Come to think of it, I did. 'Is he heading over to Queenstown to be nearer Gaby's parents?'

'Yeah. They've jacked him up with a job, and Gaby's mum will look after Angel for him during the day. A new start.'

Good, I thought. They'd have great support in Queenstown, and Leonore would love having her granddaughter close to hand.

'Greetings, young Sam.' I looked up to see Smithy arrive at the table, beer in hand. 'Am I interrupting?'

'Smithy, hi, no. Come, join us.' I didn't think these two had met, so I did the introductions. 'Detective Malcolm Smith, this is Detective Paul Frost, an old colleague from Gore.' The men shook hands and I was amused to note they completed the usual caveman sizing-up exercise that went with these occasions.

'You're a long way from home, detective. What brings you to Dunedin?' Smithy asked, rather formally.

'Please, call me Paul. I'm up for a court case, fraud, so who knows how long it could take. Hopefully no longer than a week, so I don't have to bug Sam here by hanging around her too much.'

'I can see how that would be a trial.' They shared a look, and Smithy almost smiled.

'You're familiar with her charms, then. Are you the poor unfortunate that has to babysit her and hold her hand?'

'Paul,' I interjected, 'be nice, I don't need to be babysat by anyone, thank you very much.'

'I don't know, I seem to recall you're pretty good at getting yourself into trouble. I bet she's done that up here too,' he said to Smithy. 'Has she gotten up everyone's nose yet?'

'Rubbish. And I don't get up people's noses.'

'How do you explain that DI Johns guy, then? I seem to recall you were so far up his nose all people could see were your shoes sticking out of his nostrils.'

'You are so full of crap, Paul Frost. I get on fine with DI Johns, thank you.' A Pinocchio porky if ever there was one. 'I think I've — '

'Ahem,' Smithy cleared his throat. 'I think I'll leave you two to it, then. You seem to have a bit to talk about. Nice to meet you, Paul.' With that he picked up his glass, gave me an odd look I couldn't quite interpret and disappeared into the crowd.

Paul was wearing a smug expression when I turned my attention back to him. 'He fancies you,' he said.

'Who? Smithy?'

'Who else? Of course Smithy. He likes you. He was jealous.'

'Don't be so bloody absurd. Who'd be jealous of you?' I had to admit he had seemed a bit frosty towards Paul, which wasn't like him at all. 'Anyway, he's happily married, and got kids.'

'That doesn't mean a thing. I tell you, you need to watch him. He's got the hots for you.'

That notion was straight-out daft. 'Paul Frost, don't be so juvenile. You are so full of crap. Just because you can't keep your hormones under control doesn't mean that every man out there is on the prowl for anything in a skirt.' The alcohol must have loosened my tongue a tad. Considering I didn't know Paul that well, I was giving him a fair amount of rather personal stick. But he deserved it, making stupid allegations like that. Smithy was a work colleague and a friend. So was his wife. He was an honourable kind of a guy. Of course he wasn't interested in me like that.

'Oh, you are defensive. Hit a raw nerve, did I?' I gave him a look that could have withered an ocean. He must have realised he'd pushed this one a bit far because he quickly picked up his beer and looked elsewhere as he took a draught. 'I hear you guys may have something big on your hands. The case sounds interesting.'

Nice save.

'You got that one right.'

'We should hook up while I'm in town, go grab dinner or something. We could talk about what's happening in your case. It's got to be more fun than my fraud caper.'

It was my turn to laugh. He'd got me a bit too riled even to contemplate the notion. Why would I want to spend time with a juvenile, egotistical larrikin like him? All he seemed to do was irritate the crap out of me.

I slid down off my stool, grabbed my drink from the table and gave him a parting shot as I went to search out Maggie. 'No way. You've gone and stuffed yourself way too far up my nose for that.'

22

'How's the head this morning?' Maggie asked, as I walked into the kitchen to hunt out breakfast and a serious dose of caffeine.

'It's fine, I didn't have that much to drink. Weeknight. Besides, I need to keep a clear head, or more to the point keep awake, with more of those flaming interviews today. Yesterday's dragged on for ever. It's going to be a long haul.' I looked in Maggie's direction and made an appraisal of last night's effects. She didn't look too shabby. Mind you, her version of looking like a wreck was more chic than I could muster on a good day. 'What about you?'

'Oh, I'm good,' she said. 'Raring to go, in fact. Got the fun stuff happening today. We're into the forensic psychology part of the course where we get to see what makes the nutters tick.'

That actually sounded appealing.

'Do you want to swap? I'll go check out the inner workings of the nutters and you can listen to the lurid confessions of the circus folk.' Anything to help me figure out what was going on in the head of the nutter who took it upon himself to violently kill and dump a young woman in a river. The vision of Rose-Marie, face down in the Leith popped into my head and my body responded with its obligatory shudder.

'Oh, Sam, someone walk on your grave?' Aunty Jude wandered into the kitchen, a vision

111

of meticulous style and grooming. I wish my family carried the gene responsible for that degree of elegance.

'No, not mine,' I said, as I sorted out an industrial-size coffee, the dreaded instant variety, not the flash stuff. 'You're looking lovely, where are you off to today?'

The responding bashful smile showed she wasn't immune to the admiration. 'I'm doing my stint at the hospice this morning. And, thank you for the compliment. She's such a nice girl, isn't she, Maggie? You can stay in our home as long as you like.' Jude had filled her days up admirably since the girls had flown for foreign shores, leaving a corresponding twin-shaped hole in her life. There was the volunteering at the hospice, she delivered Meals on Wheels once a week in the Mercedes and she'd become heavily involved with Altrusa, the community service organisation populated by already overworked professional and business women. She was also a lady who lunched and seemed to have an inordinate number of friends on the wine-and-dine or coffee-and-catch-up circuit.

'Sam met up with a tall, handsome stranger at the bar last night,' Maggie said, with a positively salacious tone.

'Ooh, Sam, tell me more. This sounds good,' Aunty Jude said.

'Don't believe a word she says. Anyway, he wasn't a stranger.'

'But he was handsome?'

'Well, kind of.' Paul Frost seemed to think he was, so that was all that mattered. 'One of the

Gore guys was up, that was all, and Maggie's being a stirrer. She can't comment because she was being rather chatty with a few of my colleagues, if I recall correctly. A number of them were giving her the eye.'

'Maggie? It's about time you had a boyfriend again; pretty girl like you shouldn't be alone.' A touch of pink infused Maggie's face. I was pleased to see that aunts could be just as embarrassing as mothers. 'I'm sure Sam's workmates are nice young men. When do we get to meet one?'

'Not in a million years. Uh-uh, not ever,' Maggie said, shaking her head. 'I don't do policemen.'

'Who *do* you do, then, Maggs?' Aunty Jude asked with a mischievous glint.

Maggie's feigned shock and that question — delivered in Aunty Jude's posh voice — made me laugh, unfortunately with a snort.

'God,' she sighed. 'It's been so long I'd settle for anyone with a pulse.'

'Surely there must be some earnest, brooding student types that take your fancy?' I asked. 'All foppish hair and piercing, intelligent eyes.'

'Yes, the campus is littered with them. But the psych ones take themselves so damned seriously. And they're a bit skinny and pasty looking — too many Dunedin suntans. I need to find me some bronzed Grecian God with buns of steel.'

'Can't say I've seen many of those around here, and if I did, I'd race you for him.'

'Well, you can't be looking that hard, then. Haven't you checked out the butt attached to your Detective Frost?'

'Firstly, he's not my Detective Frost, and secondly, I wasn't looking at his butt.' I had actually noted its merits, but I was never going to admit it to Maggie, or him for that matter. 'If he does it for you, you're most welcome to him. I don't think he's attached. I could set you up on a date, if you like.'

'Like I said, I don't do cops, and I believe his gaze falls elsewhere.'

★ ★ ★

If I had any sense, I thought, I'd walk down to work. It would only take twenty minutes or so. It would also save the usual parking drama at the other end. But, damn it, I owned my own car for the first time in my life and by God I was going to use it. My zippy black Honda Hatch was parked a block away and around the corner from the house, due to the usual scrum for parking and the heap of crap still hogging the space out the front, despite my best efforts. I hopped in the driver's seat and was putting the keys in the ignition when I spotted the piece of paper tucked under the windscreen wiper. Driving with it wedged there, flapping in the breeze, would annoy the crap out of me, so I got out and grabbed it from under the wiper. I unfolded it, curious as to what vacuum cleaner, Dunedin band or home beauty product was being peddled this time.

Fuck you bitch.

I was so taken aback I almost dropped it. I

114

checked over my shoulder, pulse racing, and then screwed the note up and tossed it into the gutter before jumping back into the safety of the car. Who on earth would write something that awful? Then I remembered the little note I had left under someone else's wiper blade. Surely not? I'd been very polite and signed it from the general household, not specifically from me. It was carefully non-confrontational, so as not to offend. This was personal. Besides, my car was parked around the corner from the house, so the owner of the crap-heap wouldn't know it was mine. Maybe it was random?

Or not.

This was stupid; it was just a note, someone having a sick joke. The way my heart was thumping away in my chest was plain ridiculous. Maybe I should tell someone? Nah, this was small fry in light of the murders and everything else going on around here. Some idiot's idea of fun wasn't worth a mention. In fact, the guys at work would probably just laugh and tell me not to be such a sissy. That logic didn't do anything to quell my hyperactive nervous system though.

I got out of the car, and with slightly shaky hands, went over to the gutter and retrieved the screwed-up note. Maybe it would pay to keep hold of it, just in case.

23

There was something about Zarvo the clown that set my crap-o-meter jangling. He was hiding something. A lot of them had been hiding something, you could tell that by the overt signs of nervousness, sweating, hand rubbing, strained laughter. It was to be expected of people, many foreign, caught up in a large police investigation. I'd be feeling edgy too. But with him there was something else. He was a clown in the show, but didn't look very clown-like today, a clean-shaven (over his entire head except for the eyebrows), unremarkable-looking man dressed in a clean white T-shirt and blue jeans. Like all the circus people we'd encountered so far, with the exception of Terry Bennett and the fat lady, he had a fit and muscular physique. He was probably accustomed to hiding under half an inch of make-up and an absurd wig, so maybe conversation undisguised made him uncomfortable. But he still seemed too measured, too careful in his choice of words. I didn't think it could be put down entirely to language difficulties. He hadn't requested a translator and his Slavic accent was pretty broad, which the others didn't seem to have noticed.

I listened as Smithy asked the now familiar string of questions about his whereabouts.

'I was at rehearsals in afternoon, then I was doing dogs. My job is look after dogs. They part of my act. Then we eat, then do show.'

The dogs in question came into the way-too-cute category. White balls of charming fluff Bichon Frise. I recalled seeing three of the little blighters attired in hats and waistcoats rehearsing some pretty slick moves. I was sure they'd be a hit with the crowd.

'Is there anyone else who could vouch for your whereabouts?'

'Serge with me the whole time. He do dogs too. We in same caravan.'

It had been pretty much the same for all of the interviews. The circus was a close-knit place and it was all business. I'd often fantasised about running off to the circus when I was a girl, anything to get me out of helping with the milking and the inhumane early-morning starts, or my worst of the worst, docking the lambs. Seeing these guys in action had changed my mind about it being the great romantic adventure. They worked bloody hard. There were constant rehearsals, cleaning, looking after the grounds and maintenance. Terry Bennett ran a tight ship and kept them busy. Which was a good thing for most of them, as they were busy together. Constant companionship meant rock-solid alibis. There wasn't much time for privacy, rest and relaxation, let alone slipping off to kill young women.

The other thing that had been bugging me, apart from Zarvo, was that Rose-Marie's body had been found in a place that seemed carefully chosen. I ran past there at least once a week, and I had never taken any notice of the path down to the river, which suggested a bit of local knowledge on the part of the killer. The circus had only been in town two days when she was murdered. Those two days would have been full on with setting up camp and preparing for the first show on the Friday night. It had been a busy night in Dunedin: rugby at the stadium, circus at the Oval, body in the Leith. The walk from the circus to the Botanic Garden would easily take half an hour at least, probably closer to forty minutes. When would one of them have had the time? And how would they know to take her there in the first place? I made a note to myself to check out each person for previous visits or knowledge of Dunedin. Or even friends or relatives here. Perhaps they had help. Perhaps they drove or biked.

Zarvo's interview was over. His photograph was taken and then he was exchanged for yet another member of the company.

Why did I feel like this was getting us nowhere, fast?

24

'So, when are you going to realise this is all a bloody great waste of time?' Terry Bennett had come over to watch as I finished giving Cassie the elephant a rub down, under the wary supervision of Jamal, her keeper. He'd been rather surprised at my request to get so up close and personal, but, after consulting with the boss, had consented. It was good public relations, after all. And for my part, after having my hand cramped around a pen and my brain cramped around mind-numbing tedium, it felt good to stretch my fingers and tune out with the rhythm of rubbing.

'Cassie doesn't think it's a waste. I think she's enjoying it, Mr Bennett. Aren't you, Cassie?' I knew she was enjoying it. She was leaning into the brushstrokes and I could feel a deep vibration coming from her body that reminded me of a cat purring. She seemed a lot more relaxed. So was I. It was mutually beneficial. It wasn't quite the same as rubbing down a horse and admittedly, seeing as I wasn't the tallest of people and she was fairly sizeable, I was only reaching the lower half of her body for now. But I loved the feel of Cassie's skin, dry, rough and with the texture of cabbage-tree bark. She smelled kind of warm and earthy.

Terry Bennett managed a smile before continuing on his purpose. He wasn't easily deflected. 'I told you I keep a tight watch on my crew, there are no shirkers. We've nothing to do with these murders. You haven't found anything, have you? You're on the wrong trail here and you know it.'

I put down the brush, patted Cassie on the rump and moved over to where he was standing. 'Well, Mr Bennett, even you would have to admit some in your company are not entirely blameless. There's been a fair amount of narcotics and banned substances found and some very unsavoury behaviour towards some of your animals.'

His face creased into a scowl and I noted his fists clenching and reclenching. I was expecting a tirade back when I felt a soft thump on my shoulder. I turned my head to the left and saw a slightly bristly, mottled-looking proboscis parked there. I laughed. I didn't know elephants could sneak up. When I turned right around to look, Cassie had stretched out to the full extent of her chain to reach me.

'You feeling left out, old girl?' I gave her trunk a wee tickle.

'Looks like you've made a friend,' Bennett said. He cocked his head. 'Maybe I underestimated you. Elephants aren't too bad a judge of character.'

'I'll take that as a compliment,' I said, ridiculously pleased with Cassie's gesture. 'Look, the bottom line is a young woman is dead, as are several other people that could be related to this case. We will follow every lead to its conclusion to find the killer or killers. We would be doing the victim a huge wrong if we didn't. This isn't about you or your circus, and you know it. It's about accountability. Whoever did this has to be brought to justice. Surely you must understand that.'

'Of course I do. Someone's got to pay, My concern is that my circus gets trampled on in the process. Public image is a fickle thing. You've seen it yourself with the protesters and stupid bloody pranksters. The circus gets a bum enough rap anyway. We don't need to give them any more ammunition. I just want to make sure we get the same courtesy as any other group of people in this situation. You know, innocent until proven guilty, which we won't be. The last thing we need is any more bloody media attention to fuel the fire.'

25

'The thick and smelly stuff has truly hit the fan this morning,' Smithy said as I arrived in the squad room ready for another fun-filled day at the office. It remained to be seen whether the office in question would be here or in a tent. 'Your Mr Bennett's going to be a bit pissed off.'

'Why, what's happened?' I asked.

Smithy held up the front page of the *Otago Daily Times* and there, splattered across it, was the headline: 'Circus makes a killing'

'Oh crap, that can't be good.' We had the paper delivered at home and I usually checked the headlines and laid claim to the cryptic crossword puzzle before heading off to work, but I'd been late back from my run this morning and missed the juicy bits.

I went over and grabbed the proffered paper to read some more. 'Jesus, they've even said that the murder may be related to the string of unsolveds up the country. How the hell did they find out about that? I thought that information was top secret.' This added to the twisting sensation in my gut that hadn't resolved itself since I'd found a second note under my windscreen this morning. This one was the same paper, but blank. Somehow, that felt worse than being sworn at. I was considering having a quiet word to Smithy about it if the opportunity arose, but it still felt a bit wimpy to feel so fazed by such a little thing.

'It was supposed to be,' Smithy said. 'Someone's going to be very unhap — '

'Meeting, first floor, now.' DI Johns' manner gave no room for discussion as he leaned around our doorway and roared. Even the big boys flinched. 'Move it.' That was all the instruction we got — and all we needed.

'I'd guess that was the unhappy someone.' I said, after I'd scraped myself off the ceiling.

We followed the stream of obedient CIB folk down the stairwell to the first-floor briefing room. The chairs were already taken, so we stood around the side. Looked as though everyone in the building had been summoned for this one. The lights, which were usually dimmed in here for presentations, glared relentlessly.

DI Johns stormed up to the front, then, with great drama, unfurled his copy of the newspaper with a whip-like crack and held it up for all to see. 'Now what the bloody hell is this?'

Even I was shocked to hear him use that kind of language in front of the whole staff. He looked as though he could blow a vein.

'How the hell did the press find out about this?'

Silence.

'Someone has been talking and I want to know who.'

I had a flashback to school assembly and Principal McLeary holding up a cigarette butt, demanding: 'Someone has been smoking around the bike sheds and I want to know who.' Would we be made to sit here for an hour in silence until someone owned up?

'I know news of the circus investigation was bound to get out eventually, but the media have stated that we are looking into other unsolved murders in relation to this case.' He jabbed his finger into the page for effect. 'That is sensitive information and was strictly to be held within these walls. For God's sake, they've even used the words 'serial killer'.'

A murmur went around the room from those who hadn't caught the news themselves this morning.

'Do you realise how much more difficult this makes our job? Now we're going to have public panic and the national spotlight on us. There is going to be a media scrum out there. Not to mention government pressure to get this solved. If there are leaks coming from this building, by God, I will find out who it is and their job will be gone. They'll be booted out faster than any of you can draw breath.' He stopped then, and glared out into the room as if waiting for a confession. He eyeballed individuals in the room, including what felt like a particularly long stare at me. Several heads turned to see who the focus of attention was. I longed for the normal low lighting in the room as I felt the heat rise up my face, even though I knew I had no cause to feel guilty. The intensity of his anger had made many in the room suddenly fascinated by their shoelaces. Mine looked like they could do with replacement soon. The silence had become excruciating. Just when the tension was almost asphyxiating he spoke, with a quiet voice of steel.

'The game has changed. The remaining interviews of circus staff will take place at the station. We are in the headlines now. No one, but no one will talk to the media except me. I want a uniform branch presence down at that circus now. This is bound to draw out the crackpots again. I don't want any incidents.' He shook the paper in the air again. 'If you were responsible for this, you can expect to hear from me personally, and soon.' He paused, waiting for the veiled threat to sink in. 'You are dismissed.'

You could feel the collective sense of relief at those three words.

'That man should be an actor,' I whispered to Smithy, 'such a sense for the dramatic.'

'Damned right, that flourish would be hard to beat — talk about playing the crowd. I pity the poor sod who let that information slip.'

The room erupted into action, but just as bums had started to rise from seats, he bellowed out one more command. Everyone froze mid-manoeuvre.

'DC Shephard, I want to see you, now.'

26

All heads turned to stare as I walked back into the squad room. I paused, not quite sure what to do or say when Smithy came straight out with the question that was no doubt in all their minds.

'So have you still got a job? What did he want to see you about?'

My shoulders slumped and my voice reflected my enthusiasm.

'Nothing, absolutely nothing. All he wanted was to tell me to go down to the circus this morning, seeing as I'm their requested liaison, and oversee the transport of the last members to the station for questioning. Oh, and to iron out any issues Mr Bennett might have after the newspaper revelations, of which I'm sure there'll be plenty.'

'Sorry?' David Reihana said from the corner of the room. 'He singled you out in front of everyone just for that? God, I thought he'd decided you were the leak and was going to fry your arse.'

'You and everyone else there. You should have seen some of the filthy looks I got on the way back here. He may as well have had me fingerprinted, processed and proclaimed guilty as charged.' I swallowed down the small lump in my throat, but couldn't hide the tell-tale crackle. 'Why the hell did he have to do that?'

After this morning's blank note under the wipers, this added yet another layer of distaste to my day. My usual chirp was shot.

'Don't take it personally, Shep. That was low, even for him,' Smithy said, as he came over and gave me a pat on the shoulder.

'What do you mean?' I asked.

'What Smithy's trying to tell you,' Reihana said, 'is that the DI has a bit of a reputation for being a bully. You probably haven't been here long enough to notice, but he always likes to have someone to torment. Otto had the pleasure for a short time there, didn't you, mate?'

'Unfortunately,' was the one-word reply.

'You seem to have been promoted to the position of his favourite punching bag.'

Actually, I had noticed. 'Oh, bloody terrific.' Like that made me feel any better. 'I thought it was because of what happened in Mataura. We didn't exactly see eye to eye.'

'So we heard. I'm sure that helped. He doesn't like to be shown up by anyone and is pretty good at holding a grudge.' Reihana paused, as if debating whether to say something.

'Is there something else I should know?'

'I don't think he was very pleased about you being fast-tracked into the CIB.' Again, the considered pause. 'To be honest, it didn't go down well with a number of people here, especially some downstairs.'

I felt the full attention of the room on me again. It was true that after what happened at Mataura someone in the hierarchy saw fit to assist my cause and get me into detective training sooner rather than later. I knew full well places were limited and there were those in the uniform branch who had been waiting for years to get the nod. I had expected to have to wait too, so was pleasantly surprised by the speed of it all. It wasn't a popular decision among the troops though and my presence was barely tolerated by some. A memory jumped to mind of one Chardonnay-fuelled female officer informing everyone at Friday-night drinks that I must have slept with the right people to get there. I had often wondered what some of my colleagues in this room thought about it. Now I knew.

'I worked damned hard to get in and I pull my weight. I've got as much right to be here as anyone else,' I said, jumping on the defensive. Despite trying to convince myself otherwise, I really cared what people thought of me, and the backward glances and snide comments I sometimes got chipped away at my self-confidence.

'We know you do, and it's nothing against you personally. But what I'm saying is, you should tread careful. There are some people around here who would love to see you take a fall. You should watch your back, especially now.'

27

Before I went and did my duty at the circus, there was a small task pressing on my mind. It remained to be seen how my request would go down, but I took a breath and tried anyway.

'Hi, Jeff,' I said, as I hung around the corner of the door into Forensics Services. Jeff Arnott was one of the police photographers and shared office space with the SOCOs. They occupied the farthest corner of the building.

'DC Shephard, we don't usually see you down here. What can I do for you?' Jeff was a genial character and greying a bit around the edges. When he wasn't busy photographing blood and guts and the detritus of crime, he was out shooting birds, of the feathered variety, with his camera. He'd done quite well at it, especially with the native birds — won some comps and a vibrant shot of a tui had even graced the cover of a magazine. I hoped he'd be sympathetic to my cause, but these days one couldn't make assumptions.

'Have you processed the personnel photos from Operation Sparrow yet?' That name grated every time I used it, which wasn't often.

'They're next on the agenda. Why? Was there something specific you were looking for?'

'There's something about one of the circus crew, a man named Zarvo the clown, or Zarvo Krunic, that rang a few alarms.'

'He's not on the list of possibles. What was the problem with him?'

How did you describe woman's intuition and a finely attuned bullshit-o-meter? 'I don't know exactly. He seemed to have something to hide, made me feel suspicious.'

'By the sounds of it, half of them did. Why do you want to single him out?'

My gut instincts were usually pretty sharp and this chap had set things jangling for me, for whatever reason. But I could tell that a definite answer here was more likely to get cooperation, so I said the first thing that jumped to mind. 'He looked vaguely familiar, so I was wanting to check his photo out against wanted lists and missing persons.'

'Does the head guy know you're doing this?' He inclined his head in the general direction of my tormenter's office. I wondered if every detective in Dunedin had their lines of enquiry queried like this or if it was a special treat reserved just for me? All this extra attention was getting tedious, so I took the direct approach.

'No, he doesn't specifically know I'm checking this individual out. It's a bit of an initiative of my own. Why, are you going to dob me in?'

He gave me an appraising kind of a look, then smiled — the warm, genuine variety. 'Nah, he's been a right royal arsehole towards you. Come back in an hour and I'll have it ready.'

28

What a shit of a morning.

I needed therapy.

There was always chocolate, but my stash of portable therapy was in the glovebox of my car, and that was too far away to merit the effort.

Retail therapy might work. But there was that little prerequisite of money.

It was a bit early in the day for a good stiff drink, and anyway, I still had to go back to work this afternoon.

There was nothing for it; I pulled out my cellphone and texted Maggie: *Meet at the Good Oil in 10 for lunch?* I was one of those strange creatures that couldn't bear to disembowel words in text messages. It was full spelling, grammar and punctuation for me. Maggie's reaction to my long-winded missives involved the words 'anal' and 'retentive'. She had no such qualms, as indicated by her rapid-response reply: *(-:*

Twenty minutes later and I had my laughing gear wrapped around a bagel filled with roast lamb and token green stuff. Maggie had gone for the more civilised smoked-salmon option. We both had our standard flat white, except I adulterated mine with sugar; she didn't. There was an enormous slice of raspberry and coconut cake in the middle, with two forks, and yoghurt rather than cream — our nod to healthy eating.

'You know,' Maggie said, around a mouthful. 'You could go for harassment, if he continues to pick on you like that.'

'Yeah, right. He'd deny it for a start, and probably chip in that it was all my doing and that I was incompetent. He acts like he's God, and knows it all. Just because he's got a flash paper degree and they've given him some rank, he seems to think he can ride roughshod over everyone.'

'Smithy and your workmates would back you up though?'

'Maybe, maybe not. I get the feeling it would be like career suicide to stand up and take him on. No one's ever done it before, and it sounds like there have been plenty of officers who have experienced his special brand of attention. They're all scared of him.'

'The class bully?'

'The class bully,' I agreed. 'But with the strategic advantage of being the boss.'

'Bugger. There's no easy answer, then.'

'No, I just have to grin and bear it.'

'That's just so wrong.'

'Yup.'

Maggie dealt with another mouthful of cake and then pointed the fork in my direction. 'Tell you something: the Sam I know wouldn't take that kind of crap from anybody.'

I smiled. 'That's true, but this Sam is feeling a bit ground down by it all.'

'That's never held you back before. You've always been the champion of the downtrodden, the fighter for justice. That's why you joined the police in the first place. Don't you think it's time you championed yourself?'

She had a point.

'Are you saying I should push back?'

'Someone's got to. What have you got to lose?'

I could think of quite a substantial list of things to lose, but bugger it, Maggie was right. If I didn't stand up for myself, no one was going to do it for me, and that arsehole would continue to think it was acceptable to treat people like shit. Although it could end in disaster, and scared the bejesus out of me, it was time I put my big girl pants on and called him out.

29

The unexpected assault of the cellphone going off next to my head wrenched me violently into the here and now. I'd been in the middle of a rather unpleasant dream involving me, the police-squad room and the sudden realisation I wasn't wearing any pants. This would be bad at the best of times, but in this dream, I was addressing my colleagues about the Bateman case. They hadn't noticed yet, and my mind had been going rapid-fire, trying to think of a way to get out of the predicament before I made a total fool of myself. My panic was reflected in the twisted mangle of sheets I found myself entwined in on waking. It was dark, my heart rate was through the roof and my hands shook like a druggie on a severe downer. Despite this, the cellphone's intrusion had done me a favour.

The time on the display screen glared 5.14 a.m. Who the hell rang anyone at this time of the morning? Good news never came at this hour. My mind leaped immediately to Dad.

'Hello?' I said, my voice foreign and raspy.

'DC Shephard?' Oh God, that sounded formal.

'Yes.'

'Dunedin Watch House.' The chest tightness eased a fraction, but the other ill effects of the adrenaline rush remained. 'Look, there's been a bit of a development at the circus.'

'What's happened?' It must have been bad for them to be calling in off-duty officers at this time of day.

'A fire, someone's torched the place. It's pandemonium, you need to get there straight away. The owner specifically requested you.'

Shit.

'I'm on my way.'

★ ★ ★

It was quite possibly the strangest and most surreal sight I'd ever witnessed. It would have been oddly beautiful if the ramifications weren't so hideous.

The orange and red hues of the still-leaping flames shimmered through a billowing pall of black smoke and cast the pre-dawn sky aglow in a Dante-esque vision. The now-exposed poles of the big top, jutting up like bones amid the still-burning carcass of the tent, reflected the staccato flashes of red and blue made by the fire units and police cars crowding the scene. The flames hadn't restricted themselves to the main attraction and I could make out two trailer homes and the ticket office alight as I pulled up to the scene.

The sight was bad enough, but when I opened the car door and got a hit of the audio track, my blood ran cold. The sound of the animals screaming yanked at some primitive part of my being and I found myself running towards the conflagration as fast as I was able. Fire fighters, police and staff were swarming like ants in seeming disorder, I saw a face I recognised from the previous day's interviews and grabbed at her arm as she ran past, terrified.

'Where's Bennett?' I yelled.

She tried to pull out of my grasp, before recognition crossed her face and she stopped still, sobbing. 'Cassie, he's after Cassie.'

Shit, the elephant. I sprinted around the side of the main area to where she'd been secured when I last saw her. The area was full of roadies, frantically moving the animals away to safety, but I could see no sign of Cassie. The air was rank with the stench of burning plastic, a lung-searing, eye-watering miasma. It must have been the seating in the big top that was fuelling the flames.

I grabbed at another hand and yelled, 'Bennett, where's Bennett?'

My eyes followed the pointing arm and I got a glimpse of the man-mountain heading away in the opposite direction. I ran after him, weaving through the throng of desperate, wild-eyed people. After colliding with a semi-clad man also at full tilt, I picked myself back up off the ground, the air knocked out of me. The sound of the monkeys' screeching grated at every nerve ending in my body like a thousand nails scratching blackboards. I tried to ignore that and the pain in my knee and continued on.

'Terry,' I yelled out, 'Terry, wait.'

His head swung around and I saw desolation etched into his face. He grabbed me by the shoulders when I caught up to him.

'Cassie, she's gone berserk, you've got to help me.'

'What do you mean she's gone berserk?'

Tears rolled down his stricken face. 'A burning chunk of tent canvas landed on her. She's pulled her chain, she's hurt and panicked. She's already trampled someone.'

Shit.

'What can I do?' I asked, not having any clue as to how he thought I could deal with a four-tonne rampaging elephant. It was then I noticed that he'd been trying to hide something under his coat. He pulled out a shotgun, a single-shot, 12-gauge shotgun. My eyes dropped to the gun, then raised back to his face.

'We've got to catch up with her.'

'Which way?'

He pointed across the Oval towards the highway bordering the far side and the major intersection on to the Southern Motorway. It didn't take much imagination to work out how much havoc she could cause there even at this hour of the morning. I took off running across the sports ground and assumed from the heavy footfalls behind me that Terry Bennett was following. I hoped she hadn't travelled too far, as once she got out to the road there were a myriad of directions she could go in. I wondered what Terry meant by 'trampled'. Accidentally hurt in the rush to escape? Or had she been driven to do someone serious harm?

Evidence of her path was nearby as I broke through by the low hedge bordering the road.

I ran up to the van, which was tipped over on

the driver's side. The windscreen was broken and a man was scrambling out through the shattered glass.

I helped him get to his feet. There was a sizable dent in the side of the vehicle, now pointing skywards.

'Are you alright?' I asked. There was blood running down the side of his head, but otherwise he seemed uninjured.

'Huh? Bugger me, I just got hit by a fucking elephant. I'm sure it was an elephant. What the fuck's an elephant doing in the middle of the road?' Under normal circumstances if any driver had uttered those words to me, I would have had them lined up for an evidential breath test.

'Which way?' I asked. 'Which way did she go?' I heard Terry thunder up behind me, breathing so hard I thought his lungs would explode.

'That way, I think.' He pointed further south along Anderson's Bay road towards the peninsula. 'Fuck me, that was an elephant, right?'

'Yup.'

She had headed towards the most-open ground. It should make her easier to find than if she'd gone into the industrial area, where there were lots of places to lose her. It seemed absurd to think of losing something the size of an elephant, but then, this was turning into one hell of a strange day. I peered up the road and saw a distant set of headlights make a sudden swerve to the right. There was only one thing I could think of that would cause that kind of manoeuvre.

'Come on, she's this way.' I took off on foot

138

again. Thank God, it was early morning and there weren't many cars around. I did a quick check then darted across the huge intersection that led onto the motorway on my right. The chaos she could cause in peak traffic didn't bear thinking about. The rail overpass loomed ahead and I got about fifty metres further up the road when I heard a strangled shout from behind me. I swung around in time to see Terry Bennett hit the ground and roll, hands clutching at his chest. By the time I got back to him his breaths were laboured and gasping, his ashen colour obvious despite the orange cast thrown by the overhead sodium street lights. Beads of perspiration joined to form small rivulets of sweat running down the sides of his face.

'Shit, Terry, hang on, I'll go get help.'

'No, no.' He clutched for his chest again and then my arm. 'Sorry, arggghh.' With his other hand he thrust the shotgun at me. 'I'll be okay, go.' He tried to nod in the direction of Cassie. 'You have to,' he gasped.

'No, I can't do that. Don't ask me to shoot her.'

'She killed people. She's injured, she's panicked and she's dangerous. You have to do it. You have to.' He grit his teeth, sucking in air between them, while tears flowed from the corners of his eyes.

He was right, and it had to be done before she did more harm. I could hear sirens in the distance, as more emergency services headed for the scene. But there was no one else here now who could deal with this except me.

'How?' I said quietly. 'Head or heart?'

'Head.'

'With a shotgun?'

'They're rifled slugs, they can do the job.'

'How many rounds do I have?'

'Two. One's already loaded, the other's in my coat pocket.'

Jesus.

I felt in his pocket until I found the other round. The size of it gave some reassurance.

'You'll be okay?'

He nodded, the movement clearly causing pain. 'You have to get this done before she hurts someone else.' His breathing, already laboured, shuddered with sobs. 'I'm so sorry.'

The sight of this broken man and the thought of the task ahead led me to do something I would never have believed possible, considering my feelings towards him. I bent down and kissed Terry Bennett on the forehead. When I looked up, I could see the van man running towards us. Hopefully, he'd be able to get some help. Right now, my priorities were elsewhere. I got up, and holding the shotgun army-style in front of me, began to run up the road. Despite the nearness of so many police and emergency staff, I'd never felt quite so alone. I'd often gone out hunting with my dad and brothers on the farm, but there was one hell of a difference between potting a few possums and the odd deer, to having to hunt down an elephant — an elephant I considered to be a friend.

The night sky tinged watery blue at the horizon, which along with the orange fiery glow to the north, the distant sirens and the toots from passing motorists added to the surreal nature of the situation. I supposed, to people who had just seen an elephant on the road, the sight of a woman running with a bloody great gun was not so out of the ordinary.

How would Cassie react to the sight of me? Would she recognise me? I thought elephants were supposed to have poor vision, and it was still pretty dark. Could she smell me? Would she recognise a gun, see me as a threat? Maybe, with the state she was in she'd see any human as a threat. If the first round missed or didn't drop her I was going to have to reload real fast. If I stuffed this up completely, there was no plan B, and I could be left with an injured and very pissed-off elephant. 'Stop it, Shep,' I muttered aloud. I was thinking too much. I had to focus, trust my instincts and not succumb to analysis paralysis.

Suddenly, there she was: two hundred metres ahead of me, standing in the middle of the road, her back towards me, seemingly mesmerised by the headlights of oncoming traffic. Several cars had pulled over onto the side of the road — I only hoped no one would be stupid enough to get out of their car and approach her.

'Don't be dumb, please don't be dumb,' I said to myself as I upped my pace. Now I was closer I could see she was waving her head and trunk from side to side. She slapped at the ground with her trunk. I read that as not a good thing.

I approached the first pulled-over car. The occupants looked panicked and I realised they weren't comforted by the presence of a chick with a firearm. Wearing civvies didn't help there. I'd just grabbed what was on the floor when I got the call — a red top from the night before and jeans. I reached into my pocket and pulled out my warrant card, holding it up for them to see as I got to the driver's window. He was on his cellphone, and I could guess to whom.

'You talking to the police?' I asked.

He nodded.

'Please, I need to talk to them.' He dutifully opened the window and handed the phone over. 'Detective Constable Samantha Shephard, Dunedin CIB.'

'Central despatch. What's the situation?'

'I'm tracking an escaped elephant from the visiting circus. The circus has been set alight and the animal is injured and panicked. It has killed people already and I am armed with a rifle and intend to destroy the animal.' I heard the driver of the car utter an expletive.

'Do you need an Armed Offenders call-out?' Could I do this by myself? I didn't want to, but I could see Cassie had turned and was moving in this direction. I was going to have to act now.

'I'll need back-up, but the situation is urgent and I'm going to have to do this now.' I handed the phone back to the bewildered-looking man. 'Tell them exactly where we are and get the hell out of here.'

A nerve-shattering screech erupted from Cassie, sending my heart rate into the stratosphere. She was on the move and in my direction. Did she recognise my voice? Something had sparked her interest enough to get her headed this way. I'd been kind to her, given her some company and attention. Surely that would work in my favour. But something about her body language suggested otherwise.

I didn't want to have to do this in full view of the cars that had pulled up for the spectacle. They had no idea how real the danger was, but I didn't have the time to trot backwards and forwards across the road to tell them to bugger off. I wondered if I could get her into a side street, or even the warehouse car park, but I didn't have enough ammunition to fire into the air to get her moving and anyway, it looked like time was running out.

She was a hundred metres away and picking up pace. Shit she could move fast.

Head shot, Terry had said. Easier said than done when she was thundering straight for me. Stand or kneel? Stand, in case I missed and had to run and reload. I thanked my lucky stars for a misspent youth having shooting competitions with my brothers. But even though I rated my skills as a marksman, the fact I only had one back-up round made me more than a little nervous. Okay, she was fifty metres now, and whatever was happening in her head, it was very apparent she'd decided I was the one she wanted to see, and I was pretty sure it wasn't for a pat and a rub. Her head was up, her ears out and she meant business. A dark stain that must have been blood was spreading down the front of her head. How close did I let her get? Forty metres. I could hear her footsteps and her exaggerated huffing.

All other noise disappeared as I honed my attention in on the centre of her head, tracking her movements. My brain registered her speed, made the calculation and estimate of seconds before she was on me.

I pulled the shotgun up to a shooting position, heard the loud click as I cocked the hammer, sighted over the top of the barrel. She was so close.

Her footsteps vibrated through the ground and up my legs.

My heartbeat pulsed through my ears.

I sighted down the barrel.

Finger on the trigger.

My heart beat.

Cassie's face.

Heartbeat.

Footsteps, closer.

Heartbeat.

I breathed out.

Sighted

Squeezed.

30

The report shattered the vacuum of silence that had encompassed my world. In a seeming pinprick of time everything happened.

The kickback of the shotgun as the recoil pad slammed into my shoulder.

My gasp as my body recognised the need to breathe again.

The jarring of the earth as the elephant collapsed to the ground, a colossal wreck, her forward momentum leaving her only ten metres from where I stood.

The sharp smell of gunpowder.

Then stillness.

Then sound. My rasping breath, the pulsing of blood in my head, sirens in the distance. Whirring, jangling noise.

Worst of all, I could hear her, hear her sucking in huge, lurching gasps of air. I hadn't killed her. It wasn't over. I approached with caution, feeling the ball of hot acid rising in my stomach, not knowing how incapacitated she was or how fast a prone elephant could rise to its feet. She had slid onto her knees then over onto her side, her vast rib cage rising with every shuddering breath. The bullet wound in her head swelled with blood that ran to co-mingle with that I'd seen earlier. She could see me, she watched me approach. I could not break away from her gaze. That eye that seconds ago had been so crazed now carried its melancholy cast, the same sadness I'd witnessed when I first saw her. That sadness stabbed me in the heart. I had one round left and knew what I had to do. Would she let me?

'Oh, Cassie,' I said, my voice cracked and laden. 'You'll be alright, I'll take care of you and everything will be alright.'

I walked around her and stood behind her head, still talking to her softly, trying to keep us both calm. I leaned forward and touched her, she lifted her trunk slightly in acknowledgement but there would be no resistance, no fight.

She didn't even flinch at the sound of my breaking the shotgun, ejecting the spent cartridge and clicking it shut with the next round.

Once again, I pulled back the hammer.

I pressed the barrel flush against her flesh. My vision blurred as the tears flowed down my cheeks.

Another shot rent the night.

31

'Lay down your weapon.'

'Huh?' The intrusion of the voice snapped me back to the now. How long had I been sitting here, leaning back to back against the now lifeless form of what I considered one of God's most magnificent creations? A creation I had just killed.

'Sam, we need you to lay down the weapon.' A different voice, softer, and one I recognised.

I looked up through tear-hazed vision and saw Smithy standing nearby, accompanied by another two officers with weapons drawn and pointed in my direction. Why the hell would they need to do that? I was an officer. Then I realised I was a non-uniformed officer with a non-issue weapon. I shoved at the shotgun that lay across my lap and it skittered across the asphalt, spinning a slow arc as it scraped to a halt.

The officers immediately dropped their stance and holstered their Glocks.

While one of them attended to the shotgun, Smithy came over and crouched down on his haunches next to me, placing a hand on my knee. 'Sam, are you hurt? Are you okay?'

I couldn't bring myself to speak, so just shook my head slowly, side to side. I wasn't hurt, but I sure as hell wasn't okay. The shaking in my hands had started the moment I fired that second shot, and it hadn't abated. In fact, I felt

147

chilled — chilled in so many ways.

'Jesus, if this isn't the strangest thing I've ever seen in my life,' he said, shaking his head. He reached out and ran his hand across Cassie's spine. 'First a burning bloody circus and now this. Are you sure you're okay? The guy over there said the elephant was running straight for you, said it was mad. You're lucky you killed the thing.'

Yeah, real lucky.

'Come on, let's get you up from here and out of the spotlight.'

Spotlight? I looked around me for the first time and realised I'd attracted a bit of a crowd. Well, not me, I supposed. Then there was the stage lighting from above. The noise of an overhead helicopter registered to my addled senses. Police, I assumed. I accepted the proffered hand and got to my feet, swaying a bit with the resultant head rush. For the first time, I got to fully take in the scene around me. Cassie's life had ended in the middle of an intersection. This creature, which to my mind should have been living out her days in the lush jungles and wetlands of India, had instead ended them on a sea of asphalt, in the heart of the commercial sector. The irony of that wasn't lost on me. The continuing cycle of glowing green, orange and red of the traffic lights seemed incongruous with the sight of this enormous mammal strewn across the carriageway. The effort required for me to hold it all together was immense.

'Here, you're shaking.' Smithy pulled off his jacket and draped it across my shoulders. My eyes were drawn back to Cassie and were trapped.

There was so little blood. Surely there should be more blood? Instead, Cassie looked deceptively peaceful, as though she hadn't spent the last moments of her life in blind panic and rage. I had done that. I'd done that to her.

Smithy's arm went across my shoulder and gently moved me in the direction of a squad car. My eyes stayed on Cassie as long as they physically could before pain forced them to the front. In the far distance, beyond the police car, I could see an ambulance.

Terry Bennett.

He would have heard the shots. He would have understood their cruel message. He had lost everything tonight.

By now, the noises I had so successfully filtered out were an incessant assault upon my ears. The helicopter rotors, the sirens, the animal shrieks, the shouts, the voices. I closed my eyes against the counterpoint flashing of red and blue as every sense went into overload. It was only when I felt the cool vinyl of the seat beneath me and heard the click of the car door closing beside me, shutting out the world, that I found the ability to breathe.

Smithy must have sensed my need to be left alone. He didn't say a word as he slid into the driver's seat and drove me away. The police radio crackled rapid-fire orders and updates until he reached over and turned it off. Then there was no siren, no speech, just the murmur of the engine and hum of rubber on tarmac. He slowed down as we passed the point where the ambulance was attending to Terry Bennett. I caught a fleeting glimpse of a form on a gurney, sheet pulled up and over its head before the tears flowed again.

32

The polystyrene cup contained a hit of coffee sweet enough to make my face twitch. Even so, I could only just feel the benefits of the caffeine infusing its way through my system. A gin would have been more helpful. My head was a jumble of flashbacks: ear-shattering gunfire, the metallic smell of blood intermingled with the acrid stench of burning plastic, the mountain of enraged flesh bearing down upon me, the shockwave up my legs as her bulk hit the asphalt, the flashing lights of the emergency vehicles, the thrum of rotor blades. A continuous assault of images strobed through my mind. Closing my eyes to them made it worse, so instead I stared out the window, trying to blot them out with the stream of morning rush-hour traffic and pedestrians swarming like ants below me. Life ground on as normal for so many; most were oblivious to the devastating and downright bizarre start to this day.

Smithy had dropped me off here earlier before returning to the scene. Now I could hear the movement and rustlings of my fellow detectives as they came into the office. Word must have filtered through as thus far they had skirted around and left me be. The enormity of what I'd just done was dawning and a maelstrom of emotions was threatening to explode. I took another large breath and started counting cars again in a futile attempt to blot out the playback.

Four sets of feet had entered the room so far and I could hear another approach, and fast. It was funny how you could recognise someone by the cadence of their walk.

'Sam? How are you holding up?' I swung around to see Smithy striding towards me. Before I'd even had the chance to put the coffee down he'd enveloped me in a big hug. I had to gulp hard to stop the tears from bursting out as one-handed I gripped him fiercely around his waist. He stepped back before sitting on top of the desk. 'You feeling any better now?'

'Not really, I could do with a stiff drink.'

'I'm not surprised. That is the damnedest thing I've ever seen in my life. You must have balls of steel to stand there and take down a charging bloody elephant.'

I didn't feel like I had anything of steel right now. In fact, my innards had the consistency of underdone custard. And they developed a viscosity more like water when I recognised the next set of footsteps storming towards the room. Oh God, not now.

DI Johns stopped in the doorway, targeted his sights on me, then braced his hands against the doorframe. 'What the hell did you think you were doing?' he bellowed. Every head in the room jolted around and a charged silence descended. His cheeks puffed out several times before he found the words to continue his tirade. 'Why did you have to kill the frigging elephant? Don't you realise how bad that makes us look?

Jesus, you have got a lot to answer for, young lady.'

I dropped my head and focused on breathing and keeping the bile down that threatened to join an old food stain on the carpet. He couldn't do this to me, not now.

'Well, come on, then.' He banged his fist against the doorjamb, jerking my eyes back up. 'Answer me. How the hell are we supposed to clean up after this bloody great cock-up? What are you? Fucking stupid or something?'

That was one step too far. The dam that fought to hold back all my anger and grief failed, threatening to overwhelm me and anyone else in the flood path.

'I did what I had to do.' I spat out each word. 'How bad do you think it would have made the police look if it had rolled another van and killed more people? She was going berserk. I had no other choice.' I made no attempt to modulate my voice. I yelled back and I didn't give a flying flick who heard me. 'It wasn't like I could just walk up and stick a bloody halter on her. It was a bit beyond leading her away to a nice safe area out of everybody's way. Of course I had to bloody well shoot her.'

'Well you didn't have to kill it there. We'll have to get a flaming crane in to clear the road. And it wasn't even an official weapon you used. Where the hell did you get the shotgun? Do you realise how much trouble you'll be in for that?'

'I grabbed whatever was to hand. What was I supposed to do? Say, 'Oh, Cassie, can you pause your little murderous rampage while I pop back to the station, fill out the paperwork and get a police-issue weapon?' Get fucking real.' I felt the crack of the polystyrene cup as it crushed in my hand and felt the remaining warm liquid run through my fingers, making its way to the floor. 'You weren't there and you didn't have to make the call. I was there. I had to decide, I had to kill her. Me. Do you have any idea how bloody hard that was? Do you?' By now, the tears were rolling down my face and my voice was laboured, laden with hurt and emotion. 'Do you have any idea what it felt like to kill that beautiful, beautiful creature? Her name was Cassie, God damn it. Cassie. She was . . . ' I groped for words that could convey how I felt about her, but in my rage they proved elusive. 'Bennett couldn't do it, he fell, and if I didn't shoot her, she could have bloody well killed someone else. I had no fucking choice. Get that into your thick head and for God's sake just leave me alone.'

I threw what was left of the cup to the floor and stormed towards the door. The stupid bugger didn't move out of the way so I shoved both hands hard into his chest and sent him reeling backwards before I escaped out the door and bolted for the stairs.

'You come back here right now, you little bitch,' I heard him bellow and then Smithy's angry voice yelling, 'DI Johns, you are out of order . . . ' before the doors clicked behind me and the only sound was my footsteps, running.

33

'Well, you certainly know how to make a scene.' Smithy had tracked me down to my unlikely place of sanctuary. I'd wondered if anyone would come looking and was almost glad to see him. Half an hour of silence and stillness had calmed some of the physical manifestations of my rage, but had done nothing for my mental health. I wiped away the blood on my hand from the scab I'd been harassing.

'He started it.'

'Yeah, he did.' Smithy leaned against the doorway, head cocked to the side, observing me with a frown wrinkling across his brows. 'He was way out of line, Sam, and everyone in that room would say so. He had no right to treat you like that.'

No, he didn't have the right, but it didn't stop him. He seemed to take great pleasure in singling me out for attention regardless. Reihana was on to it when he said I seemed to be the DI's punching bag of choice. How on earth could I relinquish that position? No idea. I was powerless, in every way. I recalled the snatch of angry words I'd heard between Smithy and the DI during my bolt for freedom.

'Thanks for standing up for me, I appreciate that.'

Smithy came over and sat beside me on the bench, elbows on his knees, his dry skin making tin-whistle scales as he rubbed his hands together.

'It was all I could do not to deck him one. Let's just say it got a bit ugly in the room after you left and I think our DI is in no doubt as to whose side we're all on.' I managed a smile. 'Interesting choice of bolt-hole by the way. It took me a bit to find you.' We were sitting in one of the empty cells in the basement. It had been a quiet night, so there were plenty to spare. I'd craved somewhere small and quiet and dark and my feet had directed me here. There was something cave-like about the room and I needed that security of cool concrete against my back.

'Not very cosy, but I thought no one would look for me here.'

'You got that right. Most people like to avoid imprisonment.'

'I'm not most people.'

His hands stopped. 'Maybe you should go home for the rest of the day, have a break. You've been through a hell of a lot.'

'But they'll want a statement and I'm sure I haven't seen the last of the DI. I'd only get into more trouble if I left now. It's probably better I stick around for a while.'

'Don't you worry about him. I'll have a word with higher powers because I don't think he's being objective or fair. You did a good job out there this morning, Sam, under bloody awful circumstances.'

Having some positive affirmation of my morning's work set the waterworks off again and

I wiped away at the tears, annoyed at how easily they betrayed me.

'They captured the whole thing on video.'

My eyes slammed shut. Oh God, just what I needed. The thrum of the helicopter rotors re-invaded my headspace. Not only would I have to recount the event in detail for the inevitable enquiry, I'd get to see it all from God's point of view in marvellous technicolour. That awful moment replayed again and again, and not just in my mind. Smithy put a hand out to steady my legs as they twitched.

'They?'

'News crew, I'm afraid. I've seen the footage. You were incredible, I'm . . . well, we're all in awe. You don't have anything to worry about. Despite what Johns said, no one's going to have you up for what you did. It's obvious you had no choice. We're just all glad we weren't in your place.'

Tiredness was taking over and my body was losing the battle against gravity. I slumped further against the wall. Maybe it would be a good idea to go home, try and forget it all for a few hours. There would be the unavoidable internal investigation, and I didn't expect DI Johns would let my outburst slide. And then there was finding where this all fit in the context of the murder investigation. I couldn't let this distract me from the fact that a young woman was dead. And now there were more deaths to add to the tally, even if by an indirect cause.

'Do you think they'd miss me for a few hours?'

'Of course, but we'll cope without you.' He

was being facetious and I gave him a thump on the leg for his trouble. It did draw a smile from me, which quickly lapsed back into a frown as another thought came to mind.

'Oh, crap. My car's down at the Oval.' Returning to the scene and seeing the carnage at the circus was the last thing I felt like right now. Too raw, too much. 'Can you give me a lift home?'

'No prob.'

34

It took a moment to register the knock at the door over the melodic strains soothing my mind via my phone. I didn't normally like to use earplugs unless running, but this morning the need for all-encompassing sound to drown out the memories overrode any concerns about hearing preservation. I couldn't find anything obnoxious and thrashy enough, so instead had opted for mellow and chill. It had backfired a bit because now all I felt was numb. I pulled the plugs out and went to the lounge window to peek and see who it was. The front door was made of glass, so if you could see them, they could see you, but spying from the side of the bay window gave a view of the visitor and therefore the option of hiding. When I saw who it was, I skipped that option, pulled my clothes into some semblance of order and headed around to greet him.

'Paul. Hi. What are you doing here?' I asked as I tucked a wayward lock of hair behind my ear. 'How did you know where I live?'

Paul Frost stood dominating the doorway, hands in pockets, a quizzical look flickering across his face. 'I'm a detective, Sam. It would be a bit pathetic if I couldn't find out your address.'

Valid point. He hadn't answered the first question though.

'Was there something I could help you with? I

thought you were supposed to be in court.'

'No, no, court's finished for the day, I'm a free agent. No, I just heard about your exploits this morning and thought I'd pop around to make sure you were okay.'

'Oh. Thank you, I'm fine.' I can't have been a convincing liar as he stood there, with one eyebrow cocked up. Oh, what the heck, company might be good, even if it was him. Paul, for all his obnoxiousness, was one of those men who seemed to feel the need to protect me. I remembered him doing it in my Mataura days and he obviously couldn't control the urge here either. It was annoying in a gratifying kind of a way.

'Did you want a cup of tea or coffee?' I asked as I led him down the hallway.

'Coffee would be good, thanks.'

I bypassed the lounge and headed straight down into the kitchen to make the drinks. Paul followed along behind, pausing here and there to take in the original artwork on the hallway walls.

'There're some rather well-known names on the paintings,' he said. 'Is that a Ralph Hotere?'

If he was impressed with the hallway gallery, he'd be blown away by the works in the lounge. Aunty Jude and Uncle Phil's approach to art was to buy works they loved from emerging artists. The pay-off was they got to enjoy living with pieces that gave them pleasure, and over time, some of those emerging artists had turned into stars. They also had friends in the right places.

'Whoa, great view.' In the kitchen, Paul headed straight to the vast picture window. The

Kershaws' ridge-top house had a million-dollar view, and that was probably not much less than the price tag of the house. From the rooms on this side you could see down across the dense green belt and to the central city, then on to the glittering harbour and peninsula, with the Pacific Ocean in the distance. Nightfall removed the water vista, but added a new dimension of beauty with the sprinkling of city lights moulded into the contours of the hills. It was one of the things I loved about this city. Every corner turned brought with it a new pocket vista, whether it be the harbour, peninsula, green belt or historic architecture. Even the clagged-in drizzly days were somehow spectacular.

'It must be tough having to look at this every day,' Paul said. 'And it's Maggie's aunt's house? They must have a bit of dough.' I hadn't really thought about it that much, but I suppose they must be pretty well off, considering the art collection and antique furniture and the address. Highgate. A grand old house on Highgate. Expensive real estate, even if the parking was crap.

'It is rather posh, I suppose. Uncle Phil's a lecturer at the university and I think he inherited quite nicely when his father died. Aunty Jude came from a bit of old money too. When in doubt, marry rich.' I fossicked around in the pantry until I found the open packet of Toffee Pops to offer, and then sat down at the kitchen table, opposite where Paul had already plonked himself. He had the knack for making himself at home in any situation.

'So, why do you call them aunt and uncle if they're Maggie's relatives?'

'You don't come from a big family, do you? Lots of relatives, cousins?' He shook his head. 'When you do, everyone a generation older than you who's not your parent becomes aunt or uncle. The habit's stuck.'

'I take it your family breeds well, then?'

'We're farming stock, what else can I say?' I slid a mug across the table and under his nose.

'Thanks,' he said. 'Looks like there'd be plenty of space to squeeze you and Maggie in. What is this place, six, seven bedrooms?'

'Eight,' I said, while munching on a biscuit. 'Well, originally, but Aunt and Unc have a den each, they converted one into an en-suite and walk-in wardrobe off the master bedroom — got to have the mod-cons. There's a permanent guest room, the twins had a room each and the last one's been turned into a sun room.'

'Great what money can buy,' he said, with only a hint of envy.

'Yeah. Haven't had the chance to find that out yet, personally. I have to say though, it must have felt a bit empty here when the twins left home, before we came along. It was all a bit echoing hallways and vast spaces. I think they were quite pleased to have a couple of extra warm bodies in the house.' They were certainly gracious and accommodating hosts.

'I bet you're in no hurry to go. Bit of board money in exchange for the Ritz.'

'Oh yes, a girl knows a good thing when she's on to it, and Aunty Jude's a fabulous cook. 'Why

162

would you leave that? Anyway, they charge mates' rates and I couldn't afford to live anywhere else. I lost everything in the fire in Mataura, remember?'

'Maybe you should have been insured, then.'

Like I needed to be reminded. I shot him a look that left no doubt about what I thought of his insensitivity. 'Why did you come here again?'

He had the grace to look abashed and held his hands up in supplication. 'I'm sorry Sam, that was a bit low.' He turned on the full-beam look. 'I was worried about you.' That look might have got my pulse up a bit on another day, but I was too numb for it to even elicit a token twitch.

'Well, you've got a funny way of showing it,' I said and wrapped my hands around my hot mug.

'What can I say, my charm doesn't always work. But really, how are you, anyway?'

'You mean for someone who had to shoot an elephant this morning? Oh, just fine and dandy.'

He smiled at the sarcasm. 'I heard about the thing with Dickhead Johns.'

'Yeah, well, you got his title right. I don't get where he gets off treating me like that.' I took a gulp of the too-hot tea, to try and prevent the waterworks from starting. I felt it burn its way down my throat. Made a change from acid burning its way up. 'It was bloody awful having to kill her. I've had to destroy animals before, on the farm. Dad made sure I got to do some of the hard jobs, lessons in life, and all. You have to do the hard jobs as well as the good ones, he always said. Builds character. But it was nothing like this.'

'Sam, you had, what, a four-tonne elephant charging at you? Of course it was hard. Most of us would have shat ourselves.'

'I know, but it's not that. Well, it was a bit. But I'd spent some time with her, you know. When I was at the circus for the interviews I always made a point of going over to give her a pat and a rub down. She seemed so sad, and I felt sorry for her, chained up like that, dragged out like a performing monkey, and yes, I felt sorry for them too. It probably sounds weird, but it was like shooting a friend.'

He reached across and put his hand over mine. 'For all your bravado, you're a bit of a softie, aren't you, Sam?'

'Don't I know it?' I looked down at the table before girding up the strength to ask the next question. 'Did he die?'

Full points to Paul in that he knew exactly who I was talking about. 'Yeah, sorry, Sam. A massive heart attack, they think, and hardly surprising under the circumstances.'

My eyes were misting up and I reclaimed my hand, using it to take another slug of my drink in an attempt to fight back the tears. So much for the saying you can't cry if you're drinking. What a bloody mess. How many lives had been lost because some git, probably drunk git, had decided to mete out their own form of justice and torch the circus?

My hands started to shake again.

35

My cellphone rang and saved me the indignity of completely falling apart in front of Paul. Not that it was a call I valued. It was time to front up at the station and answer the hard questions while they performed a post-mortem on my actions. I wondered who 'they' would be. The thought of DI Johns being on the panel turned my innards into a seething mass of worms again. Mind you, Smithy had said he'd have a word to higher powers. I prayed to God he had, and that Johns would be off my case and off my back.

Paul had offered me a lift down to the station and had been astute enough not to bother with idle chitchat along the way. Instead, my mind drifted to the strains of the Rolling Stones. I was relieved he had classic taste in music. His home town was Gore, home of Country and Western, but he didn't subscribe to their favourites. Small mercies.

He pulled up outside the station and turned to me as I undid the seat belt. 'All the best with the debrief. You'll be fine, you've got nothing to worry about.' That's what everyone was telling me, but it was scant comfort. It was me, not them, who had to front up and bear the scrutiny. Another burden on an already crap day.

'I hope you're right. Hey, thanks for checking up on me, and thanks for the lift.'

Before I could move to get out of the car, he

leaned over and gave me a quick kiss on the cheek. 'Tell it exactly like it happened, keep it simple and drop in key words like 'public safety' and 'risk'. And if you feel like going out later to drown your sorrows and need some company, give me a call.' Tonight was the last thing on my mind, but I was touched by the sentiment.

'I don't know what I feel like at this stage, but thanks anyway.'

I got out of the car and heard him call out, 'Look after yourself, Sam,' before I closed the door and with stomach churning, turned to face the music.

★ ★ ★

'Sam, can I have a word?' It was Sergeant Watson, one of the Intelligence officers.

'Yeah, sure, Bruce. What's up?'

He'd caught me in the second-foor hallway, on my way to the interview room.

'You know that fellow you asked us to check out from the circus, Zarvo Krunic? We've turned up something rather interesting.' He opened the manila folder he was holding and rearranged the contents so there were two photographs side by side. The first one I recognised as the picture taken yesterday of a serious-looking Zarvo that Jeff Arnott had supplied me with. The second picture was of a grinning, olive-skinned man, European, curly brown hair, mid-thirties I'd guess and not too bad looking.

My eyes flicked back and forth between the two, comparing features. Zarvo's shaved head, his nose, chin shape, eyes and eye shape. Pad the face out with an extra ten or more kilos and add some hair, a suntan, and a smile and it was the same man.

'Not called Zarvo, I take it?'

'No. Meet Jason William McDonald. Reported missing from Tauranga in 2004. Missing, assumed dead. Left behind a wife and then four-month-old son. Went to work on Tuesday night, late shift at the hospital as usual. He was a nurse. Never arrived at work, never came home. His car was found, burned out near Te Puke. Police speculated he had been robbed and murdered, but his body was never found. Now we know why. DNA testing will confirm it.'

'Wow, how do you go from being Jason McDonald to Zarvo the Clown? I've heard of people running away to the circus, but he seems to have gone to extreme measures to hide himself. Mind you, slathered in clown make-up, it would be like hiding in full sight. Did he have any form?' Perhaps he'd run away to escape past crimes, and in his new life had resumed his old hobbies.

'No, nothing, not even a parking ticket. Basically, your bog-standard, working-class family man. No priors, no known enemies, loved his wife and kid.'

He can't have loved them that much if he'd run away and hidden in the relative anonymity of the circus. It did make you ask questions as to why, especially in light of the string of murders that had tailed this particular circus around the countryside. I couldn't imagine boredom would drive someone to abandon their family and do something so extreme. This information certainly placed him firmly back in the running as a suspect in Operation Sparrow. It also meant there was a family in Tauranga that may or may not be thrilled to receive news of their lost loved one.

'Thanks for that, Bruce. Can I keep this? I'm on my way to see the boss.' Unfortunately, for me. 'I'll pass this on.'

'That's your copy. Well spotted.' He hesitated a moment before adding, 'Good luck with . . . ' He inclined his head towards my pending interrogation. 'You know.'

*   *   *

I was accustomed to being in the interview room delivering the questions, not being in the firing line. I rubbed my hands up and down my trousers and measured my breaths while I waited for them to take their positions. DI Johns was there, bugger it, but avoided eye contact. There was also the big gun, the Southern District Commander, Ian Frederickson. Normally, one of the detective senior sergeants would conduct this, but they must have decided the situation warranted more power. I was getting the full treatment. Ian had interviewed me when I was under suspicion in Mataura, but despite the bad memories that brought back, he was what I classed a goodie. I hoped I wouldn't be proven wrong. He started the proceedings.

'Detective Constable, thank you for coming in

for debrief. I hope you've had a chance to rest after this morning's events. This interview is for the purposes of the station and is being recorded. Also, be aware that you will be questioned later for the Police Complaints Authority, as is standard for this kind of incident.'

I wasn't aware that this kind of incident, as he put it, happened frequently enough for there to be a standard. It certainly hadn't come up in any manual I'd seen. At least it appeared the District Commander would be asking the questions this afternoon rather than my arch-nemesis. The knot in my stomach loosened a little.

'Did you wish to have any representation present?'

'Is this a disciplinary hearing?' I asked.

'No, it is purely for the purposes of recording and reporting the incident. We have video footage, which will help verify the sequence of events, but as there was a firearm discharged and public safety put at risk we need to have a formal interview.' He was being very proper in his language, but the tone of his voice and the relaxed nature of his posture told me this was no witch-hunt and my anxiety levels dropped another notch.

'Then no, I don't need any representation.'

'Very good. Would you like to see the helicopter video footage?'

I couldn't help the shudder and knew there was no way in hell I was ready to see that yet. 'No thank you, sir. Maybe at a later date.' Much, much later.

DI Johns still had not spoken and I noted he was sitting like someone had rammed a steel bar up his arse. My guess was Smithy had been true to his word about reporting his behaviour. Good. It was nice to see him looking so damned uncomfortable for a change.

There were no unpleasant surprises in the line of questioning. Why I had been present at the circus, the order of events, where I had gotten the firearm, why I deemed it necessary to shoot the elephant, what risk I had seen to public safety, and my own. The District Commander asked all the questions and DI Johns sat there like Big Chief Thundercloud. I surprised myself at how calm I remained throughout and how my emotions stayed in some semblance of control.

At the end of the interview the District Commander asked if I had any questions. I had one, but I didn't really want to hear the answer.

'How many died?'

The memory of the circus aflame and that noise reverberated in my mind. I had to close my eyes to blot it out as I clarified the question. 'I mean people and animals, how many died because of that fire?'

Frederickson let out a weary sigh. The muscles tightened across his jaw.

'We've got the people who started it. One of the bast — , I mean, men couldn't live with the guilt of what happened and turned them all in. Vigilantes. Decided to take matters into their own hands and punish the circus after reading in the newspaper the so-called serial killer was one of the company. The culprits did a hit and run, as it were. Ran in, doused petrol, lit it and ran, so they avoided the security. They thought they'd send them a message. Some message. It's cost six lives, so far. Your elephant. A vet had to be called in to put down a monkey and one of the lions after they critically injured themselves thrashing about in panic in their cages. Terry Bennett died as a result of a suspected heart attack.' My breath drew in, involuntarily. 'And the elephant killed two of the circus workers in its panic to escape. Apparently, they were trying to free it. That tally doesn't include the other people injured trying to save and rescue the animals. There are a number of people in the hospital right now. One is seriously burned and may not pull through.'

Bloody hell. All that because some dickheads decided to take the law into their own hands and mete out mob justice. I hoped they were happy with the result.

'Which of the circus people were killed?' I asked. After days of interviews, I knew all their faces. The District Commander checked on one of the files in front of him.

'Jamal Kumar, the elephant's keeper. It struck him down with its trunk, according to witnesses; and Zarvo the clown or Zarvo Krunic. He died instantly too, apparently — trampled.'

'Oh, shit.'

The expletive slipped out before I could stop myself and DI Johns felt obliged to give me a warning growl. 'Mind your language, constable.'

Frederickson held up a hand to stop him

admonishing further. 'Why? Was there an issue with that man?'

'Yes.' I replied and passed over the brown manila folder I'd put on the chair beside me. The District Commander opened it and I leaned forward to place the two images side by side. 'I think he was one of our potential murder suspects. Zarvo the clown, Jason McDonald, reported missing, presumed dead in 2004.'

Dead again, permanently.

36

Smithy had done the chivalrous thing and brought my car back to the station from the Oval to spare me the aftermath of the circus fire while my nerves were still shot. He'd had the sense to extract the car keys from me earlier, thank God, because my mind was too addled to think of it, and to make me remove my house key first. I decided my mentor was nothing short of brilliant.

It was the first, and probably the last time my car would ever get to see the inside of the station's parking garage. The sense of grandeur I had, in pulling out of the police gates in the Honda didn't, alas, extend to being able to magically find a space for my car once I got home. The crap-heap was still rotting outside the house and my already volatile temper was disproportionately rankled by the sight of the damned thing. The temptation to ram it was immense — I was insured now and was sure I'd have been able to make up a feasible story. Swerving to avoid a cat? Or a child? The only thing that stopped me was the fact I was rather fond of my car and couldn't be stuffed with any resulting panel-beating hassle.

I couldn't resist giving the Mini's front tyre a kick or two on the way past though, and I didn't bloody well care who saw me, although I did note a young woman with a pushchair crossed the road as soon as I started lavishing attention on the hunk of junk. Once my foot started hurting though, I gave up on retribution and stormed into the house and up the stairs to my room.

Maggie must have heard my entrance; anyone within a five-kilometre radius would have, courtesy of the stomping and colourful muttering. She arrived in a flash and before I could say anything she strode over and enveloped me in a huge hug. The effect was like sucking oxygen from a fire. All day I had laboured at holding myself together, trying to be the staunch, strong woman my colleagues expected. I had succeeded, mostly, but the sheer effort of that had taken its toll. The façade crumbled and I felt Maggie rocking me as I bawled all over her shoulder.

'God, Sam, that must have been so awful for you,' she said while rubbing my back the way Dad used to when I was a girl if I'd hurt myself and he was trying to soothe away the pain. 'I've been in a lab all day and it's like a vacuum from the outside world. I had no idea, otherwise I would have come and found you earlier. I've only just turned my phone back on and got your messages, I'm so sorry.'

'That's okay,' I said and stood up straight to reach for some tissues to deal with the snot. Unfortunately, I'd also left a bit on Maggie's shoulder and she laughed at my inept efforts at cleaning it up. It was pretty ludicrous and I managed to half-laugh, half-sob, which sounded so silly that Maggie laughed even more.

'Well, Sam,' she said as she held up the

rubbish bin for the sodden tissues. 'What are we going to do with you?'

I tossed them towards the basket and missed badly. The floor caught them. 'Shoot me and put me out of my misery.'

'After that fine display, if you tried it yourself, you'd probably miss. Just as well you had a damned big target this morning.' I tried to smile, but the tears welled up again, instead and I could feel my face crumple.

'Oh, sweetie, come back here,' Maggie said, and wrapped her arm around my shoulders again, giving them a squeeze. 'Besides, my snivelling little friend, if I shot you, it would make a hell of a mess on Aunt and Unc's carpet. Anyway, I kind of like having you around, you keep me amused. Got any other suggestions?'

'Am I allowed to suggest anything involving large quantities of alcohol?'

'Only if I'm invited.'

'You're invited.'

'I thought you'd say that, but I have to be honest. I don't know if I want to be seen in public with someone whose eyes make her look like she's spent the day smoking illegal plant life. I mean this in the nicest possibly way, but honey, you look like crap.'

'Thanks, I needed that.'

'You're welcome. So, the first thing I'm going to do is take you downstairs and feed you up on some of Aunty Jude's fabulous leftover lasagne, and I'll even let you have the last bread bun, cos I'm generous like that.'

'Gee whiz, ta.'

'But wait, there's more. I'll even make you a cup of super-duper espresso coffee with the fresh roast beans I acquired from the Fix today.'

That got me smiling again. This house had all the mod cons, which included a Rocket Coffee machine that scared the bejesus out of me. That thing looked like a chromed miniature oil refinery, with pipes and gauges and steam venting in an alarming fashion. Maggie wasn't afraid to use it. She could make that thing sing.

'You got my attention with the coffee. I'll pass on the food, although I appreciate the gesture, but where does the alcohol bit come in?'

'Patience, child. I was going to suggest that after a bite to eat — I'm insisting on that, by the way — and a spruce up, we pop down into town and have a quiet one. Unless you wanted to go up to the police bar instead?'

We usually popped into the bar on the fourth floor, saluted the Queen and settled in for a couple on a Friday evening. But tonight, for some strange reason, I didn't quite feel up to reminders of work — or the possibility of running into a particular someone, not that he drank with the plebs.

'No, I think I'll give that a miss, thanks. A quiet one or five in town sounds good.'

'Did you want me to invite anyone else along? Smithy? Paul Frost? He's still in town, isn't he?'

Paul had offered, and I knew Smithy would come, if asked. But in reality, the last thing I felt like was having to be sociable with blokes. Who could be bothered?

'Nah, a girls' night out would be good.'

Maggie was creating wondrous smells from the kitchen. Aunt and Unc had just arrived home and we were discussing the latest email from the girls, who were at a ski race event near Lake Tahoe in the US of A. Mercifully, they seemed unaware of some of the nastier events in Dunedin today, or had chosen not to mention them. Aunty Jude had been filling me in on the twins' successes when Uncle Phil flicked on the television.

The images froze my blood. The aerial view was jumpy and the noise of the helicopter filled the room. Under the alien flicker of orange street lamps and shuddering white spotlight a lone, pathetically small figure stood its ground under the relentless approach of the lumbering beast. Pulsating sound from inside my head inter-mingled with the thrumming of the helicopter blades. A furious heat rushed up my body. My eyes saw the figure — the ant — pull the shotgun up to sight, the elephant getting closer, closer, and when the behemoth seemed impossibly close, bang. The shot caused my head to jerk back, my breath suck in and my world stand still. I could not tear my eyes away from the scene, as I knew the next move in this unlikely drama. Muffled voices caught at the edge of my hearing, but my mind was transfixed by the screen. The creature collapsed, its momentum carrying it forward to within metres of the figure. Fast forward, the figure standing behind the beast, shotgun muzzle to the head. Another shot, another jolt. Saliva flooded into my mouth. I slapped my hand over it to hold it in and bolted for the toilet.

37

'Are you sure you're up to this?' Maggie asked as we wandered into the Sanctum. The Octagon in Dunedin was like Grand Bar Central with way too many drinking establishments to choose from. Not a place for the indecisive. My vote had been for one that didn't have any televisions, so we'd had to case out and leave two before settling in here. Sure, the massive screens had been devoted to rugby matches, but I wasn't going to chance someone flipping channels to check out the news.

'Ask me that question again when I've got a big glass of red in my hand,' I said. 'Or even better, only half a glass of red left in my hand.'

'Your wish is my command,' she said, with a bow. 'You find a seat, I'll get the drinks.'

It was a bit chilly to sit at one of the outdoor tables, even if they did provide cuddly rugs, and besides, that was where the smokers were quarantined to and I didn't feel like breathing in any of their second-hand crap. I wandered down the back and found a booth. It was perfect — comfortable, cocoon-like and with a sense of seclusion. A good hidey-hole. Dunedin hadn't been my home long enough for me to keep bumping into people I knew. In fact, after growing up in small towns, and then being sole-charge police presence in Mataura, I was glad of the anonymity Dunedin offered. In

Mataura, people could probably tell you what colour underwear you were wearing from what they'd seen hanging on your clothes line. Here, no one knew my business and I liked it that way.

It had taken me a good hour to get myself together after the shock of seeing the television footage. It wasn't only the brutality of seeing me shoot poor Cassie. It was the second shot, so much like an execution, that was too much. Uncle Phil told me they had shown me slide down to the ground, leaning against the back of the elephant, just sitting there, head in my hands. He said they'd shown the humanity; that it hadn't come across as a cold-blooded killing. That was no consolation. The footage had also been an eye-opener, made me realise just how close to disaster I'd come. At the time, everything happened too fast to think; I hadn't contemplated the potential dangers. I was on automatic. What if I'd missed? I shuddered.

'Here we go.' Maggie was back bearing gifts of my favourite land of fruit — the squashed and fermented variety. 'I splurged and got us a decent Central Otago Pinot Noir. Enjoy.'

She slid a glass of deep, luscious burgundy-coloured liquid under my nose.

'So it's not for quaffing?' I'd had something cheap and cheerful in mind, and lots of it.

'Sorry. I thought the best way to make you pace yourself would be to get something civilised.'

I swirled the wine around the glass and inhaled the aroma. 'Ooh, you're right, this is good.' I took a sip and savoured the mellow, warm flavour. 'All we need's a cheese board and it would be perfect.'

'It's on its way,' Maggie said and tipped her glass. 'I think of everything. Although, perfection would involve me, George, you and Brad, but I couldn't quite swing that one, not even with my miracle-inducing superpowers.'

'George and Brad?'

'Clooney and Pitt.'

'Ah, yes, they would complement the wine nicely. But it always gets ugly when you have to fend off all those other adoring women, and the paparazzi. I'll make do with a quiet night and your charming company,' I said, as I tipped my glass in her direction. 'Thanks, Maggs.'

'A toast,' Maggie said. 'Here's to a glorious, humdrum, ordinary, stupefyingly dull and uneventful week ahead.'

'Hear, hear,' I said and clinked glasses.

My head had a pleasant buzz thing happening as the wine kicked in and its warmth softened the edges of the frozen ball in the pit of my stomach. My state of mellowness dissipated pretty quickly, however, when it was my turn to attend to the drinks. One of the pitfalls of being a bit on the short side is that people tend to overlook you. The situation wasn't helped by bloody great lug-heads who pushed in front of me at the bar. By the time the bar-chick noticed me, which was an eternity — amazing how all the guys got served first — I was more than a little septic. I bit back the urge to point out her shortcomings. It was probably wasted on someone who wore one of those god-awful studs below her lower lip. I hated to think what it did to her teeth. But I almost forgave all when she filled the glasses to a generous level.

I turned around and made my way gingerly back through the throng. The place had filled up considerably and the volume had escalated with it. I had a couple of close calls as I made my way towards the back and had almost reached safety when a hand plonked onto my shoulder, near giving me a coronary. I held my breath as the wine sloshed to the rim of the glass.

'Fancy seeing you here. So, you decided to come out, after all — and you didn't even invite me.' I half turned and there was Paul Frost with some stupid, mocked-up hurt look on his face. My eyes darted over to where Maggie was sitting and the cow gave me a wink.

'Oh, spare me the pathetic looks, why don't you. Are you stalking me, Paul? And don't give me your cute 'I'm-a-detective' line again.'

He laughed, deep and melodic. 'Sorry to disappoint you, Sam, but no, you don't quite rate high enough on my obsessions for a good stalking. Almost, but not quite.' I supposed he thought that smile could charm all the girls. I wondered when he'd realise it wasn't having the desired effect on me. 'I'd arranged to meet some people here, but they haven't turned up yet. I see Maggie's over there.' He waved to her and she gave a cheerful little wave back, before he returned his attention to me. His voice changed to his I'm-all-concerned one and his eyes focused in like I was the only person in the room. It suddenly felt a lot warmer in here. 'How did your interview go? I hope they were sensible and didn't give you a hard time.' The crush of the crowd meant he was leaning over me, close enough for me to smell him. He had something nice on, but a bit too much of it. 'Oh, you'd better watch your butt, its sticking out — someone can't get past, behind you.'

'It's not that big,' I said as I shuffled forward a bit, to let the guy past. Unfortunately, Paul got a shove from behind at the same time, forcing him forward into me. His body pushed against the glasses, the contents sloshed up and I watched aghast as two crimson stains ran down my best merino top in the most prominent of places. Paul's hands grabbed first onto my shoulders to stabilise himself, and then behind my elbows to rescue the glasses.

'Oh, bloody hell,' I said. 'Look what you've gone and done.' Like I needed this right now. 'Can't you be more bloody careful?'

'Shit, do you want me to wipe your boobs?' he asked as he let go of me and looked around for something to repair the damage.

'Nuh, uh, don't you dare. You've done enough already.' I thrust a glass into one of his hands, grabbed the serviette he'd swiped off a table, and then handed him the other glass. I made a futile effort at mopping up the spillage.

'Hey, that wasn't my fault,' he said. 'Between your bum, boobs and the crowd in here, it's no wonder we got jostled.'

I sucked in a big breath. I didn't think they were that big and how dare he talk like that. My internal barometer was on the rise again, assisted by the pressure of a truly awful day.

'Oh, so it was my fault, was it? Well, Paul,' my voice loud and laden. 'See these? They're called hips.' I gave mine a Polynesian wiggle. 'And they actually belong on a real woman. See these?' I said as I pointed to my wine-stained chest. 'They are breasts, not boobs. A boob is a mistake. There is nothing mistaken about these babies. In fact, some women pay to have them bigger — that's very deliberate — no errors there, except in judgement. They are *not* boobs.' His eyes were still fixated on my chest, which fuelled the fire all the more. 'God, you men are all the same.'

With this rant of mine in full swing, Paul looked at first astonished, then bemused and as I finished the last, and I thought well-delivered line, he let out a loud laugh, and to my utter astonishment, stepped forward and kissed me squarely on the lips.

He stepped back, still laughing. 'Good God, woman, do you ever shut up?'

I lifted my hand to my mouth. Did that just happen?

'If I'm not allowed to use such blokish and apparently derogatory terms as boobs and bum, what am I allowed to use? Some sterile terminology?' He put on a hoity-toity voice. 'Why, what a lovely pelvic cradle you have. So perfectly balanced with your mammaries.' It was my turn to stand, mouth agape. 'I don't think so. Sorry, Sam, but seeing as you hadn't noticed, I'm a guy. If I like what I see I'm going to say something along the lines of 'phorrrrrrgh, nice arse' to go along with, 'great rack'. It's genetically imprinted in my DNA, along with that of every other red-blooded male in the world. So you need to lighten up and get over yourself. For Christ's sake, what is happening in the world if a guy can't give a girl a compliment?'

I gulped a bit more air before replying: 'Compliment? Huh.' Seeing as witty repartee failed me, I resorted to that other frequently used item in a girl's arsenal and turned around and stormed off, well as much as you could storm through a crowded room. Maggie looked like she was about to wet herself, she was laughing so much.

'I suppose you heard all that?' I asked, as I reached over and grabbed my bag. Hopefully I'd find something in there that could deal with the spillage.

'Above this din? Not a word. I didn't need too. As they say, a picture tells a thousand words,' She nodded in the direction I'd come from. 'Don't you think you've forgotten something?'

Ah, crap, the wine. I slowly turned my head and there was Paul, making his way over, a smug grin on his face. I turned and looked pointedly at the wall.

'Ladies,' he said, and I heard two clinks as he placed the glasses on the table.

'Why thank you, kind sir,' Maggie replied. I could only guess at the theatrics, as I wasn't going to grace it with a glance.

'Always a pleasure,' he said and then I heard the gentle chuckling recede.

I turned back to see Maggie looking at me with the land of amused expression that made you want to forcibly wipe it off.

'That was entertaining, I didn't know they provided a floor show here.'

'Ah, shut ya face.' I took a slug of what was left of my wine, and then headed off to the bathroom.

38

The cellphone rang while I was back, once again, in the Sanctum's bathrooms, trying to blot with wet toilet paper the wine spilled on my top, but succeeding only in leaving a little white paper trail where I'd dabbed, in turn, drawing more attention to my chest.

'Hello?'

'Samantha? It's Mum.'

Oh, crap. With everything that had been happening, I'd forgotten to ring the olds and let them know what was going on. After the Mataura fiasco, and associated ladled-on guilt, I had promised to call more often and keep them in the loop, especially when things got interesting. They must have seen the news, figured out it was me and Mum was ringing to give me one of her little speeches again.

'Hi, Mum. Gosh, I was just about to ring you guys.' I cringed and slapped my forehead as I realised it was 11 p.m. and no sane person would be ringing their parents at that hour. There was a long pause and I braced myself for the onslaught.

'Sam, it's about your Dad.' The cold knot re-formed in the pit of my stomach.

'What's happened?'

'It looks like he'll be okay, but he's had a bit of a turn. We're at the hospital in Invercargill.' My mind sprinted through all the options to get myself down there. After three glasses of wine, driving was out of the question, even though the call had sobered me up in an instant. I was sure to be legally under the limit, but I knew my liver's tolerances, and I wouldn't be safe behind the wheel. I could get someone to take me. But who? Maggie had been drinking as well and, like me, always erred on the side of caution. It was a two-and-a-half to three-hour drive and a big ask to impose on a friend. There wouldn't be any buses or flights until the morning.

'I'll try and get there as soon as I can,' I said, my brain still calculating the logistics.

'You don't need to do that. We'll be fine. Stephen and Sheryl are here, thank heavens. Sheryl's been great, explaining what's going on to me.' Of course Saint Steve and Saint Francis Sherylgale would be there. Fortunately for Mum, Steve had married her perfect daughter — a nurse and devoted mother of her grandchildren. Not like her wayward one doing a man's job. How could I ever compete? I sighed, the weight of the day descending on me like a vanload of unexpected relatives at Christmas.

'I can be there tomorrow morning, Mum.' I'd go home, try and get a few hours' sleep, then set out early, five o'clock.

'No, don't you worry, you don't need to do that.' There she went again. I knew damned well if I didn't go I'd be forever reminded of my lack of support when they needed me most. I was on a hiding to nothing.

'What's wrong? Do they think it's his heart again?'

'That's part of it, but they think there maybe something else.'

'What kind of thing?' I asked.

'They want to do some more tests, they want to fly him over to Dunedin.'

Shit, it must have been serious if they were going to do that. The hospital in Invercargill could handle most things.

'What kind of tests?' I asked. I heard her talking to someone in the background.

'Look, Sam, I've got to go. Steve needs his phone back to call the babysitter. I'll ring you tomorrow.'

Before I had a chance for a 'But . . . ' or a 'Take care' or a 'Love you', she'd hung up, leaving me standing in the bathroom, clutching wet toilet paper and feeling utterly alone.

39

It was Saturday morning, and I was feeling the effects of the night before. None of my cruddiness was due to alcohol. The wine was too good and there hadn't been enough of it for that, more's the pity. The news of Dad being ill, on top of destroying elephants, flaming circuses and too many dead people, had left me feeling like I'd had the life sucked out of me leaving a pale-faced shell of a thing doing an impersonation of Sam Shephard. And a piss-poor one at that.

There had been no point in getting up at a sparrow's fart and driving to Invercargill. Dad might be transferred here and Mum's 'I'll ring you' had put her firmly in the controlling seat, while ensuring she could still play her trump 'You're-never-there-when-I-need-you' card. She was ever the master at these games.

I heard the pad of feet approaching me from behind. 'What on earth are you doing in the laundry at this hour of the morning?' Maggie asked, stifling a yawn with the back of her hand, a picture of elegance in a once-white dressing gown and with shambolic morning hair. 'You look a fright.' There was the pot calling the proverbial kettle names.

'I couldn't be fagged dealing with my top last night, so I just bunged it in some water. I hope it's not ruined. I was looking for stain soaker, but there's so much crap in here.' The Kershaws' laundry cupboard was full of unidentifiable boxes and ancient-looking concoctions. The washing powder lived on the shelf above the tub, but if you needed anything a little more specialist, a bit of archaeology was in order. I picked up a box that looked the right shape for stain soaker and lifted the lid. It was a powder, but the colour was a bit dodgy. 'What is this stuff?'

Maggie peered over, her expression somewhere between a grimace and a laugh. 'Eew, no, for Gods sake put that away, that's Great-Uncle George.'

'What do you mean, Great-Uncle George?' I said, giving it a little shake.

'I mean, that is, literally, Great-Uncle George. Those are his ashes.'

The dawning realisation I was holding someone's remains in my hands gave me a major case of the heebie-jeebies. I flipped the lid back down and hastily put him back on the shelf where I found him.

'Who the hell keeps their relatives in the laundry cupboard?' I asked as I rubbed my hands down my pyjama pants. Then, deciding that wasn't quite good enough, I reached over and washed them in the sink, with an excessive amount of soap.

'He's been there for years. He's Uncle Phil's father. Apparently, they didn't get along too well, so when he died, Uncle Phil put him the laundry cupboard and he's stayed there ever since.'

'Why didn't they just scatter him somewhere or bury him?'

'Aunty Jude wants to, make it decent and proper. In fact, she was the one who caved in and picked him up from the Kremlin.'

'Kremlin?'

'Crematorium. Uncle Phil wasn't very impressed at her meddling. He'd wanted to leave them there, uncollected. So now the ashes are here, George takes pride of place in the laundry.' I know my old flame Lockie's parents had their English pointer cremated when he died, and the dog's remains were kept in the lounge on a bookshelf until he was planted under a memorial pohutukawa tree in the garden. That was creepy enough. We always just dug a bloody big hole when one of the farm dogs died; we didn't waste money on cremation. Anyway, if a dog wasn't allowed in the house when it was alive, why the hell would you change the rules, just because it was dead? I'd thought they were a bit strange. Although, this took the cake.

'But surely he'd see them all the time in the laundry; it would be a continuous reminder under his nose, every day. The old guy must have really pissed Uncle Phil off to end up in some cupboard.'

'It's a bit of a sore point and no one will talk about it. Besides, I think the ashes are quite invisible to him in the laundry. I mean to say, how often does your dad do the washing?' As soon as the words came out of her mouth, I could see Maggie regretted the reference to my dad. 'Oh God, Sam, I'm sorry, I didn't mean to, I know you're worried, I — '

'It's okay, I know what you mean, and it was a

fair comment. I don't think Dad's seen the inside of our laundry for decades.'

Maggie smiled and gave me a tug on my sleeve. 'Come on, leave that for now. Another hour won't hurt it. I need a cup of tea and some breakfast — we've got fruit toast, if you're interested.'

She knew damned well a promise of fruit toast and tea would get my attention. I trailed her out to the kitchen and plonked myself down at the table, so I could stare out of the window. The morning light was reflecting off the still water of the harbour. It was breathtaking. It was moments like this that had me thanking my lucky stars I'd made the decision to up sticks and move here.

Maggie filled the kettle and flicked it on, a magical sound. The next piece of magic was the sound of the toaster clicking with its cargo of fruit bread.

'So what's your plan of attack today?' she asked.

I hadn't really thought that hard about what I'd do. It was Saturday. I had the day off work, so was a free agent, but I felt shackled by the need to know what was happening with Dad. It was 7.15 a.m. and Mum hadn't rung. Surprise. I could ring Stephen on his cellphone, but that might wake them up if they'd had a late night at the hospital and Mum would probably get snarky because she'd think I didn't trust her to ring me. Family politics could do your head in. It would be a waiting game, and patience wasn't one of my strong points. I needed a good distraction, which got me to contemplating something that had been waving for attention at the back of my mind.

With all the events of yesterday, my mind had veered off target. I realised I'd lost sight of a beautiful young girl, murdered, dumped in a river, who needed justice.

It was time I turned my attention back to Rose-Marie.

40

It was still obscenely early for a Saturday morning, but I decided to make a trip down to work and pick up some notes on the Bateman case. With luck, the antisocial hour would lessen my chances of bumping into anyone. The plan was I'd join the milling hordes at the farmers' market at the railway station and grab a coffee and a fresh pastry, then tootle into work, grab the information I needed, dump the notes back at the house, force myself to go for a run to clear the cobwebs and make the most of the splendid morning, then set my mind to the riddle of Rose-Marie's death and those who had preceded her. Solid plan.

Mum had finally rung and told me Dad was being transferred by helicopter to Dunedin hospital in the afternoon. I was going to meet her there at 2 p.m. He'd had a good night and was stable, which was reassuring.

I didn't notice the note on the windscreen until I was in the driver's seat. I stared at it for several moments, trying to get my heart rate back under control, before throwing the door open, getting back out and tearing it from under the wiper blade. Now what?

Bang, bang.

I tasted the acid tang of bile in the back of my throat and a surge of fire in my veins. Someone was playing a stupid little game and I wasn't in the mood. I pulled a pen and notebook out of my bag and marched back down to the hunk of junk outside our house. My initial pang of apprehension had been overwritten by indignation. Stuff this. It was time I did something. I was going to check out the number plate and find out who the shit-heap belonged to, then it was time to pay a little visit.

But once at the office, all thoughts of retribution against note-writing idiots flew out of my head the moment the lift doors opened. For despite my theory of getting in early to avoid any inopportune meetings, I was presented with the worst-case scenario. Oh, fuckity fuck.

What do you do when trapped in a small steel box and find yourself face to face with an arsehole boss? It wasn't like I could take evasive action.

DI Johns took one look at me and glowered. I took one look at him and felt an overwhelming need to go to the loo.

'Good morning, sir,' I said, forcing a hopefully friendly-looking smile on my dial. In training, they always said the best thing to do in a confrontational situation was to talk calmly to an aggressor.

'Shephard,' he said, before an uncomfortable pause. 'I think we need to have a little chat, down in my office, now.'

Shit. The last thing I wanted to be was enclosed in a small room with him and no witnesses, but what choice did I have? The temptation was to let the lift doors close and pretend I was never there. Didn't think that would help my cause, though. There were no other detectives around to divert attention — my plan had worked perfectly there — and I didn't want the DI to think I didn't have the guts to front up. So I stepped out of the lift and took what felt like a very long walk down the corridor to his domain. The sound of his door clicking shut as he closed it caused a corresponding lurch in my stomach. I folded my arms across my chest and stood, braced, waiting for it.

'Take a seat.' He indicated towards the chair and went and sat behind his desk. I did as requested. His eyes engaged mine for what felt like minutes, not seconds, until I had to break away to examine the few wisps of cloud in the otherwise azure sky behind him.

'Ahem.' The sound of him clearing his throat drew my attention back to him. 'I'll be completely honest with you, Detective Constable, and say I think you are an irresponsible and foolhardy officer and I think you are an impediment to this team.'

That was certainly honest, brutally so. Despite chewing on the inside of my lip, I could feel the tell-tale tears spring to my eyes.

'I opposed your inclusion in the detective programme, but for whatever reason, others thought you were of the right material. As far as I'm concerned, your actions have only gone to prove that they made the wrong decision. But I have been instructed', he spat out the word instructed with sneering distaste, 'to allow you to continue in this case in an active role.'

At least there were higher powers on my side.

197

'So against my better judgement, I will allow you to assist in the murder investigation, but I will not tolerate any unorthodox behaviour or meddling on your part. Do you understand me?'

'Yes sir,' I said, my voice hoarse.

'I will be watching everything you do, and the moment you step out of line, or screw up, I will be down on you like a ton of bricks and you won't know what's hit you. And this time, there will be no one to save you. You might have everyone else fooled, but I know what you're really like young lady. You seem to think you're above the rules and everyone else here, and I will not hesitate to take you down and kick your arse back to the boohai where you belong. The only reason you're still here is because you're someone's pet. I don't know who you fucked to get here, but don't think you'll get any special attention from me.' Jesus Christ, all I'd ever had was special attention from him. 'Do you have anything to say?'

Actually, I did.

I cleared my throat and spoke, my voice still gravelly, but quiet and clear. 'If we're going to be brutally honest, sir, then I have to say I feel that you've had it in for me from the moment we met at Mataura. I don't think I ever had a chance in your eyes because you already had me pegged and labelled and that's not going to change, no matter what I do.' My eyes flicked up from the desktop to his eyes and saw them, cold and narrowed. I paused a moment, anticipating the rebuttal, but he didn't interject. 'Despite what you seem to think, I am a good detective and a good investigator', I continued, daring to look him straight in the eye, 'if you'd only give me a chance to do my job, instead of throwing up these constant barriers and impediments. You have to admit I have come up with the main leads in this case.'

'Yeah, and the circus lead looks like it was one great red herring. You've wasted everyone's time, and not to mention, lives.'

He knew how to throw the cruellest barbs, and once I was able to continue talking, I couldn't disguise the hurt.

'You can't lay the blame for that on me, and the coincidences there are too great to ignore. There is a connection between the circus and those murders, you know there is.'

'Why don't we have any firm suspects, then?' he asked, leaning forward over the desk. 'Sometimes coincidence is just that.'

'Because we haven't looked hard enough. We haven't given the processes enough time. We've been too distracted by everything else.'

'And whose fault is that?'

God, he was good. My mother finally had some serious competition when it came to applying guilt, but I was damned if I was going to accept this load. I leaped to my feet and leaned forward with my hands planted on his desk.

'In case you hadn't noticed, I am not the only one on this investigation and it is certainly not my job to lead it, so don't look at me for the shortcomings in the whole bloody thing. Leadership comes from the top. Your performance hasn't been exactly stellar. You need to take a good hard look at yourself instead of looking for scapegoats elsewhere.' The fuse-wire holding my temper in check had shorted and my voice rose to the occasion.

He smiled, lips slowly exposing a row of perfect teeth and the image of a shark again jumped into my mind. I felt like a minnow under his gaze. I think the bastard was enjoying this.

'Sit back down.' He gestured with his hands and I, face burning, did as I was told. 'Well, Shephard,' he said, slowing his voice to a drawl. 'I've got to give you credit for having balls. Not many people would dare talk to me like that and keep their job. But I'll take that one on the chin, for now. So if you're so well positioned to make an opinion, where do you think the investigation should go? I'm curious. What would you do?'

My opinion was the last thing I expected to be asked for and I wavered for a moment.

He pounced. 'See, you can't tell me. You have no idea, do you? So maybe you should — '

'No, wait, before you write me off, give me chance to speak.' My hand had shot up, gesturing him to stop and he looked at it and then at me with a look of condescending amusement. I felt like a mouse, being batted around by the cat until it tired of the game.

'I think we need to go back to the beginning, Rose-Marie's friends, flatmates, family, boy-friend, look into her life, her university studies, the things we started on before the circus connection became apparent. Get back to basics. We need to look over the other murders, similarities, differences, any connection between the victims.'

'Yes, well this isn't telling me anything your average schoolkid couldn't figure out. You'll have to do better than that.'

'It hinges on the circus. If our murderer isn't a member of the crew, then someone has gone out of their way to set them up, use them as a smokescreen. But who would do that and why? Is this something personal against the circus or a person in it? Did someone hate Terry Bennett, for example — enough to try and set him up for murder? Were all these victims random collateral damage for someone's elaborate plan? Or is this about them as individuals, specifically targeted?'

I could see him mulling it over, his fingers tapping his lips. 'I hadn't thought about this being a personal vendetta against the circus. If it was, they've achieved results in spectacular fashion. It makes me want to look at some of those animal-rights activists a bit more closely.'

Me too. I'd heard of instances overseas where the activists had crossed the line from peaceful protest into wanton crime — the worst case involving desecrating some poor woman's grave because her son-in-law bred guinea pigs for medical research. Could someone have gone so far as to commit murder — make that multiple murders — to get at a perceived animal abuser? That smacked of obsession bordering insanity.

He looked up at me, this time minus the sneer. 'Is that why you're in here this morning? To look at the Bateman case?'

'Yes,' I said, simply.

'After everything that's happened, and in your own time?'

'Yes.'

He tapped his fingers against his lips some more. 'What do you need?'

My God, was I actually going to get some support from the man? I wouldn't get my hopes up. 'Files on the investigation to date, access to the videoed interviews and transcripts of the ones that weren't. Opportunity to talk to some of the parties involved.'

Seeing as all cards seemed to be on the table, I dared another direct question.

'How do I know you're going to let me get on with this and not withhold information or interfere? How do I know you're not setting me up to fail?'

'You're just going to have to trust me,' he said, deadpan.

'Well I don't, so that's going to be a problem.'

The right side of his face twitched, but his voice remained even. 'The feeling is quite mutual. I will give you the opportunity to prove my opinion of you wrong. But if, for any reason, you let me down, or make me look bad, no amount of help from above will keep your arse in this job. Understood?'

'Perfectly.'

41

I was back at square one, and after the events of the last week — my God, had it only been a week? — I felt sluggish, as though I was trying to shake off the effects of a persistent head cold. I slowed down from jogging pace and stood, breathing heavily, under the spider-like tree that marked the last moments of Rose-Marie Bateman's journey. Her friends all called her Rosie, but somehow calling her Rosie didn't sit right with me. It didn't afford her the respect she deserved.

Death. The shudder my body gave wasn't just a result of the sweat cooling on my heated skin. This walkway used to be a favourite route. Now, even on a sunny day, it gave me the creeps.

I'd felt compelled to come past here on my run, revisit the place, remind myself of what was at the heart of the matter. The path down to the spot where Rose-Marie was found still sported the remnants of crime-scene tape, although someone had chosen to ignore it and it lay discarded to one side. What would one more set of footprints matter? I checked around to ensure I had no company, then walked down the path and along the riverside until I reached the spot where I'd stood guard over her body. Today the site seemed innocent, even cheerful with sunlight glinting off the water's surface and the musical soft murmuring of the Water of Leith. The exuberant warbles of a bell-bird, which would on any other day elicit a smile, seemed to add to the injustice. All traces of Rose-Marie's passage and struggle for life had disappeared. How quickly nature erased and the world forgot.

Her murder had led to a cascade of events that had resulted in more death, destruction and misery. Just ask Terry Bennett, or Jamal, or Zarvo, no, Jason as he was known and his once hopeful and now devastated family. Just ask fifty-odd displaced circus performers and workers, jobless and many of them stranded in a foreign country. Then there were the murders that preceded all this. What a bloody mess to sort out. My brain was stuffed full of the facts of the investigation I'd been working through. I'd hoped the run would spur my subconscious into processing it all, picking out the bits that jarred, the bits that gelled. What I needed most was to talk with someone about it all to help order my thoughts, structure the bedlam. Smithy? I'd considered ringing him, but he was a family man and I was sure being in the force put enough pressures on his domestic life without me adding to them by dragging him away from what little time he had with them. I couldn't do that to Veronica and the kids. As for the others? I didn't really feel I knew any of them well enough to impinge on them like that. There was Paul. He was still in town, but I wasn't sure I'd be able to have a good work session without him being his usual chauvinistic self and irritating the crap out of me. My threshold for tolerating his rubbish was a bit low right now. Maggie was always good; maybe Maggie.

It was all a moot point though. There were other priorities for the moment. I checked my watch; I'd have to rattle my dags. Mum would be expecting me at the hospital soon and it didn't pay to keep her waiting.

My sense of urgency had returned.

42

'Hi Sam-a-lamb, fancy seeing you here.' Dad looked wired for sound with a drip going in one arm and ECG stickies poking through the grey mat of hair on his chest. I wasn't quite sure what state I expected to find him in, but was relieved that he seemed perky and hadn't lost that twinkle in his eye. He was sharing a room with two empty beds and a striped-pyjama-clad elderly chap who seemed to be trying to watch the very loud television through his eyelids.

'Hey, Dad.' I leaned over and gave him a kiss on his stubbly cheek. 'Standards are slipping, I see,' I said, giving the stubble a scritch with my knuckles. 'Stick you in a chopper and send you to the big smoke and you think you're on holiday.'

'Some holiday, the room service is terrible and as for the food. Don't they know a man needs a real lunch? Where's the meat?'

'I think that brown stuff *is* meat, Dad.'

'Really? If it is, it's having an identity crisis. And as for this other stuff,' he said, poking at some greens with a fork. 'None of this limp-salad-and-orange-juice business. What the hell would I want with salad? Salad is for rabbits. That kind of diet will only make you sick.'

'Glad to see there's some fight left in the old boy. How are you anyway? What's up with all this attention-seeking behaviour?' I asked, indicating the array of hardware he was attached to. The lovely thing about Dad was you could be direct. He didn't go for tiptoeing around the facts. No games, no bullshit, unlike someone else in the family.

'You want to know the truth,' he said quietly while looking around to check the coast was clear. He leaned forward and reached up to pull me close. Even at sixty-five he was a large and fit man, although, he did look a bit thinner than when I'd last seen him. I could see his abdominal muscles tighten as he sat up. When I had bent down near enough, he whispered in my ear. 'I'm just doing it to annoy your mum.' We both enjoyed a good laugh before the devil herself entered the room.

'What's so funny?'

'Dad told me he had three days to live and he wanted his ashes to be blasted into space like that guy from *Star Trek*.' We both laughed all the more, while Mum stood there, not so amused. She was what people described as a handsome woman, and having filled out slightly with age, she was a stocky, handsome woman. I did wish she'd upgrade her wardrobe, or at least go buy some Trinny and Susannah books to try and be a modern, stocky, handsome woman.

'Samantha, don't be so crass,' she said, hands on hips. 'You don't make jokes about that kind of thing.' The woman really needed to go buy herself a sense of humour too. One look at Dad told me it wasn't so bad; he wasn't about to drop dead. And he plainly thought he was okay, so that was the most important thing.

'Can you come down with me to the nurses' station, they want your cellphone number or something.' She grabbed me by the arm and escorted me out of the room. I blew Dad a kiss on the way out the door.

Once we were a safe distance along the corridor, she spun around and got started. Mum was a shorty, like me. In fact, she was one of the few people I knew who I could talk to at eye level. But where her altitude may have equalled mine, the attitude was poles apart and she took great pains to let me know my station in life and how great a disappointment I was for her. She gave new meaning to the term battleaxe and made Boadicea look like a big girls' blouse. 'You shouldn't say things like that, Samantha. What if he's really sick? How would you feel then, making light of everything?'

'Well, is he? Is he really sick?'

'That's what we're here to find out. They don't fly people from here to there for nothing you know. They must be concerned about something.'

'What have they told you?'

'They want to do more tests on his heart. But they also want to do an MRI scan on him. They're concerned something else is putting pressure on it, so want to check his whole chest.'

'What makes them think that?'

'I don't know. Sheryl explained it to me, but I can't recall all the details. I wish she'd been able to come over, but she couldn't get anyone to look after the kids. She'd have been a great comfort for us all.'

Because I wasn't?

'Where do I go to give the nursing staff my number?' I asked, changing tack before I got to hear of Sheryl's many virtues and get pinged some more.

'Oh, they've already got it. I just needed to have a word with you, alone.' That sounded ominous. 'Look, I didn't want to upset your dad, so I haven't told him about you killing that elephant. He knows nothing about it.' She made it sound so premeditated. 'The last thing he needs right now is to hear about your latest escapade. I guess I've got used to you not wanting to tell me about these things by now. But your father would be really hurt if he knew you'd excluded us again.'

Oh, Jesus, she knew exactly where to punch. Any debate was pointless. She was the queen of pique and I didn't think there was anything I could ever do that would win her seal of approval. Even if I gave it all up to dedicate my life to saving AIDS orphans in Rwanda, she'd find fault, or tell me how Saint Sheryl would do it better. The chance of getting any sympathy for my misadventures was zip.

I tried to change the subject before she let loose with another barb.

'Where are you staying tonight? Do you want me to ask Jude if you could stay with us?' The spare bedroom was made up, ready for such impromptu needs, although the thought of being under the same roof . . .

'I wouldn't want to be any trouble.'

'She'd love to have you. In fact, she'd be

mortified if you didn't stay.'

Mum wavered for a moment then gave a big sigh, as though it was such a tough decision. 'Well, okay then, that would be very helpful. I'll be at the hospital for most of the time, so I won't get in anyone's way.'

'You wouldn't be in the way. Come stay, then you won't have to worry about accommodation or food and you can concentrate on looking after Dad.'

'Tell her not to worry about me for meals or anything, I'll pick things up from the hospital café. I wouldn't want to be a bother.'

My mother, ever the martyr.

43

This really was tragic. It was a hazy autumn afternoon with no breeze, the kind of Dunedin Saturday that settled over you like a warm grass-scented blanket. It was begging for a walk along the beach, or a bike ride up the peninsula, or even a chance to lounge outside with friends and share a good bottle of wine. But no, what was I doing? I was sequestered in my room, surrounded by an avalanche of notes, thinking of murder, not the season of mellow fruitfulness. My brain was flitting from Rose-Marie Bateman to Dad, to Terry Bennett, to the trail of death, to killing elephants, to any stupid, random thought that entered my head.

I shoved aside the folder I had tuned out of, climbed off my bed and ambled over to the window. At this time of day my room didn't get the sun, but I did have the consolation of the view. Somehow though, today, even that didn't offer solace. I had an almighty case of the blahs. Blah, blah, blah. My head felt like someone had pulled my hair into a vicious ponytail and was insisting on making it tighter, my eyeballs had a sandpapery texture, which seemed odd considering how much spontaneous lubricating they'd been getting over the course of the day. I looked down at the red-brick-paved courtyard and watched as the Kershaws' overweight fluffball excuse for a cat tried, very optimistically, to stalk a bird. It was about as subtle as a traction engine, and just as graceful. It wasn't much of a surprise when the fantail flew off up into the safety of a kowhai tree, probably laughing. I enjoyed a derisive snort at the cat's expense myself.

My scheme of initiating positive action to distract myself wasn't working. And, as much as I hated to admit it, what I really needed was company. Maggs, doing the studious thing, was down at the University Central Library on a hunt for references for an assignment due next week. Aunty Jude was at some Altrusa fundraising event. Mum was at the hospital, and wasn't planning on getting in until later this evening. That only left Uncle Phil — and as much as I liked him, and he was always good for a chat, I didn't feel I could interrupt his work because I had a case of the lonelies to go with the blahs.

Unappealing as it was, the only remedy I could think of would involve me having to swallow pride.

And pride was never a sugar-coated tablet.

44

Humble pie. Perhaps it wasn't so bad, although this one did have a sharp aftertaste. When I'd rung to ask if he'd come round and discuss the case, Paul couldn't resist getting a dig in about my needing him, after all. I didn't expect anything less. Lucky for him I valued his opinion in a professional sense, so I allowed him his mileage, if it made him feel better and massaged his little ego.

So here we were, closeted indoors at the kitchen table, late on one of Dunedin's finest Saturday afternoons, discussing death, murder, doom and gloom. Me, Paul and Fluffy the vanquished bird-slayer, with a pile of photocopied notes and a continuous supply of tea and coffee. We were chain-caffeining.

'So,' I said, my hands enjoying the last skerrick of warmth from being wrapped around my now empty mug of tea. 'I don't think anyone in the circus had anything to do with it. Well, not directly, anyway.'

'But you think they did indirectly?'

'Yes. It could be someone who wanted to set them up, destroy them. What better way than to label them as killers and get them under the scrutiny of the police and the media. They'd be guaranteed front-page news in every newspaper in the country and I imagine the gate sales would dry up a bit after that. Mr and Mrs Joe Average

213

Kiwi wouldn't be inclined to take little Johnny and Jill to the circus to see the big bad murderers.'

'Yeah, but that's a little extreme. I still think we need to keep an open mind on the circus folk. What about the guy that died? Zarvo?'

'He has no form at all, under either name. It seems his greatest crime was being a spineless wonder. His poor family — not only have they found out he was alive and well and had just abandoned them, but they find out he's now dead and they won't get the chance for an explanation or even to give him an earful and a boot up the arse. What a cowardly thing to do, to take off like that and fake death, rather than own up and admit you weren't happy. What kind of legacy is that to leave your kid? The only consolation is there doesn't seem to have been another woman involved.'

'Maybe he felt backed into a corner and he couldn't think of any other way out. Some people don't cope with stress or confrontation well and make dumb decisions.'

'Oh, so you're defending his actions, are you? Is that what you'd do, run away from your responsibilities?'

'No,' he said and smiled at me. 'I would take my responsibilities very seriously.'

I dropped my eyes and, feeling a blush start to sneak up my face, I got to my feet with a big scrape of chair legs on the floor and made to refill the kettle with water. Not that we needed any more.

'Well, I think running away from your

problems is gutless, but hardly the actions of a cold-blooded killer. And someone who would risk their life for some dumb animal would hardly be the type to murder.'

'There are plenty of examples out there of people who value their pets more than their own family, so don't be fooled by some apparently kind-hearted or even spur-of-the-moment gesture.' I gestured to Paul to see if he wanted another cuppa. He shook his head and continued. 'And you'd said you'd had a run-in with some people the other day who seem to value animals over humans.'

'The activists?' I said.

'The activists.'

'Yeah, they made quite a spectacle. Their leader fit the description of rabid quite nicely, I thought. But even the most rabid animal-rights activists wouldn't stoop to murder humans to protect animals. And most certainly not in this country; we're all a bit too laid-back for mass-protest civil disobedience. They might get a bit heated — there was certainly plenty of vitriol over those native giant snails being moved because of that coal mine on the West Coast — but sanctity of life and all that. Unless someone had well and truly lost their marbles, they wouldn't kill a human over it.'

'It has happened before, Sam, and you of all people should know that. Sometimes I think you have too much faith in human nature.'

'Better that than being cynical and suspecting everyone who breathes.'

'I'm not meaning it as a criticism. I prefer your

view on people too, but they aren't always what they seem, and, newsflash, some even lie.' He did the newsflash with hand actions that made me laugh.

'Other than speculate, I can't investigate the activists as DI Johns is following up that line of inquiry and I'm not about to step on his toes.'

'Strange, that. So why am I here? Other than you were desperate to see me and couldn't think of any other way to lure me here and save face . . . ' I reached over and thumped him on the arm. 'Ow. Hit a raw spot, did I?' he said, with a laugh.

'Don't flatter yourself, sunshine. You're not that appealing.'

'That's not what I've been told.'

'They say nice things to your face, then get real behind your back.'

'That's what you say. Go on, admit it, you think I'm charming.'

'Oh, for God's sake. You're so damned persistent. You must have a titanium hide. Don't you know when you're being spurned?'

'No.'

'Duh,' I said and threw a teaspoon at him. 'Okay, I'll make it perfectly clear for you, then, in words of one syllable. No, I didn't invite you here so I could sleep with you just because I've had a hard time and was a bit upset, so you can tuck your ego away. I invited you here to help with the case, so let's get back to the point, shall we?'

At this, he opened up with the kind of laugh that originated from the depths of his boots and

216

resonated off the walls. Even the cat lifted her dreamy head to see what caused the hilarity. 'Not even a birthday bonk?'

'No,' I said, searching for something on the bench to throw. 'As I just said, can we get back to the point, please?'

'Alright then, enlighten me on your theories, oh great one. Where do you think we need to look? And yes please, I've changed my mind, I will have another coffee.'

I could have reacted to the goading, but wasn't going to give him the satisfaction, so instead fussed around with making the drinks and trying to compose myself. I hated the way he could bait me and I always rose to it. I resolved to be a grown up and not play his silly little games.

'I think we need to get back to basics and look at each of the murders and victims, similarities, commonalities. Find out how they are linked, other than the obvious, and work from there.'

'Yes, well a five-year-old would realise this.'

'No need to be sarky.'

'Okay, truce,' he said, hands up. 'Fire away, one by one with the murders. Who was first?'

I brought the drinks over, and then spread the files out on the table, out of spill range. DI Johns had allowed me to bring the copies home, but I had to admit to feeling suspicious about his sudden change of heart, and the cynical part of me wondered when it would come back to bite me. Prejudice aside, I was determined to make the most of the situation. Under normal circumstances, my practice was that work life stayed at work, home life at home, all things in their rightful place, but I was way too involved here, and it felt personal. This case had intruded into my life on too many levels.

'First victim, Christchurch, first of March, Erica Jane Moorhouse, twenty-four years old.' I handed Paul a photo of a fresh-faced, pony-tailed brunette wearing waders and holding a sizeable trout. My heart gave a lurch, water again, although this young woman hadn't died in it.

'Pretty girl, nice fish.'

'Yes,' I agreed. 'She died as a result of an overdose.'

'Not self-inflicted, I take it?'

'No. Damned scary, actually. She was out at a bar-cum-nightclubby place with a group of girlfriends for their usual Saturday night out. They believe her drink was spiked while they were up dancing.'

'Oh, yes, I remember that one now. Police were putting out extra warnings to people to never leave their drinks unattended. What do they say? Victims make mistakes that put them in danger, make them targets. We'd been running a safety-education campaign anyway with pub patrons because of concerns over drinks being spiked with date-rape drugs, but this was something else — spiked to kill.'

'Yeah, massive dose of GHB. They never caught the killer. By the time she died in hospital, and people realised the most likely source, the nightclub had closed for the night, patrons gone home to bed and the glassware had been cleaned. Nothing in the way of evidence other than some grainy security video which wasn't of much use.'

'Sad. Bring on victim number two.'

'This one was thought to be an unfortunate hunting accident that no one ever owned up to. William James Brody, aged fifty-one, was angling on the Ashburton river when he was shot, in the back with a .303.' I handed Paul a photograph of a solid, slightly balding and jovial-looking man. He reminded me a bit of Dad with his standard farming uniform of checked shirt, shorts and floppy hat. He didn't have a fish. 'A nearby angler saw him drop and ran over thinking he'd had a heart attack or something. He pulled him out of the river, but Mr Brody died before medical help could arrive. No weapon was found, and there was no obvious motive for foul play, so it was thought perhaps to be a stray shot from a hunter who never owned up, or never made the connection between the death and their activities.'

'Didn't the other guy hear the shot?'

'No, it was pretty noisy because there were trail-bike riders nearby.'

'And they didn't see anything unusual or anyone with a gun?'

'The riders were on the opposite side of the river and obscured from view. They're there most weekends apparently, some form of club. So with all the din they were making, they didn't hear or see a thing. The shot appears to have come from behind the anglers, where the terrain varied from paddocks, to stands of bush, to flood-protection willows. They couldn't determine the angle the shot came from because the victim fell and floated a bit before his waders filled up. It was pure guesswork. The police speculated it could have come from someone potting rabbits or something.'

'And you think this is linked to the other murders?'

'Only because it occurred when the Darling Brothers Circus was in town, on the sixteenth of March, and was an unexplained death. It seems too coincidental to leave out.'

'Fair enough. Who's next?'

'Timaru, Monday, the twenty-fourth of March, exact date of death unknown. This is another in that didn't-look-like-a-murder, but-now-I-wonder category. Michael George Anderson, AKA Mick, a well-known drunk and bum. A bit of a local icon for all the wrong reasons. Found drowned off the wharf at the port. People assumed he got himself pissed and fell in. His blood alcohol was high enough to start the embalming process prior to death. His was one of those sad lives, made sadder by the fact it would now appear he had been murdered and people didn't take much note of his death other than to think the local bum fell in the drink.'

'I suppose he'd be an easy target.'

'And he was targeted, frequently. The local skinheads used to take particular pleasure in tormenting him. For someone determined to finish him off, all they'd need to do was feed him a big bottle of grog and give him a bit of a push — no worries. The world's easiest killing, all for the price of some cheap whisky.'

'He probably even thanked his murderer.'

'Probably toasted his good health.' Mick's picture was of a scrawny, bearded, stooped-looking creature in an oversized coat, with too-long trousers draping over sandalled feet with scary toenails. The officer holding him up looked dressed for Arctic conditions, My eyes kept pulling back to Mick's exposed feet.

In contrast, the next photo got me all teary again. Sparkling eyes shining out of a slightly acned face, braced teeth showing no signs of self-consciousness and bared in a huge grin. The school uniform another telling giveaway as to this victim's youth. I handed the picture to Paul and watched as his expression too, darkened.

'God, how?' He asked.

'Yeah, a waste, eh?'

'I'll say. A sure murder?'

'Unfortunately. This one shocked the community and there was a great hue and cry. Levi Edward Jones, aged fourteen. Two weeks shy of his fifteenth birthday. He appears to have been clubbed from behind with some kind of bat or pole. He dropped and was then clubbed again while on the ground. Post-mortem shows the first hit would have been enough to mortally wound him. The killer took no chances and finished him off.'

'Yeah, that's right. I remember it now. Where did this happen?'

'In Oamaru, the historic precinct, early morning, Sunday the sixth of April. Most of the light industrial places around there were closed, so the area would have been fairly quiet. He was found by a tourist. His parents owned a business in the area, which is why he was hanging around there on a Sunday morning. No sign of a struggle and no murder weapon.'

'He wouldn't have known what hit him.'

'Not a hope in hell.'

'Which leads us down the road to Dunedin.'

'To Dunedin, and Rose-Marie Bateman, Friday the eleventh of April, and what was an obviously premeditated murder.'

Paul had placed the photographs in a row and was looking from one to the other.

'What's the first thing that strikes you about these deaths?' he asked.

'Apart from the circus being in town, they have absolutely nothing in common.'

'Exactly. There's a mix of male and female victims, different ages, different cause of death for each. Did the victims know each other at all?'

'So far into investigations, it appears not. Smithy, actually, the one I introduced you to . . . '

'The one who fancies you.'

'He does not, and don't be so gross.'

'Whatever you choose to believe, Sam.' I gave him a boot under the table. 'Ow! Is that how you deal with everything challenging? Resorting to violence?'

'Only towards those who are too thick to respond to reason.'

'It's just an observation, stating what I saw.'

A bit too late, I remembered my resolution not to bite. 'Well, keep those astute observations to yourself. So as I was saying before I was so rudely interrupted, Smithy has been looking into possible connections between the victims and has come up blank. In fact, they seem pretty random.'

'Purposefully random?' Paul asked.

'Yes, my thoughts exactly. They don't draw attention to each other, so unless you were specifically looking for the circus connection, you'd never realise they could be related. And no one in their right mind would now turn around and say it was pure coincidence that these people died when the circus was in town.'

'Some geeky statistician would probably try. Which brings us back to the circus. Five different murders, five different killers?'

'Or five different murders, one killer trying to make it look like five different killers.' A big hand grasped onto my knee, gave me a hell of a fright.

'What?'

'You're jiggling.'

'Oh, sorry.' When my brain is going, I need to be moving. Normally I'd be pacing around the room. I didn't even realise I'd been doing the old jiggly thing. I stood up and took to the floor. Paul watched with a bemused expression on his face.

'Do you want me to join you up there?'

I shot him a look and continued on my way. 'There is no single obvious suspect on the circus crew. Their timetabling, the nature of their close proximity to each other all of the time and the sheer menace of Terry Bennett meant almost everyone had an alibi and those that didn't, didn't count — children, a few of the women and a dwarf.'

'Hey, don't discount the women, the fairer sex is quite capable of murder.'

'Yes, and I'm glad you acknowledge we're the fairer sex. If you met these ladies you'd understand. One was the size of one of their house buses, and the other very petite. Ditto, the dwarf. It would take height and strength to physically assault those last few, particularly the young man who . . . oh.' A thought had sprung to mind and I moved around behind Paul to take another look at the victim photos. Of course. Why hadn't I noticed it earlier? One of those nasty crawling sensations began to work its way up my spine and across my scalp.

'What have you spotted?'

'It's a progression, they're a progression,' I said, tapping my finger from photo to photo. 'Look at the victims, and the killings. No wonder they seem random. They're not, they were quite carefully selected, I'd bet, except perhaps the first one. Look at them. Erica Moorhouse, poisoned. The killer spiked the drink, then probably left. Didn't have to see it, didn't have to watch his victim die. Killed anonymously, as it were. Next, William Brody. Shot. Killed from a distance. Shot in the back. If you think about it, the shooter didn't even have to look him in the face as he pulled the trigger. Quite clever too, choosing a victim who was fishing. If his shot was off, and he only injured him, then there was still a high probability the victim would fall into the water and drown anyway.'

Paul caught on to my train of thought. 'The next one, drunk old bugger, a gentle push, no chance of a struggle, so no real risk for the killer. Murder for dummies.'

'Fourth, Levi Jones, hit from behind. Much more personal, but although the victim was a male, he was physically small and young, so an easier target, and again, there was the element of surprise. Low risk. And then we get to Rose-Marie. Face to face, up close and personal, but incapacitated first with the wrist ties and the taped mouth, so again fairly low risk. It's almost as though the killer was serving an apprenticeship, Practical Killing 101. A different technique each time, which is smart, because it would make them seem unrelated. We always think of a serial killer as having a MO or set patterns. That's what the criminal profilers tell us. There aren't any here, or if there are, we haven't realised it yet. We'll have to go back and check these cases for even the most trivial-seeming details. This is the work of someone who has planned and worked hard to fool the police.'

'And each time they've killed, they've got closer, more personal and more confident. That's one hell of a creepy learning curve. Then, of course, you have to ask yourself who is going to be next, and how? What is the whole point of this spree?' It was a damned good question.

'I would place a bet on the murders continuing on if we hadn't made the circus connection here. Balclutha is the next scheduled stop. Then Invercargill. But yes, you have to ask why? What is the trigger and what is the goal?

Revolting as it may appear, it's almost like someone's doing it to see if they can. Which is too simplistic a view, I know. But look at it. They've set it up for the murders to seem completely unrelated, then if someone does get curious, or make a connection or two, then it looks like the culprit has to be in the circus, so all attention on them. Short of a personal vendetta against the circus or someone in it — in which case you'd think they'd just deal to the person they were pissed off with — or animal-rights activists gone feral, which I doubt, someone has created one hell of a smokescreen for their activities.'

'And with everything that's happened to the circus,' said Paul, 'they've achieved that emphatically.'

'Hell, yes.' Didn't I know it?

45

'Howdy, pardners,' Maggie said as she breezed into the kitchen and dumped her backpack on to the floor. 'Who's for a cuppa?'

'Thanks, but no thanks, if I had any more it would come out my ears.'

'Paul?'

'Ditto.'

Maggie headed over to the kettle and gave it a cursory water-level check before flicking the switch. I checked my watch. Shit, it was after 6 p.m. We must have been engrossed.

'You two look like you've found the perfect way to spoil a beautiful afternoon.'

'Sam's company wasn't quite that bad,' Paul said, and shuffled his chair back out of lacking range.

'You can hardly talk,' I said and pointed to the abandoned bag. 'I'd hazard a guess you've been a zot down at the library?'

'Assignments don't have an if-it's-a-sunny-day-you-can-skive-off-to-the-beach-and-make-the-most-of-it-instead clause. I wish they did.' Maggie looked dressed for just such a sunny-day clause, complete with knotted hibiscus-patterned sarong skirt and white-rimmed Jackie-O style sunglasses balanced jauntily atop her head. 'There were plenty of other poor unfortunates to keep me company in purgatory. And there was one positive — I got asked out on a date.'

227

'Ooh, by who? Tell me more.'

'You'll laugh.'

'He's in the police?' I said.

'No, I'm not that desperate,' she remembered the company and made a hasty apology. 'Sorry, Paul.' He waved her off. 'Besides, when was the last time you saw a policeman in the university library?'

'Considering I've never set foot in the place, that would be fairly obvious.'

'They might have been doing a drugs raid,' Paul said. 'You know what they say about students.'

'Rampant stereotypes aside, I got asked out by one of those earnest, long-haired, pale-faced, skinny, studious types.'

'And what did you say?'

'Well, considering he is drop-dead gorgeous, tall and, despite being a bit skinny, has broad shoulders and a make-your-insides-melt voice, I had no choice but to say yes.'

'*Doop, doop, doop,* back up the bus a moment. Didn't we have this conversation a few days ago and didn't you say, in rather absolute terms, never the earnest types?'

Maggie shrugged her shoulders and said in a way that made it look like she was powerless to resist, 'Lust: what can I tell you? It's a fickle thing.'

'So that's where I've been going wrong,' Paul said. 'All this time I've been thinking the chicks go for the macho types, and it's the pasty, nerdy boys who you girls dig. Maybe I should grow my hair long, stay indoors and get me some glasses.'

'Oh no, I think Sam goes for the hunky outdoor type. Stick with that strategy, you'll be alright.'

'So if I keep up the tan and the workouts, I'm in with a chance?'

'Yeah, she's a buns-and-abs girl. Yours look mighty fine to me, so just pile on the charm and you'll crack her.'

'Excuse me,' I said, amazed at the course of conversation. 'I am in the room, you know.'

'Yeah, yeah, we know,' Maggie said, before turning her attention back to Paul. 'Where are you going to take her for dinner tonight?'

'I thought Nova looked good.'

'You're making a few assumptions here, aren't you?' I piped up from the cheap seats.

'Shhhh.' Maggie frowned in my direction. 'Nova's good. Good food, great wine list.'

'She'll like that, then?'

'Sure bet.'

'Hello, do I get any say in this?'

A simultaneous 'No' was accompanied by conspiratorial grins.

'Oh, for God's sake. What's the point in arguing? Okay, whatever.'

46

This wasn't so bad, after all. My left hand held a superb Central Otago Pinot Noir, while my right attended to the selection of breads and dips. I would never have imagined the humble beetroot could manage such an amazing transformation — my mother being from the just-pickle-those-suckers school of thought, I'd only ever encountered them sliced and diced.

Speaking of my mother, my only stipulation to agreeing to dinner was a stop at the hospital to catch up with Dad and check in with Mum. That was me doing the catch-up. Paul waited in the car.

The old boy had seemed in good form, although he was still complaining about the food. Mum was Mum and ensured I was warmly wrapped in guilt to go out.

I took another slug of wine.

'You'd better pace yourself, Sam.' Paul said, having observed my slightly generous quaff. 'It's a bit early for sliding under the table.'

'Sorry, shitty week, I needed to drown that thought.'

'If that was the case, I'd have brought you the cheap one.'

'Apologies again, what can I say?' I attempted diversionary tactics. 'Is it really your birthday, or were you just having me on?'

He gave a melty smile and took a sip from his

glass. 'It's really my birthday, so I appreciate you coming out and saving me the indignity of a lonely night in with delivery pizza and pay-per-view porn at the motel.'

'Too much information, Paul.' I hoped he was joking about the porn. 'I wouldn't think of me as your rescuer either because, as I recall, I didn't get much choice in the matter.'

'Oh, and it's such a hardship for you, then?'

'Not really, it was your company or my mother's.'

'Ouch. In that case, I'm glad to be of service, I think. Maggie can be fairly persuasive when she wants to be.'

'You should try living with her. So, what grand age have you reached?' I couldn't quite pick it. His face was quite youthful with only a few lines marching to the corners of his eyes, but there was a peppering of grey through his close-cropped hair that, I had to admit, suited him very well. I'd have guessed thirty-two or -three.

'I thought it was impolite to ask a person's age?'

'It's impolite to ask a lady's age. Men don't count.'

'That's a bit of a double standard.'

'Life's full of them, I thought you'd be used to that by now. So 'fess up, how old?'

'Guess.'

'Forty-five?' I put on my best wide-eyed look.

He laughed at my transparency. 'Funny, but not that far off. I'm thirty-eight.'

'Really?' I'd have never guessed. 'You don't act it.'

'Thank you. I'll take that as a compliment.'

'And you've never married?' His eyebrows shot up at the rather personal nature of the question. I'm not quite sure where it popped out from. Must have been the wine.

'No. Does that seem so strange to you?'

'No. Well, yes.'

'Why?'

'Come on, Paul — you make yourself out to be a bit of a ladies' man, you're always flirting with the girls. I mean look how you're always joking around with me. I'd have thought a guy like you would have caught himself a dolly bird and settled down by now.'

'And who said I was joking around?'

'Right,' I said, and laughed, then took another slug.

'Anyway, I'm not going to answer your question. A man's got to maintain an air of mystery, after all.'

'Who do you think you are? James Bond?'

'Taught him everything he knows.' He leaned forward, even closer. 'Maybe I've been biding my time, waiting for the right girl.' He shot his eyebrows up in query and I spluttered on my wine.

'Hey, don't look at me, mister. I don't date cops,' I said, hoping he wouldn't notice the full-on flush I could feel rising up my face.

'So you say.' He seemed amused at my reaction and took another leisurely sip of his wine. 'So what about you? What vintage are you?'

'What did I say before about that question?'

'You said it was rude to ask a lady, so I figured it's okay to ask you.'

'Funny.'

'Come on, quid pro quo. I told you.'

'This isn't an I'll-show-you-mine-if-you-show-me-yours competition.'

'Are you offering?'

'You should be so lucky. Okay, if it will make you feel better, I'm twenty-nine. My next birthday will be the big three-O and I'm planning how I can do something big to divert my attention from the fact I'll be old.'

'And you've never married?'

'You're starting to sound like my mother. No, I've never married. Come close, sort of. Well, you know all about Lockie. So far, my career's been my focus. Yes, the career thing. Even more so now I'm on the detective path. I want to do it justice, be damned good, not just ordinary. So I guess I'll be a swinging single for a bit longer.'

'I don't know if you've noticed, Sam, but there's nothing even remotely ordinary about you.' He delivered that with the kind of look and tone that created a warmth in my innards that was not entirely due to the Pinot.

Damn him.

47

A gentle snort eased me into semi-consciousness and I snuggled further into the warm arms wrapped around me.

Arms, warm, around, skin? Shit.

My eyes snapped open, my body tensed. What the hell was I doing here?

Dozy disorientation evaporated as memory flooded back. Me, Paul, oh shit.

In the dark, my eyes flicked to the red glare of the digital alarm clock: 2.14 a.m. Shit, shit, shit. I must have fallen asleep.

The next thought drove me bolt upright.

Mum.

Bloody hell.

I fair leaped out of the bed and started scrabbling around on the floor in a desperate search for my clothes. My head connected with the corner of the bedside table and the resultant yelp had Paul sitting bolt upright, patting around on the bed to find me.

'Sam?' His voice was groggy, husky and laden with confusion. 'What are you doing?'

'Fell asleep. Shit, got to get home.' I'd got one leg into my knickers, but with my foot caught with the other hole, I was unbalanced, hopping sideways three steps before crashing into the wall at the end of the bed.

'Christ, woman, you'll wake the whole building, come back to bed.' I heard him pat the mattress. My eyes were beginning to adjust to the dark, so I could make out the trail of clothes as they disappeared towards the lounge.

'Can't. Gotta go.' Staccato replies. 'Mum, shit.' I followed the trail to my jeans and bra but had to ferret around again to find my shirt and socks. 'She'll kill me.'

'I doubt that. You're a grown woman, you can do what you like.'

'You haven't met my mum. Oh, God,' I called back. My brain flashed samples of the inevitable conversations and recriminations and I had to shake my head to clear them. I brought the pile of clothes back into the room and perched on the edge of the bed while I attempted to struggle into them. The sock I'd pulled up my foot was way too big, but I stuffed it and my foot into my boot, regardless. 'Keys, keys, where did I put my car keys?' I hobbled, one-shoed, back to the bedside table. Not there. Patted my jeans pocket. No, they must have been in the lounge.

'You'll have trouble finding them,' Paul said, with more than a hint of mirth in his voice.

'Don't play games. Where are they?' I'd found the other boot by this stage. And at least the other sock was the right size.

'Who drove us here, Sam?'

Shit, piss, fuckity fuck. Paul. My car was in its usual possie, a block and a half away from the Highgate Hilton.

'Shit. I'll have to get a taxi. Where's the phone?' I was pretty sure there was one on his side of the bed.

'Don't be so bloody silly. I'll drop you back, if

235

you must insist on leaving.'

Ugh, my eyes were assaulted by the sudden light and I raised my arm up to cover them. Paul climbed out from under the covers, and even in my state of panic my heart rate ratcheted up a bit more at the sight of his physique. Hadn't quite intended for things to work out like this.

'Where's my sock?'

'On my foot.'

'Well, I'll have it back, thanks. I don't do floral, plus I don't think I'd even get my toes in this thing.' He held up my missing hosiery, and then flipped it in my direction. 'What a way to end a perfect evening,' he said and came over, cupped my cheeks and kissed me gently. 'I hope ditching me for your mother at this hour of the morning is worth it.'

Oh, God, yes. He didn't know the half of it.

48

The click of the key turning in the lock and the creak of the front floorboards sounded like gunshots to my paranoid ears as I skulked into the house. I paused, listening for any sign of life, before advancing towards the staircase. A shaft of light cut into the hallway from beyond the partially closed kitchen door. Someone must have forgotten to turn it off. I pushed the door open slightly and reached around for the switch.

'Sam, is that you?'

It was just as well I didn't have a full bladder.

I pushed the door open and was appalled to see Mum, seated at the kitchen table, wrapped in her towelling robe, hands wrapped around what looked to be an empty mug. Her eyes were bloodshot and puffy. A sharp pang hit me in the stomach.

'Oh, God, Mum, what's happened? What's wrong?' I asked, afraid of what news that kind of face must surely convey. I came around and pulled up a chair beside her, reached out my hands, one on her knee, one on her shoulder. My heart pounded, not wanting to hear, not that.

'What's wrong?' she asked, between sniffs. 'You have the cheek to ask me what's wrong? Your father is lying in hospital, ill, dying for all we know and my daughter cares so little for him, for us, that she won't even grace us with her presence, slinking in at some ungodly hour of the morning, and you ask me what's wrong?'

I felt a surge of heat as it rushed up my face and I leaned back into my chair.

'My God, Sam. What's happened to you that you don't even care about your own family? What if we'd needed you? Your father would be heartbroken if he knew we mattered so little to you that you'd rather spend your time out partying or doing God knows what, rather than support your family.' She had to play the Dad card. 'You could've at least dressed yourself properly after sleeping with God only knows who.' I didn't think my mortification could creep any deeper. Wrong. My eyes dropped down and I was sickened to see I'd put my top on inside out. Betrayed by side seams. 'Have you got a boyfriend, or is this what you do now you're a big-city girl, go out and sleep with any guy who comes along? This would kill your father, you know that.'

I had mentioned to them I was going out to dinner when at the hospital earlier, but I'd embellished the truth somewhat and said it was with some of the girls to avoid the 'boyfriend' interrogation. Not my best call, it would now seem. I didn't bother to mount a defence, or even an attempt at an offence. Besides my being too flabbergasted and embarrassed to speak, any effort would be futile. In my mother's eyes, I was tarred, feathered and performing the chicken dance.

And there was no recovery from the chicken dance.

49

'That was a nice atmosphere down there over breakfast. What did you do to piss your mother off this time?' Maggie asked. We were in the relative sanctuary of the upstairs bathroom.

'I think the fact I breathe pisses her off sometimes.' I turned to face Maggs, rather than talk to her reflection in the mirror. 'I know she's worried about Dad, and I tend to cop the backlash sometimes, but hell, she sure knows how to turn on the guilt.'

'You still haven't answered my question.'

'I got in a little late last night.'

'How late is a little late?'

'Half-two.' I still cringed in the telling.

'But you were out with Paul.' A huge grin spread across her face. 'Does that mean you two . . . ?'

'Ugh.' I leaned my head against the wall, but slightly misjudged, so there was a fairly hefty bang.

'What happened to Miss-I-don't-screw-the-crew?'

'It seemed like a good idea at the time.'

'But I take it from the look on your face, it's not looking so good now.'

'No. Yes. I don't know.' I set my toothbrush down on the counter, trying to corral my thoughts. 'I got a bit carried away with the moment, and you know, things happen. I didn't mean to.'

'I didn't mean to. Do you realise how juvenile that sounds?'

'Unfortunately, yes. And now, I don't know quite what to do about it.' Life was complicated enough already, and I'd gone and made it a whole heap more challenging.

'I can't see the problem. Come on, admit it, you really like him. You two have been doing the ol' pull-ponytails-and-poke-out-tongues ritual for ages. And you have to admit, he is hot.'

'Yes, but . . . ' That wasn't the problem.

'What's the matter, then? Was he lousy in bed?'

My face broke into a sheepish grin, despite myself. 'Ah, no, hell no.' I even blushed. 'No problems in that department.'

'Okay, so he's fun, he's hot, got a great bod and rocked in bed. What's not to like? Don't you think your standards might be getting a little high if you're prepared to throw this one back into the ocean?'

'You've heard of buyer's remorse? I have bonker's remorse.' I did a slow-motion face-palm. 'What was I thinking? For heaven's sake, I have to work with the guy. That's always going to end in tears. Things will get awkward and messy, people will talk.'

'Sam, in case you didn't realise it, he lives in another town. It's not like you're going to be tripping over him every day. In fact, it's perfect, really. Work hard during the week, catch up and shag each other silly on the weekends. You don't even have to commit yourself. Anyway, since when did you worry about what people say?' she asked, between flossing her teeth.

'Woah, let's not talk commitment. It was only one spur-of-the-moment, unexpected shag. In fact, knowing Paul, now that he's conquered me, so to speak, he'll lose all interest and move on to the next challenge.'

'Ouch, that's a bit harsh. Not much faith there. He might surprise you.'

'Trust me, I've been dealing with him for years, I know his type. He hunts for the thrill of the chase. Now he can tick me off his list. I bet he doesn't even call.'

'Bet you he does. In fact, I bet you coffee and a Modak's cinnamon pinwheel you see him today.' That was high stakes.

'You're on. You better get your money ready though; you're destined to lose.'

I checked my watch. 'I suppose I'd better get my act together and go face the music at the hospital.'

'You never did explain why your mum was so frosty with you at breakfast. How did she know about Paul?'

I raised my eyebrows and added a wee eye-roll.

'What? Was she waiting up for you like you were some sixteen-year-old out on a date, or something?'

I gave a slow nod. 'Or something.'

Maggie's face gaped. 'You're kidding me. She really was waiting up for you?'

'Caught in the act of slinking in. Although, to give her credit, it was an unhappy coincidence she was up at the time. Unhappy being the

241

operative word. And let's just say someone noticed my attire was somewhat askew.'

'Oh. That explains a bit.'

'Yeah. Hence the frosty nostril this morning and her hasty retreat to the hospital. Apparently, I am the worst daughter in the world.'

'So what are you going to do to redeem yourself?'

'She's not the type of woman to be swayed by gestures, no matter how grand, so I shall have to suck it up, take my punishment as it comes and go face the consequences.'

50

'Shit.' I fair jumped out of my skin when my cellphone double-bleeped the arrival of a text message. Heart still racing, I looked at the screen. It was almost noon. I must have been absorbed — I'd been working almost two hours. So much for a lazy Sunday morning.

Rapunzel, Rapunzel, let down your hair. It was Paul. I texted back the obvious one-symbol answer,*?* and put the phone down on the desk beside me.

Even though I expected the reply, its arrival still near sent me through the roof. My neurones seemed to be set to frazzle. I'd forgotten how much a wooden surface amplified sound, especially as the phone was set to vibrate mode too and danced a wee jive across the table. So much for technology being our friend.

Am outside. Let me in.

Oh. Bugger. Maggie, as usual, was right; she'd get her flaming cinnamon pinwheel, after all. Okay. I could always ignore him, but that would be the height of rudeness. Then it hit me. He was probably outside home, not realising I had turned into one of those sad creatures that went into work on a Sunday for something to do. Brill. I texted back *At work.* But I couldn't just leave it at that, so extended a tentative invitation: *Catch up later?*

The reply boomeranged back fast. He must be

a damned sight better than I was at pushing the right buttons.

Look out the window.

I went over to the window and had to stick my face right up to the glass and stand on tiptoes to get the right angle to see out front of the building. But yes, there he was, making a dick of himself, waving in my general direction from the other side of the road. There was no avoiding him any longer, so I headed for the stairwell and trotted down to the Watch House to greet him.

He stood in the foyer, looking at the flash artwork on the wall. 'Gidday,' he said, exaggerating the word's Kiwiness and accompanying it with a wink. It sounded more Aussie than Kiwi.

'Gidday, yourself,' I replied, without the wink and raised my eyebrows.

'Are you going to invite me up or are you going to just stand around here getting weird looks from the sergeant over there?'

I toyed with the continued-weird-looks option, but thought better of it. 'You'd better come up, then.'

He pointed behind him, in the direction of the entranceway at the cause of a fair amount of amusement for the last few days — God knew, we'd all needed a spot of comic relief, even if it was from a recalcitrant gatecrasher. 'What's the story with that frigging seagull and the door? I just about stood on the thing and killed it.'

'Station mascot,' I said, with a smile. I swiped my card and let him into the main area of the building. 'Rapunzel?' I asked.

'Well, this place is kind of like a castle.'

'But I don't have long hair.'

He reached out to touch it in a way that was a bit too familiar, so I made to turn and headed towards the stairs.

'You know, some refer to it as the Dunedin Hilton,' I called behind me. 'Urban myth has it that a number of tourists over the years have rocked up to the front counter to enquire after a room for the night.'

'I'm guessing the cells weren't what they had in mind.'

'Correctamundo.' The Dunedin Central Police Station with its grand-looking entrance and marble finish was one of the flashiest buildings in the city. I didn't mock it though, because, all told — well, if you removed a few individuals — it was a terrific working environment. After the tiny little box of a station at Mataura, this was the Ritz. Modern, light, good views, gym, staffroom and bar; other than said individuals and the lack of cutting-edge technology, it was nigh-on perfect.

'Hasn't this place got a lift?' he asked

'Yes, but that's for unfit lazybones.'

That said, my words came back to bite me and I was slightly peeved to see it wasn't Paul puffing the most when we got to the second floor. I put that down to the fact his legs were twice as long as mine, so I had to work harder. Bastard had a smug look on his face. 'Do I get a good morning kiss now?' he asked, pulling me in close. I could hardly not, so gave him a cursory peck before pulling back.

'Not here, someone might see us.' I was a bit annoyed at how even the little peck had rendered my tummy warm and fuzzy.

There was no sign of DI Johns, much to my relief. A few bods were around, but mostly we had the place to ourselves. I plonked myself down at a desk, and logged back into the network to check some details.

'I see you've been elevated to getting a desk with a computer,' Paul said.

'Not quite.' There were only two computers in an office shared by five detectives and I sure as heck didn't qualify for one. Budgets didn't extend to the so-called luxury of a computer each. 'This is Smithy's desk. I'm still the underling.'

I'd been reading the reports and statements completed by the end of the week. Other work was continuing over the weekend — I was aware of DI Johns and others following up on the animal-rights activists — but the typing pool got Saturday and Sunday off, so any interview transcripts wouldn't be available till Monday.

It had been an exercise in futility. There were no obvious suspects, several different lines of enquiry and a growing sense that this was going to be one hell of a long investigation. We were just going to have to cover all bases and be thorough. The killer would make a mistake. We would spot it. Media attention on the case had brought forward more people with information on the murders in the other towns, which offered some hope of fresh leads. All it needed was one person with the right piece of information to make it all come together. Legwork and persistence were what would crack this one. It wasn't glamorous, and it wouldn't keep the top brass and politicians braying for a quick result happy, but thems was the breaks.

It would be easy to get distracted by all the satellite issues, spreading my mental resources too thin, so I was back to concentrating on Rose-Marie, setting aside thoughts of any connection to the other murders. For me, for now, it was all about her.

Paul had wandered off, I presumed to the loo. I'd been so engrossed in looking over the photos of Rose-Marie's bedroom and belongings that I hadn't realised it had been longer than a comfort stop until he announced, 'I'm back'. I swung the chair around and resisted crushing his ego by admitting I hadn't noticed he'd gone. He had something hidden behind his back and was looking quite pleased with himself.

'Here, close your eyes, hold out your hands.' I obliged and held my hands out cupped together, eyes closed and fervently hoping it was something involving chocolate. I felt something warm lower into my hands and at the same moment felt a cold chill shoot down my spine. The chill spread to my face and I gasped in surprise as my hands flew apart and my eyes flashed open in time to see the takeaway coffee succumb to gravity, bouncing off my knees and hitting the floor rolling.

Simultaneous 'shit's exploded into the air and Paul dropped to his knees in a mad scramble to rescue the cup before too much spilled on to the carpet. Thank God, the lid had stayed on. He grabbed the offending container and plonked it back on to the desk beside me. 'There's gratitude for you. A simple 'no thanks' would have sufficed.'

'God, Paul, I'm sorry, I didn't mean to. Shit.' My mind groped at the mental images running through my head. Replays of Rose-Marie's body in the Leith, the photos I'd been poring over, the scene that had just played out in this room. 'He knew her, that's how he . . . he must have, oh my God . . . he did it.'

Paul, still on his knees, placed his hands on mine and said, 'Slow down, Sam. What? Who?' The transient look of anger on his face was replaced by confusion.

'The killer. That's how he could have got the tie around her wrists with no struggle.' I thrust my hands out towards him again, palms uppermost, cupped side by side, like they had been, obediently waiting for my surprise.

Paul looked from my face, to my hands and back to my face again, and the sight of him on his knees before me, hands resting on my legs, eyes burning into mine, brought another awful realisation.

'Oh, Jesus,' I uttered in a whisper. He leaned forward, even closer. 'It was a proposal, I bet it was a proposal. She wouldn't have had a chance. She was with someone she trusted, someone she loved. We'd all said she probably knew him, but she *knew* him, Paul. He would have asked her to close her eyes, just like you did, hold out her hands and she would have, holding her hands

248

together, expecting a gift, a ring, anything — not betrayal, not death.'

My brain tried to comprehend what Rose-Marie would have gone through, her emotions leaping from exquisite joy to utter terror in one mind-blowing moment, and my heart couldn't cope. I shook my head to try and ward off the tears, but they came all the same.

'That bastard, that utter, utter bastard,' I said, voice hoarse.

'Bloody hell.' Paul's voice echoed my disbelief. 'The boyfriend. He's had everyone fooled all along with his grief-stricken act.'

Something else clicked into place as another mental image vied for attention. 'No, not that boyfriend. There was someone else.' I stood up from the chair and reached over to grab one of the photographs I'd been studying. 'Check this out.' By now, Paul was back on his feet and beside me. 'Look at her personal belongings.' I pointed to a tell-tale sheet of tablets.

'Oral contraceptives, which you'd expect, since she had the boyfriend.'

'Yes, but the boyfriend maintained that they were a good little Christian couple and weren't having sex. They were doing the saving-it-for-marriage thing. So if she was saving it for marriage with him, why did she need these?'

'He could have been lying, just another part of the act — throw doubt.'

'If you'd seen him, you'd realise he was telling the truth. He comes across as rather . . . flaky, I suppose. Very Christian.' I was sure there were plenty of good Christian folk out there who would resent that comment, but it was the best description. 'She was on the Pill for a reason. It wouldn't be for fun, believe me. Those things screw your body up.'

He gave me an indecipherable look. 'Don't some women need them to regulate periods? Or even acne? Perhaps she was on them for medical reasons.' It was a good question.

'That could be the case, but I don't think so,' I said. 'The boyfriend said they hadn't seen that much of each other lately, too busy and stuff like that. Maybe they hadn't been seeing each other because she was seeing someone else, someone with a penchant for murder. She could have been weaning off contact with him or been avoiding him because she felt guilty because she was sleeping with someone else.'

'I thought it was only guys who did things like that.'

'Guys wouldn't feel guilty about it.'

'True,' he said. 'Did the post-mortem results mention any sign of sexual assault or activity?'

'Not that I'm aware of, the prelim just talked of cause of death. I can make a phone call to get more details there — I have a friend in the morgue.'

'Alive, I presume.'

'Last time I checked. Of the pathologist variety.'

'Handy. So we're back to looking at this murder in terms of her direct associates. If you're right, and she was duped by the killer because she was expecting a gift or proposal even, then relationships take time to reach that kind of level where you can look at commitment.' I could feel Paul's eyes on me, but I stared fixedly down at the desk while he continued. 'If the boyfriend talked of them being a bit distant for a while, then the relationship with the killer could have been going on for some time, which then begs the question: is this murder related to the other murders at all, or is it just a coincidence of timing? We may have completely separate cases here.'

I grabbed my head in my hands and pushed it from side to side. 'Argh, I feel like we're going in one big circle. So — well, yes, you do have to ask that question. But then, what if they *are* related? We've looked at the other deaths in terms of a progression, each being more directly physical than the previous one, the murderer getting bolder each time.' My hands made a chopping motion, marking off each death. 'By the time we got to Rose-Marie it was very up close and personal, which fits that pattern. And we predicted that if there was another, the next one could be even worse, an escalation of violence. So what if the other murders were random victims, who fitted the killer's experimental needs as a practice run in killing the ultimate target, Rose-Marie? What if she was the focal point?'

'The apprenticeship, building up the skills to deal with this young woman here in Dunedin?' I saw the shudder pass through Paul's body.

'Precisely.'

'Well, that's one special kind of sicko.'

It didn't bear thinking about that there could

be such a calculated, reptilian person out there. 'We need to look at what kind of mind could set up such an elaborate and gruesome decoy in order to hide the murder of a harmless young woman. I mean, they basically set up the circus to be their fall guy.'

'What if the young woman wasn't that harmless?' Paul said.

'What do you mean?'

'What if someone had a lot to lose because of her? She was putting on the guise of being the chaste young woman, but what if she had been having another relationship and was the other woman? Civilisations have fallen because of the other woman.'

'True,' I said. 'You'd have thought she'd have told or given some hint to her flatmates or girlfriends. No one's given any indication of even a rumour of such a possibility. A young woman in love, how could she have contained it all?' Paul's mouth curled into a smile and I regretted my poor choice of words. 'But then, if you come from a good Christian family and belong to a church, the last thing you'd want revealed is that you were shagging your boyfriend, let alone someone else's husband. They tend to frown upon such things, although, I think they've stopped the practice of stoning now.'

'Well here, at least. So the husband has enough of his young toy and needs to get rid of the evidence? Murdering the mistress, let alone four other people to hide it is a pretty extreme way of dealing with your extra-curricular problem. Most people would break it off, or pay them off, or send them all-expenses-paid overseas.'

'Why, is that how you afforded that time in Europe, Paul?'

He gave me a bum shove that sent me sideways. 'Not even going to grace that one with an answer,' he said. 'She could have been a too-significant other, or perhaps not. Perhaps we're putting too much weight on relationships here. What about her cellphone records? Was she texting anyone other than friends, family and her boyfriend?'

'No, no messages to an unidentified lover, unfortunately. But that doesn't mean anything. Hell, lots of people have two phones now, using different networks. She could have had a second phone, dedicated to him, for all we know. He could have taken it when he killed her.'

'I suppose that's possible.'

'Well, I'm certain it had to be someone she knew, someone she knew intimately. There's no other signs of a tussle, other than at the end, so whoever it was lured her down to the river with no resistance.'

'What if they'd carried her down? What if she was already tied up and unconscious and they carried her to that place to dump her?'

'For a start, someone would have noticed. The walkway is often used by students or joggers, and it would be too far to carry someone. You haven't been to the crime scene, have you?' Paul shook his head. 'She was a standard-sized girl, probably around sixty kilograms, so even someone with your build would find it difficult to carry her the hundred metres or so from Gore Place to the spot at the river. And it would be too risky. The evidence all points to a struggle at the end, skid marks in the grass, head smashed on the rock, that kind of thing. She was murdered there.'

There were simultaneous sighs. We looked at each other and exchanged smiles.

'Where to next?' he said. I was pretty sure he wasn't asking about the case, but I wasn't ready to address that other issue right now.

'Look at the circles she was moving in, where she could have met this man.'

'You're still assuming it's a man.'

'Honey,' I said to him, in a jokey voice, 'if it was a woman lover, she was hardly going to need the contraceptives, was she?'

'So I'm your honey now?'

'No,' I said and moved back to the point. 'She was involved with the university, her church and her friends and flatmates. I think I'll let someone else tackle the walking on eggshells involved in finding the possibility of a lover in her church.'

'Yeah, that would take a special kind of subtlety you lack.'

I gave him a thump on the arm for being so rude. 'That's ripe coming from Mr Overt Flirt. You wouldn't know the meaning of the word subtle.'

'It worked on you.'

I felt the heat rise up my face and once again changed the direction the conversation had taken. 'Smithy and I will probably head back to the university tomorrow, start at the place where she spent most of her time. I've met a couple of her peers and her professor — interesting dynamics there. DI Johns is working on the activists and I pity the poor sod who gets to approach her church. I'd really like to get a conversation with her boyfriend; I've seen him on video, but not face to face. But I don't know that my leash would extend that far.'

There must be a way to engineer that one, I thought. A bit of creative manoeuvring might be in order. It was a pity in a way that Paul wasn't a part of this investigation and would be back to his court case in the morning. Although I would never admit it to him, I thought we worked quite well together.

'So,' he said, wrapping his arms around my waist and giving me a kiss. 'What are our plans for tonight? Do you want to go out, catch a movie or something?'

Okay, this was awkward. Nice, but awkward. Just because I'd slept with the man — unintentionally, I might add — didn't mean I wanted to encourage any further dalliance. For once in my life my mum could do me a favour. 'Sorry, Paul, considering the grief I got last night, I think I'd better put in some time with the old girl.'

'Fair enough. What about lunch tomorrow, then?'

It did have appeal, but a part of me was in denial that Paul and I were now a bit more than friends, and another part of me wanted to be the one calling the shots. Did that make me a bad person?

'The case is getting quite complicated, so I don't know where I'll be at tomorrow. Can I get back to you on that one?'

51

It was Monday morning, and for some strange reason it felt like the weekend had been cancelled, and not due to lack of interest. My body was on a go-slow and everything had been a struggle. In fact, it felt like life was conspiring against me.

First, I had to tip toe around The Mother, which, at least, did go better than anticipated. But from there it all descended into crud. There was no wholegrain bread left and I had to eat white-crap toast. I was last to the shower and it was only lukewarm. Then my hairdryer wouldn't work, and now I couldn't find my flaming car keys. Consequently, I was running late, which wasn't a good thing when the first item in my diary was an audience with DI Johns. He wanted an update on what I'd covered over the weekend, which was shark talk for keeping an eye on me. I supposed it was progress that he now had enough respect for me to give me the time of day, but my bowels seemed to disagree.

After the second time around the house checking the likely spots, I finally found my keys under the newspaper, on the kitchen bench. My eyes did a spot of spontaneous leaking at the sight of the photograph of Rose-Marie and another of the fire-ravaged circus on the front page of the *Otago Daily Times*. The paper was folded in half, banner headline uppermost, and I wasn't about to flip it over to see if there was a photo of an elephant on the other side. The odds were pretty high. Instead, I grabbed the keys and hightailed it out of there.

Decorum went by the wayside and I ran down the street to my car. But my rush was brought to an abrupt halt by the sight of the folded piece of paper tucked under the windscreen wiper. I sighed what felt like all the air out of my lungs and my shoulders drooped to match my mojo. Not today. There was only so much a girl could handle and my resilience had been eroded to next to nought. I wished I'd done something about this sooner, but I truly couldn't face the hassle. It wasn't as if there had been anything else happening in my life. I picked the note out by the corner, tossed it, unread, on to the back seat and then moped my way down to town.

★ ★ ★

I needed to hear a friendly voice, so decided a phone call was in order. It wasn't purely a social call, as I was in need of information, as well as geniality.

'Pathology.'

I smiled at the sound of the familiar drawl. 'Alistair.' I drew out the last syllable.

'Samantha.' He returned the favour.

'How are you bearing up in the big smoke?' I asked.

'Oh, you know how it is. As much as I loved Invercargill, the grime, the bland flatness, the arctic southerlies, I'm coping okay, just. Some company would help. What are you up to tonight?'

Good old Alistair, always a trier. In fact, he'd been trying since I was a teenager and he was a pimply geek who spent his school holidays with our family. His parents were busy professionals who found it a bit inconvenient when boarding school emptied everyone out. Fortunately for him, my parents had a farm and were in the habit of picking up strays. Nowadays, Alistair was no longer pimply and was a pathologist at Dunedin hospital.

'Mum's in town, Dad's in hospital — nothing serious. I need to put in some contact hours. Enough said.'

'I hear you. So to what do I owe the pleasure, then? You only seem to call me when you want something, not just for my charm.' He put on a dramatic sniff.

'As much as I love the sound of your voice, you're right, I'm that transparent — I want something.'

'I knew it. So not even any small talk?'

'Not today, sorry. The room has ears.'

'Fun, how very James Bond. Fire away, then.'

'A murder case last week.'

'The young woman?'

'Yes, Rose-Marie Bateman. Did you do or attend her post-mortem? What can you tell me about it?'

'Yes, I was there. The forensic pathologist from Christchurch came down to perform it. Details? Fairly straight forward, actually. Major trauma to the head, fractured skull, intra-cranial haemorrhage which, if it didn't kill her, would have left her with far fewer faculties than she started with. But the cause of death was drowning.'

'She was a very bright girl, Ph.D. student.'

'The head injury would have taken care of that.'

I felt an angry heat forming in my guts. It was a sensation that was surreptitiously replacing the blahs as my day rode on. DI Johns had helped it along, as had thoughts about the deaths that were trailing this case, criminal, medical and animal.

'What about evidence of sexual assault or activity. Was there any semen present?'

'No physical sign of sexual assault, vaginal or anal, which doesn't mean there wasn't any activity. Normally seminal fluid would last in the vagina for at least twenty-four hours, but as she'd been in the water, there was no trace.'

'Okay. I know this probably sounds odd, but her boyfriend claimed she was a virgin. Was her hymen intact?' I found myself blushing on the end of the phone asking such a personal question. Smithy looked at me sideways from the next desk.

'Interesting question. No, but that doesn't mean anything nowadays, with women leading such active lifestyles. And if we're being frank here, there are objects of, shall we say, pleasure that can cause the hymen to tear without any actual male involvement.' I was half-expecting Smithy to comment on what must by now surely been a beetroot shade of red up my face.

Alistair gave a small chuckle, as if he could feel my discomfort. He probably enjoyed it. He always was a little off-centre.

'Okay, that came into the too-much-information category.'

'You asked.' Even more humour in his voice.

'Pregnant?'

'No, I'm not, thanks for asking, and neither was she.'

'Oh, ha, ha. What about other traces of DNA? Her mouth had been gagged by tape, so there were sure to have been skin cells from her on that. What if she'd kissed someone? Could you get a DNA sample from their skin cells or saliva in her mouth if she'd been kissed?'

'Honey, you have been watching far too much TV. In the real world, not likely. In this case, with the body in the water, impossible. Water is the enemy of evidence.'

'But wouldn't the tape have kept the water out of her mouth?'

'She had a nose.'

Good one, Sam, I hadn't thought of that.

'What about fibres stuck to the tape?'

'Can I refer back to my comment about your television viewing?'

'I can't help it, I'm an optimist, however unrealistic.'

'Which is undoubtedly the best way to be, and one of the things we love about you, Sam. The tape did go to ESR for testing, so if there was anything on it, fibres, fingerprints, DNA, you'll have to be patient and wait for them to perform their magic.'

Dunedin didn't have its own forensic laboratory, we had to send samples off to Environmental
Science and Research in Christchurch. And like
all good things, they took time.

'Anything else?' he asked.

'Nothing dodgy in her blood?'

'Nothing. No alcohol, drugs. She was slightly
anaemic — could have done with some iron
tablets or a few good steak dinners. Speaking of
which, are you sure you don't want to hop out
for a bite?'

The image of Paul, the unclad version, popped
into my mind, and for some absurd reason, even
though I'd say no to Alistair regardless — too
much like a brother — I felt obliged to say no
out of principle.

What was that all about?

52

'Don't touch that.' I clamped my hands together behind my back and did my best to look nonchalant. 'That gas-liquid chromatograph cost us forty thousand dollars, so if you don't mind, keep your hands to yourself.'

I didn't even recall touching it. I'd been listening to Smithy questioning Professor Simpson and my hand had wandered over without my knowledge. Despite my best efforts, my damned face gave me away again. Unfortunately, some things you didn't grow out of.

We were at the university again, getting back to basics with Rose-Marie's colleagues. I'd survived my early debrief with Sharkman Johns, who had let me out under Smithy's care and had been semi-civil with only a touch of condescension. Call me cynical, but I found this newfound favour disturbing.

We were standing in a laboratory in the Pharmacy Department of the university. Everywhere you went up here there seemed to be padlocked freezers sitting in dimly lit corridors. I found it an almost-depressing environment to be in, despite the pink walls. This lab was vast, with rows of working benches covered with an array of scientific-looking equipment. There was a continuous background fan hum coming from the fume hoods along one wall. Despite the air circulation, the place still had an aroma that hinted of a cross between floor polish, something acidic enough to eat your face off and weirdly, linament.

'So how would you describe your relationship with Miss Bateman?' Smithy asked, having allowed a pause for me to recover my composure.

'We had a good working relationship. I held her in very high regard, she was a fine researcher and I had no doubt she'd be a successful doctoral candidate.' The professor had turned to watch me rather than face Smithy while answering the questions. I felt distinctly squirmy under his gaze, and not just because he was keeping an eye on his property. Despite his slightly unkempt look, the man had magnetism. I wondered if the other women in the department felt it. If Rose-Marie had felt it.

'Had you noticed any changes in her behaviour or in her work recently?'

'You asked me these questions last time you were here. Look, I'm very busy at the moment. You'd be better off talking to Dr Collins who saw her every day.'

Smithy never took kindly to being fobbed oft, even less so by academics, in whom he seemed to hold an inherent distrust. 'Oh, I'm very sorry to take up your precious time, and I will be talking to the others too, but, I have questions that need to be asked, and I'm here, now.' He'd puffed up to twice his normal size, and the professor, who I took as being someone not about to be intimidated, reciprocated. He shot me a look, and I yanked back my hand that had been straying towards the chromatograph again. I had to look down at the floor to hide my smile.

'Exactly how often did you see Miss Bateman?'

'I couldn't tell you exactly, but we had a regular Thursday-morning appointment to review progress.'

'And what exactly did her work entail?'

'I won't go into details, as it's commercially sensitive and it would be too complex for you to understand.' I swear I felt the room temperature drop five degrees. 'But she was doing research into a new dosage form of insulin.'

'Who would benefit from any financial gain, and what sort of income are we talking about?' I asked this question to give Smithy a chance to breathe and prevent the possibility of physical violence. Money was as common a motive for murder as lust.

'The university would hold the rights for commercial applications of the research, and this is potentially very important and lucrative. It would revolutionise the administration of insulin to diabetics and negate the need for refrigeration. So it would have immense benefits for patients, particularly in Third World countries.'

'Thousands? Millions?'

'Millions, billions. But of course, it costs a lot of money to develop practical and commercial applications for research, and it can take years. This is early days.'

'Who pays for the costs of development? The university?'

'The university, and also grants from research

institutes. There are several stakeholders.' Commercial intricacies weren't my forte, but it didn't take a rocket scientist to see the potential for motive where vast sums of money were concerned. It still didn't make sense with respect to Rose-Marie's involvement though.

'Will this research still be able to go ahead with Miss Bateman out of the picture?'

'Of course; no one is indispensable, and I will personally ensure this vital research continues.' I'm sure he would, especially with dollars involved. The prof had no idea how much the 'indispensable' word had gotten up my back up, but Smithy sensed it and stepped back into the conversation.

'Were you aware of any tensions between the researchers on this project, any disagreements?'

The professor seemed to waver before giving his response. 'Nothing major, just the usual arguments that occur between strong-minded, focused people. Again, I would recommend you talk to Dr Collins or Dr Hawkins who had more to do with her on a day-to-day basis. Now if you don't mind,' he said, looking at his wrist watch, 'I have an appointment with the faculty head. Dr Collins should be down in his room along the hallway and to your right. If there's anything else I can help you with, please be in touch. Good day, officers,' at which he turned and left the room, leaving us standing there.

53

Where Professor Simpson had distinguished charm but a lack of manners, Dr Jeffrey Collins had a look best described as unfortunate but a natural warmth. He put me at ease from the first handshake. I'd been hauled back to the office before we had a chance to interview him last week, so Smithy did the introductions. I observed a mid-forties man whose face was dominated by a raised strawberry birthmark that spread across his right cheek and down to his jaw. He was of slim build and dressed entirely in black like a Johnny Cash wannabe. My mind immediately put him off the suspects list because he was so distinguishable. No amount of make-up could disguise his face.

'What can I help you with today?' he asked and sat down on the corner of a desk. 'Are you any closer to finding out what happened to Rosie?'

'We're going back over her work and associations at the university, so if you don't mind, I'll probably be going over some of the things I asked last time.'

'That's okay. Anything I can do to help. I saw in the papers that dreadful business with the circus. I take it if you're back here, then you no longer believe anyone in the circus is a suspect?' At his mention of the circus, my eyes filled up with tears and I turned and pretended a great interest in a poster on the wall. God, Sam. I'd thought I was getting over that. Apparently not.

'We're spreading our investigations wider and not making any assumptions at this point.' Smithy gave my hand a slight brush. 'We've talked with Professor Simpson this morning, and will be talking with Dr Hawkins after you. You worked with Miss Bateman every day, is that right?'

'Yes, she was doing her research in my lab and we were collaborating on the project. She had an amazing mind, that girl.' The tone of his voice told of his admiration for her. 'I've seen some very bright young people come through this lab, but she had not only the intelligence, but the smarts, if you see what I mean. She wasn't one of those all-brains-no-sense people. She could figure out how to tackle a problem, bring in thoughts or ideas that seemed completely unrelated or unlikely. It's like this project we're working on — such an elegant solution. It's a huge loss.'

I'd composed myself enough to turn back and join in. 'Will her loss put an end to the research she was doing?' I asked.

'Not for this specific project, as we're far enough along the track, but as far as offshoots are concerned and just the . . . her potential. It's an unbearable loss.' His face reflected his words.

'It's clear you hold her in very high regard. Was that the general feeling for everyone? We've been told that there can be a little jealousy between colleagues — was there any of that kind of friction here. Did anyone dislike her?'

'You find petty jealousies everywhere. It's human nature, isn't it? To envy those who are better, faster, more talented than you? So yes, there was a certain level of friction, professional rivalry, but basically, she was such a lovely girl, people couldn't help but like her.'

'Was there anyone in particular who comes to mind?'

'I'm sure others will tell you that there was a little tension between Rosie and Dr Hawkins. They were professional and got on with the job, but Rosie did find it difficult and couldn't understand why Penny just didn't seem to like her.' I could relate to that. Didn't everyone want to be liked? It wasn't good for your confidence to know someone hated your guts. I could imagine Rosie would have found it quite hurtful, especially if she was in contact with Dr Hawkins every day. It would be hard to escape if your nose was being rubbed in it.

'Are you aware of any romantic involvement Miss Bateman may have had within the department?' That was a rather direct question from Smithy. He was making the assumption the good doctor here wasn't a love interest, probably on face value.

'No, she had a boyfriend in the Computer Department. James Collingwood.'

'Did you see much of him?'

'No, he didn't come up to the lab. They used to meet for lunch and she'd meet him for dinner often when she was working late.'

That was curious. I recalled when watching the video of James' interview he'd said they often met for lunch but not so much in the evenings.

'Did you see them meet for dinner?'

'No, that's just what she said. I don't pay too much attention to everyone's love lives. You'd never get anything done.'

I was definitely going to have to engineer a meeting with the boyfriend. There were a few too many inconsistencies here and they all supported the idea Rose-Marie was having an extra-relationship affair.

'What can you tell me about the commercial side of your research? Professor Simpson said that there was quite a bit of money to be had from this,' Smithy said, changing tack.

'Yes, the potential commercial applications are huge, as were possible spin-off lines of research. We're talking on a global scale. So again, Rosie's death is a huge loss.'

'Did she stand to make money from the venture?'

'Not directly. The intellectual-property rights belong to the university, and Otago has the organisation in place to take advantage of them. But then, she would benefit from funding, and would be looked after by them, as it were. The University looks after its own, because it's in its best interests to do so. Otherwise, it would lose its best researchers to private enterprise.'

'So it wouldn't have been in anyone's interests here, financially speaking, to remove her from the equation.'

'Hell no. Quite the contrary, in fact.'

53

'So what have people been saying, then? That I was jealous of her? Why would I be jealous of her? Just because she was everyone's little darling and their golden child? That she was handed every opportunity on a plate, while others of us had to justify our presence every single day. That what she was working on saw the bulk of the research dollars and overshadowed any other individual projects that may have had merit because they might make some money out of hers? Why do you think that would make me jealous or angry?'

Okay, so we'd stumbled upon the department's designated bitch, but she wasn't a very smart bitch, as most people toned it down and kept it looking civil for the police. Maybe she was hormonal, or caffeine-deprived. Even Smithy looked startled. He'd interviewed Dr Penny Hawkins earlier, but I don't recall him mentioning she was this aggressive.

'I bet it was Simpson, that puffed-up, pompous git,' she ranted on, oblivious to the impression she was making. 'He'd be just the type to say something like that. Talk about the pot calling the kettle — '

'Look, I don't mean to criticise,' I interrupted. Her behaviour was way over the top and despite the Rottweiler demeanour, I had one of those nagging little feelings about her. 'But you're not

270

doing yourself any favours being so aggressive.' Smithy looked at me like I'd gone all barmy on him, so I shook my head a fraction, then stepped up to her and put my hand on her shoulder. 'Are you okay? Is everything alright?' At this, she looked as though she was going to let rip, but then she paused, stuttered, then visibly deflated like an airbed with a leak. It was as if someone had pulled the plug.

Smithy looked at me again, surprised, and even I was shocked by the transformation. 'Do you want a tissue?' I asked, concerned she was about to start blubbing all over us. If she was, in fact, hormonal, this was one hell of a mood swing.

'God, I'm sorry,' she said and fished into her pocket for a tissue. 'It's been a really bad morning, and I shouldn't have taken it out on you. Please don't hold what I said against me. My mother died two months ago, and I've just found out my brother, who had power of attorney, has systematically bled her savings dry, so I'm feeling more than a little angry and upset right now.'

And I thought my family had problems.

'Can I get you a cup of coffee or something?' I asked, then realised this wasn't my turf. She smiled at the gesture and started to move towards the door.

'I think that's a probably a good idea. Come up to the staffroom, you must need one too.'

Smithy sidled up to me and spoke low, so Dr Hawkins wouldn't hear. 'This one's yours, too damned unpredictable for me.' I loved the fact that a man of Smithy's size and disposition could be intimidated by a woman.

We were led into the corridor, where Smithy had to duck to avoid hitting his head on a shower head and emergency handle hanging from the ceiling. We walked past more locked freezers and climbed the stairs to the seventh floor. My head spun at the view, as the bank of windows alongside the metal stairwell high-lighted the precipitous drop to the courtyard below. They didn't have buildings this tall where I came from. The staffroom had the usual trappings of a communal watering hole — plenty of dirty dishes in the sink, in direct contravention of the, I thought, rather optimistic 'Please clean up after yourself' poster, complete with passive-aggressive smiley face.

'Urgh, usual mess I'm afraid. You know what these mad scientists are like, can't tie their own shoelaces, let alone clean up after themselves.' She seemed to be trying very hard to undo the first impression she'd made earlier. 'Help yourselves to a mug; the tea and coffee things are over here.'

Smithy took a bog-standard brown glass mug and started filling it up with his usual mix of one and a half teaspoons of coffee and three teaspoons of sugar. I picked up a plain purple ceramic job. I was about to toss in a tea bag when Dr Hawkins said, 'Oh.'

'Oh? Did I spill something?' I asked, checking the bench and then the floor.

'No, it's just that,' she pointed to the mug in my hand. 'That was her mug.'

'Rose-Marie's?'

'Yes.'

The mug suddenly felt heavier and I placed it back down on the bench with exaggerated care. 'Do you have a place where her personal belongings are being kept?'

'The police collected most of her things shortly after her death, but yes, there are a couple of things we've come across since that we've put in a box near her old desk.'

'What sort of things?'

'A scarf, pack of herbal teabags, odds and ends we keep discovering. Actually, it's like a little stab, every time we find something more.' For someone who was venting her spleen not too long ago, she looked genuinely sad.

'So you didn't resent her that much, then?'

She laughed, deep and throaty, and smiled in my direction. 'Oh, I resented her alright, wouldn't you? But she was a nice kid, and no one deserves to die like that.'

'What particularly griped you, then?' She seemed to be quite open, and I felt there was quite a lot of leeway for digging.

'She was young, gorgeous and brilliant.' She shrugged her shoulders like that was stating the obvious. It seemed a bit odd coming from someone who, though slightly more mature, was beautiful, Hepburnish and probably not that shabby in the intelligence stakes.

'So which part irked the most?'

'The brilliant part. You know what we academics are like. We all want to be the most clever, the most inventive, the most highly esteemed. We envy brains, not beauty, although some of the men around here seem easily distracted and find it hard to keep their hands off the beauty.'

'Is this a problem you've encountered?'

She smiled at my blatant attempt to massage her ego. 'I've had my fair share of admirers over the years, but I think the men's tastes tend towards the younger. And yes, before you ask, Rosie did attract a lot of attention.'

'Did she seem responsive to it?'

'Well, she already had a boyfriend, apparently.'

'Apparently?'

'Look, let me be frank. She didn't show that much enthusiasm towards her young man, which is a pity, because I thought he seemed very nice. I always suspected she was infatuated or involved with someone else.'

'Why was that?'

'I was a young woman once. I recognised the signs: the sighs when she thought no one was watching. She suddenly started to take more care of how she looked, hair always tidy, clothes a little more trendy, occasional make-up. She'd get evasive if you asked her about what she was doing for dinner or things like that. She was being secretive.'

That confirmed my thoughts about her having a lover other than her hapless boyfriend, and also brought the focus back to the fact that this lover was most likely her killer. Loved to death.

'Did you have any theories as to who this mystery person might be?' I asked.

'I'd initially thought she might be having it off

with her professor, but it could be someone else in this department, or the Biochemistry Department, which she had a bit to do with too.'

'Professor Simpson?' I supposed he did have that natural charm and air of allure. I could understand a young woman being drawn to his maturity. But let's face it. He was older and a really bad dresser. 'You say 'initially'. What's changed your mind?'

'The fact that Simpson is a sponging, fame-grabbing, parasitic, lazy, male-chauvinist pig.' She wasn't one for holding back.

'I take it from that you don't like him.'

'Not particularly, and I thought surely Rosie would see through him, and that he was just a leech on the back of her and all our work.'

'What do you mean?' I was beginning to realise I had no concept of the politics of academia.

'The abridged version is: Rose-Marie has the idea, makes the breakthrough, our team researches and trials and tests and retests the information, we do all the hard work, and at the end of the day, that sponging bastard's name goes first on the academic paper.'

'Why? That hardly seems fair.'

'Because, he is the Professor, the all-hallowed High and Mighty. He is supposedly the supervisor, and even though his input has only been a half-hour meeting once a week, he gets the glory. In fact, if it came down to it, he'd get the bloody Nobel.'

'That's not right. Surely the university knows about this; wouldn't they do something about it?'

'No, because it comes down to dollars. The professor is a high-profile, internationally esteemed researcher, even though he's done pathetic little in the last few years, and in order to attract outside money, you need the high-profile names. Industry isn't likely to invest money in an untried doctorate student, or a couple of lowly departmental academics, so they chuck in the big name and he gets the glory.'

'God, if it's like that, why does anyone bother?' And I thought police internal politics was bad.

'Not everyone is like that, don't get me wrong — the vast majority of professors are hands-on, in there and passionate about what they're doing. Which is why the university is flourishing. Unfortunately, we happened to get the leech.'

55

'So what do you make of all that?' I asked Smithy as we walked back to the car.

'It makes me glad I'm just a dumb-arse detective and don't have to put up with all the bickering, infighting and arrogant giant egos.'

Well actually, I'd had to put up with the arrogant-giant-ego thing, and I didn't think either of us came into the dumb-arse category. Smithy must have realised what he'd said, as he added a proviso: 'That doesn't include Dickhead Johns, of course,' and gave me a knowing grin.

'You know what I think?' I said.

'What?'

'That if you take away all the smokescreens and petty jealousies, especially after listening to Penny Hawkins, who although she comes across as a bit of a prickly bitch I think is pretty astute, Rose-Marie Bateman was having an affair with someone, who took it upon themselves to kill her. And the reason she was killed was because she'd become surplus to requirements or things were getting too complicated for the killer. Penny said she was behaving like she was in love. Perhaps the killer wasn't expecting that — or couldn't cope with it. Anyway, I don't think it has anything to do with what she was researching or her university work because everyone there had too much to lose with her gone.'

'What about the professor? Wouldn't he get

more glory with her out of the picture, one less name on the list of authors of the research paper?'

'Short term yes, but long term, if there was a lot of offshoot research because of this, she was his meal ticket. I'm quite sure he would be looking at the long-term view.'

My pontificating was abruptly cut off by the sound of my cellphone. The shock of it breaking the quiet set my heart racing. When I saw the name on the screen, it ramped up a little more.

'Shit,' I muttered and then answered. 'Hello?'

'Gidday.' He was so self-assured he didn't even say who it was. I'd fix him.

'Hi, who's this?'

'My number's programmed into your phone, Sam. You saw the name when you answered the phone. Stop playing silly buggers.'

Damn, sprung. I turned aside, so Smithy wouldn't see the embarrassed look on my face. 'Hi Paul.'

'That's better. Say, what are you doing for lunch today? Court's taking a recess, so do you want to grab a bite?'

'I'd love to, but I've already arranged to meet Maggie — I have a little debt to settle. Perhaps tomorrow. Will you still be in town?' I was quite relieved I didn't have to lie to him as, yes, I was meeting Maggie, at Modak's for a cinnamon pinwheel to make good on my gambling debt. I could work on tomorrow's excuse tomorrow. I realised I'd left an opening this evening and decided to close it. 'I'm meeting Mum for dinner tonight; it looks like they're heading home tomorrow.' Okay, so I did have to lie, after all.

'Excuses, excuses,' he said, with good humour in his voice. I felt a pang of guilt. He was a good man and he sure as hell got my pulse racing, but 'us' just didn't feel quite right. 'I'll give you a ring tomorrow and see if you've got a space in your busy schedule for lunch. Bye.'

He hung up before I had a chance to respond and I was left staring at the phone.

'That guy from Gore?' Smithy asked.

'Yeah,' I said.

'Hummph.'

56

There was a bit of a buzz on in the squad room when we got back. The atmosphere had been rather muted this morning, but now there was a new energy. Something must have happened while we were out chasing academics.

'What's all the excitement?' I asked. 'Did someone finally get rid of the seagull?'

'No, it's still crapping in the foyer. Do you want the good news, or the bad news?' Reihana asked.

'I'll vote good,' Smithy said, sticking up his hand.

'Good,' I said and raised my hand too.

'Thought you'd say that. As well as a few positive leads in Timaru, the good news is we've got a possible description of the offender in the Bateman case.'

'Fantastic. Who from and how?'

'The uniform branch guys down at the Botty Gardens. They went back to stopping everyone who used the walkway for a chat and got a hit from a student who reckons he might have seen our vic with a man on the night she was killed.'

'And?'

'Not a very detailed one, I'm afraid. The guy said the man had his back to him for most of the time, and he wasn't taking that much notice of them anyway, but he appeared to be a Caucasian, five-foot nine or ten. He guessed around thirty to forty years old.' He saw my raised eyebrows. 'Yeah, I know, not terribly helpful, but he said it was hard to tell the age because the guy was wrapped up, had a beanie, trendy hooded anorak-type jacket, scarf, jeans and the light wasn't that good. He thought it was around eight o'clock.'

'So in reality, he could have been any age. And it was definitely Rose-Marie?'

'Yes, recognised her from a photograph.'

'And his comments on their body language?'

'Said they just appeared to be having a friendly chat.'

The question that always jumped to mind in these situations popped out.

'Why's it taken so damned long for him to say something? Why didn't he come forward last week? It's been splashed all over the news and I'm sure it's been all the talk down at the uni.'

Reihana gave a snort. 'They asked him that and his dumb-nut excuse was he didn't think it would be important.'

'I'd bet he'd have thought it was important if it was his sister,' I said. Some people were so thick it defied belief.

'You said he was a student. He didn't recognise the man as someone from the university?' Smithy asked. Reihana shook his head. 'What faculty was he in?'

'Law and commerce.' Another flaming law student.

'So chances are the man wasn't a law or commerce lecturer or prof then?'

'They're big faculties, but no, most students

281

would recognise their main teaching staff.'

'Narrows the field down a bit, for our theory of her having an affair with someone at the university. And the older age group again increases the possibility of an extra-marital affair for the perpetrator,' Smithy said.

'That idea's gaining traction?'

'Yeah, we've been talking with some of her colleagues this morning.'

'Sounds like you'd better enlighten me further,' Reihana said.

'Yes, but in a minute. Has he done a compusketch?'

'As we speak.'

Yay, something positive, even if it was tenuous. How many other people were out there, harbouring pieces of information they didn't think important? I remembered the other half of Reihana's tidings.

'So what was the bad news?'

'I've been talking to the tech guys.'

'And?'

'Two bits really. Firstly, our victim had a Facebook page, Instagram and was on Snapchat. But it was just full of the usual — her friends were all students and kids of her age, or so they claimed. She avoided all that sweary, American gangsta crap-talk the kids seem to like, and the pics she posted were all rather tame and chaste. Nothing in her undies. She loved God and her mum and dad, boyfriend, cat, that kind of thing. There are a few more local names for us to follow up, but nothing spectacular. Friends have also set up a couple of tribute pages for her, which are very moving.'

'And?'

It had to be bad, judging by the expression on his face.

'Sorry, Sam. You're a star on YouTube.'

57

It was a sheer delight to slouch back into one of the low black sofas at the café and jump off the treadmill of life. My brain was on overload and my nerves wound tight, like a too-sharp guitar string. I bumped up a bit as Maggie landed next to me.

'Jolly decent of you to admit defeat and settle your score so promptly,' she said.

'He called again today, to see if I wanted to go for lunch, but I said I was meeting you instead.'

'You dope, you know I'd have been happy to be bumped to another day. You should have gone out with Paul.'

'Actually, you were a convenient excuse.'

'Lovely, I'm just an excuse. An excuse for what? I thought you liked Paul.'

'I do, but — '

'But what Sam? Stop being so stupid. He's a really nice guy, and he's clearly absolutely mad about you. Most girls would be delirious to have that kind of attention.'

'I know, and well, that's just a bit too much to deal with right now.'

'Being adored?'

'Yes. I don't want anything that intense.'

'And has he been too intense? Is he stalking you?' I cringed at her choice of words, but didn't elaborate on my other little problem.

'No, in fact he's been really good-humoured

and doesn't seem to get offended at my evasion tactics. Which, I might add, is annoying too. It's like he's just waiting for me to come round to the fact we're perfect for each other. And that's his thoughts not mine,' I added, before she made a rude comment.

Maggie just sat and smiled at me with that knowing look.

58

My head felt like a spaghetti junction of intersecting, over- and underpassing streams of information, swirling like some rush-hour maelstrom. What I needed was to get out on the road, and pace it out, let the drum of my feet and the thrum of my heart pumping get some sense of rhythm, some order to it, get the streams of data moving in parallel, so I could see where they nudged up against each other, where the connections were. Overlay the emotional toll of the last week and it was like a fog had descended on the network and I was feeling my way on my hands and knees. No wonder frustration was eating away at me. I needed to run and as soon as I got home, I was going to indulge.

Running for me was a magic elixir that tuned out my conscious thoughts, but let the subconscious work in time with my footfalls. Rhythm, order, time. But I had to get home first. I wandered back to where my car was parked the long way around, seeing as a freight train had been so kind as to accidentally remove the pedestrian footbridge that everyone used to cross the shunting yards. I wasn't stupid enough to play chicken with the trains to avoid a longer walk, unlike some idiots. I meandered along the path behind our gorgeous old railway station, reminiscent of a gigantic gingerbread house. It was frivolous and completely over the top and the thought of a city of dour Scottish Presbyterians creating a building of such frippery always made me smile. No wonder the tourists flocked to it. I strolled around, while having wistful dreams of a work parking space — like that would ever happen.

As I approached the car, I could see something stuck under the windscreen wiper. No one else had one, so I wondered how the hell I could get a parking ticket here. It was all-day, no time restrictions. I was pretty sure my warrant of fitness and registration were up to date, so surely it couldn't be an instant fine for something as dumb as that.

I tugged the paper out and opened it up, wondering how much money I was going to get stung for this time.

You can't hide from me you murdering bitch.

I swung around, my eyes rapid-fire jumping from car to car, across the railway lines, scanning the area for any sign of an observer. There was no one except a parcel-laden woman, ten cars down. My hands shook with the same rapidity as my heart and that swirling bilious feeling churned in my stomach. Jesus, this was too much. It was beyond someone's stupid idea of a joke now. Had they followed me here? Or had they chanced across my car and decided to put the wind up me? Whatever way, it was working.

Something had to be done, but what? If I told Smithy or the guys, they'd be on at me for not reporting it earlier. Could I take care of it? I checked the ground, but there were no obvious footprints in the gravel and dust mix. I could fingerprint the wiper blades and maybe get lucky.

'Jesus,' I yelled out loud, as my cellphone rang and my heart rate jerked up even more. A searing pain shot through my head and throbbed in my temples, resonating with the heavy and rapid thuds of my heart. My chest constricted and, as I gasped for oxygen, I wondered if this was what it felt like if you were having a heart attack.

I fumbled the phone out of my pocket, flicked it open, saw who it was and managed a gulped 'Paul?' before shock and physiology caught up with me and I retched over the ground next to the tyre. I spat a few times before daring to turn my attention back to the call.

'Sam? Sam? What's going on? Are you alright? Sam? Answer me.' I could hear Paul's concerned voice well before I got my ear to the speaker.

'Ugh, sorry, no, shit.' Another spit. I leaned hard against the car, then changed my mind and crouched down on my haunches, head between my knees.

'What's happening? Where are you?' he asked.

'Sorry, I just got a fright, that's all.'

'That's all? It sounded like you were throwing up. Are you okay?'

God, how much did I tell him? I didn't want him charging in and trying to fix it all for me like some knight in shining armour, though part of me realised this had gotten way out of my control, and maybe it was time to call in some outside assistance. I took a shuddery breath and confessed.

'I've had a little problem, and it just got beyond creepy.'

'What do you mean?'

So I told him, about the first note I put under the windscreen of the crap-heap car, the response, the further notes and now this.

'Sam, this is serious, someone is stalking you. Why didn't you tell anyone earlier?' Which was the question I knew everyone would ask. But how could I explain it? Initially, it seemed too silly to mention and, if I was really honest, perhaps I'd brought it upon myself, and therefore it was up to me to fix it.

'I didn't want to make a big deal out of it.' My voice sounded as feeble as the excuse.

'But it is a big deal. You of all people should know that. These sorts of people are unstable. It might have started with a few nasty notes, but now, they're following you, and it could escalate to assault, or worse. It has to be stopped.'

Paul's words seemed to hammer away any remaining shreds of resistance. What with the crap I'd had from the boss, my grief and guilt at killing Cassie, anger at the whole bloody mess of this case, worry about Dad, tiptoeing around Mum and the gnawing ache of fear, I was spent. I couldn't even reply.

'Look, Sam,' he said, tender but firm. 'Let me go into this for you. I know you probably don't want your work colleagues to get involved, I can understand that. I'm independent and can check this guy out. Let me do this. I'm rather too fond of you to let some little arsehole stalker make your life a misery or put you in danger.'

The tears warmed their way down my cheeks and then dropped, making little circular splashes in the dust at my feet. 'Okay,' I managed.

59

It seemed ridiculous for a grown woman to be wary of an inanimate object, but I gave the shit-heap a wide berth all the same as I made my way along the footpath and up to the house. The drive home had seemed surreal. I'd felt detached from reality and had driven like a drunk knowing they shouldn't be behind the wheel of a car and therefore being exquisitely careful. My hands were still shaking as I battled the key into the front door and then stumbled into the entrance as Uncle Phil opened it on his way out.

'Oh, sorry, Sam, I didn't mean to surprise you.' He steadied me to vertical, then looked at me with great concern. 'Are you okay? What's happened?' It was one friendly person too many and I found the tears making a repeat appearance down my face. I hadn't intended on telling anyone else my woes, but they came spilling out, all the same.

'I've got this awful problem,' sniff, 'there's this guy, and he's stalking me and he,' sniff, 'even followed me to work and I'm scared and I feel stupid and that's his stupid car out front and I stuck a note and he stuck a note, then it got worse and now I don't know what to do . . . ' I was blathering and I don't recall even drawing a breath as it all came stumbling out.

'Hang on, hang on, slow down,' he said and

shut the door behind me. He pushed me in the direction of the kitchen and, when he'd got me ensconced in a chair, put the kettle on. 'Now, start from the beginning. What's been happening?' So for the second time in an hour, I told my sorry story, and despite my initial reservations about telling anyone, I was starting to feel a smidgeon better about it all. Maybe the old adage of a problem shared had credence, after all. Uncle Phil was most taken aback by the situation. He seemed quite offended that anyone would do such a thing.

'Do you want me to find this person and go have a talk with them?' It was very gallant of him, but I couldn't picture Uncle Phil even raising his voice, let alone giving someone a bollocking about stalking his house guest.

'Thank you, I appreciate your offer, but I've got someone, Paul Frost, looking into it for me.'

'Is that the young man you went out to dinner with the other night?' he asked.

'Yes.' I could tell by the sparkle in his eye he knew the ructions that occurred because of that evening's events, and we both smiled. 'He's a detective too, but from out of town and he said he'd look into it, so I don't have to feel silly asking my colleagues.'

'That's good, because you must take this seriously, Sam. That could be a very sick person and you don't know where it could lead. Just look at what happened to that young student, Rosie. It's better to be safe and get this sorted out. I'd feel awful if something dreadful happened to you and I could have stopped it.

And worse, I'd hate to have to deal with your mother's wrath.'

Again, a smile.

'It's being taken care of. But thank you for looking after me and for being so sweet.' Another male to add to my list of protectors.

'What are you going to do now?'

'I was thinking of going for a run, actually. I need to clear my head.'

'But that's not safe,' he said, the concerned look back on his face. 'What if this person's watching you?'

Like that thought hadn't occurred to me. But Shephards aren't quitters, and I was damned if I was going to be cowed into hiding by some idiot. I might be tired and tearful, and even — if I admitted to the fluttery feeling in my tummy — mildly scared. But I wasn't going to be defeatist. Still, it didn't mean I was going to be dumb about it. There was no way in hell I'd be plugging music into my ears, so my iPod would be staying at home and my ears otherwise occupied, straining for the sound of approaching footsteps.

'Shouldn't you wait until Maggie gets home? She might go with you, keep you company.'

I laughed, for what felt the first time in ages. Maggie? Running? She who had an aversion to breaking a sweat other than for pleasurable reasons? I didn't think so. Uncle must have realised the unlikeliness of his suggestion and joined me in a chuckle. 'Well, maybe not,' he said. 'What was I thinking?'

'Indeed. Anyway, I need the exercise. I'll be

fine, I'll watch over my shoulder. Don't worry, I can look after myself.'

I hoped.

60

The beat of feet meeting tarmac was working its magic and I could feel the tension that had muscled its way into my shoulders and neck retreating. I closed my mind to thoughts of work and home, and instead focused on the details before me: the crunch of gravel underfoot as I paced the roadside path, the mosses and grasses infiltrating its edges. The moist smell of lush bush mixed with the rich aroma of warm earth and the sweetness of rotting leaves. The native trees adding to the soothing hues of the green belt: five finger, pittosporum, kowhai, the large flat leaves of rangiora — or loo-paper tree, as we called it in my family — the lovely fringe of tatty bark draping the tree fuchsia. But what struck me the most was the bird call. It was gorgeous, and I found a spontaneous smile forming on my face with every warble. I could make out the call of a bellbird, and a couple of fantails or piwakawaka were making a happy racket while they performed their aerodynamics-defying flitting nearby. Maybe I should ditch the iPod more often, I thought. I'd had no idea what I was missing out on.

I'd had no set route in mind when I left home, but it soon become apparent I was heading to the Botanic Garden, to the path down which Rose-Marie Bateman walked those fateful steps. The more I thought about it, the more I was convinced the other four killings, the circus diversion, everything, was all about her. Her murder wasn't an isolated event, as had been suggested by others, a coincidence of timing. I didn't believe in coincidence. It made sense that she was the ultimate victim. There was no struggle, she followed the path with someone she knew, and now — I was absolutely certain — someone she cared for. Christ, what a price she'd paid for love. The man she'd fallen for had planned her demise with meticulous care. He'd engineered the perfect smokescreen with the circus itinerary to deflect attention from his practice killings. What kind of sick individual would take the lives of strangers to ensure they had the fortitude or technique to kill their main target? And what chilled me even more was the knowledge that the first killing had taken place months before Rose-Marie was murdered, so he'd been planning her death well in advance. Yet her behaviour suggested her love for him was growing. What deception. Did he see it as sport? Was that what turned him on? Being the Ringmaster in his own personal circus, timing the acts, building up to the grand finale to see how far could he bait her, until the night of the eleventh of April, when down at the riverbank, secluded and romantic, he said, shut your eyes and hold out your hands, leading her to believe her love was giving her the ultimate gift.

That was the scene as it played out in my mind, and as I shook my head to be rid of the taint of it, I threw myself off balance, veering onto the road. He'd also played the police. We'd jumped beautifully on to his decoy. And although he could not possibly have orchestrated the vigilantes — well, at least I didn't think he could have — his diversion could not have worked out better. I wondered if he would have been disappointed if the police hadn't stumbled upon the circus. Would he have tipped us off, to make sure we knew how clever he was?

Of course, I might have been totally wrong about all of this, but my heart said I wasn't. Then another awful thought popped into my mind. Was part of his sport to seduce and deflower the good little Christian girl? See what kind of deceptions she'd pull to keep their secret, what lengths she'd go to come to him? She'd lied, she'd deceived and she'd gone against her own principles for him. Did he set out to steal her soul as well as her body? This train of thought was getting too depressing, so I blanked it all out again, by concentrating on the sound of my breathing, the feel of the air as it cooled my sweat-glistened skin.

I had reached the spidery tree on the path to destruction, and found myself checking both ways for signs of life before getting up the gall to walk down its lonely sweep. I'd said hello to the constable stationed at the garden gates to question passers-by, but still, it felt creepier than ever to be there, as I sat down on a rock, not *the* rock, with my back to the bank and my eyes to the path. When my supersensitised ears finally stopped my supersensitised brain from thinking every creak of a branch and whisper of wind was a stalker or killer, I set my mind back to the who, not the how or why.

Who could manage such a thing? For it was truly an orchestration. I wasn't a criminal psychologist, or profiler, but it didn't take a flash qualification to figure out we were dealing with someone very clever, and very intelligent. This wasn't some opportunistic thug; this was a rational, calculated act. What kind of sick individual could manage all that?

What I needed was a profiler. No doubt the best profiling minds in the country were already on the case, but I wasn't privy to that information. Which meant the nearest I had to one was Maggie. I was sure a couple of semesters of psychology would qualify her to give me an insight into the killer's mind. If anyone understood people, it was Maggie. Some people had that innate ability, and I'd swear that girl was one of them.

61

'Hello, anyone home?' I said, as I knocked on the door to Uncle Phil's study.

'Hang on, Sam, I'll be there in a second.' I heard his footsteps tread over, and he pulled the door open. 'You survived your run okay? No problems?'

'No creeps jumping out of the bushes or anything like that.' I don't know what I'd have done if they had, other than wet myself and run faster. 'I was just letting you know I'm back safe. And I was also wanting to ask you a question about the university. Thought you might be able to help me out on the whole politics side of things.'

'Heavens, I don't know if anyone could tackle that one with any certainty, but I'll do my best. It was about time I emerged for oxygen, anyway. Let's go downstairs for a drink.' He pulled the door shut behind him and we padded down the stairs. 'Look at that, it's wine o'clock.'

I didn't usually subscribe to wine as a fluid replacement after running, but after the day I'd had, I was willing to rehydrate by any means. I did give some thought to side effects though and drank a large glass of water while Uncle Phil organised the refreshments.

'University politics is fraught with danger, what did you want to know?' he asked as he set a couple of glasses of white on the table.

'This relates to the murder case, so I can't really go into specifics, but we were talking to some of Rose-Marie's colleagues about acknowledgement of research on academic papers and that land of thing. They were saying that in certain circumstances, a professor, or someone of high academic standing will put in a minimal contribution to the research, but be named as a main player, even if someone else has done the bulk of the work. Is that really what goes on?'

'Hah,' he said, with a smile. 'A difficult area, and a very grey one. I'd love to be able to say no, that doesn't go on and the people who do the work get the credit, but in reality, sometimes it happens.'

'And the university doesn't do anything about it? Surely it's bad for their credibility?'

'Yes and no. It's not good for credibility among the university folk and, as you can well imagine, it can cause a lot of resentment and discontent. But when it comes to gaining international credibility and, ultimately, funding, sometimes you need a high-profile name up there to get it noticed in the first place, to get invited to the international symposia. It's a competitive environment, and even in New Zealand, the universities compete for funding based on their research output. The government giveth, and the government taketh away, depending on your ranking each year. So it's big bikkies really.'

'Is it rife?'

'No, but I have heard of several instances. Was it happening to Rosie?'

'Yeah, looks like it. Interesting dynamics in her department. Seems she was being had in many ways. But you can be certain, we'll get the person who did this to her, to all of them.'

'So you think those other deaths are linked?'

Speculation had hit the newspapers, so I wasn't breaking any confidences. 'Looks that way.'

'Wow, that's serious. Do you think you're getting close?'

'Getting closer. The whole circus thing drew our attention in the wrong direction, I think. But we're piecing it all together, and we'll catch our man.'

'Good. Someone like that needs to be put away for everyone's safety. Does that information help?'

'It helps me understand some of the intricacies of what was going on, so thanks. It's almost as bad as police politics.'

'I doubt it,' he said, and I laughed in agreement. 'Well, if there's anything else I can help with, just ask. And I meant what I said earlier: if you want me to, I'll track down the person who's hassling you, have a word — sort it out for you.'

'Thanks,' I said, 'you're very kind, but it's being taken care of. Hopefully that's the last I'll hear.'

62

'Maggs, I need your professional opinion on something.'

It was evening. I had successfully danced the eggshell hop around my mother over dinner and something miraculous had happened. She'd managed to not say anything judgemental or guilt-inducing and I'd managed to not stick my foot in it. I'd call it a draw. She'd gone back down to the hospital to annoy Dad and the nursing staff, and I'd retired to the comfy chairs in the lounge with a mug of Milo, a packet of Toffee Pops, Fluffy the bird-slayer and Maggie. Aunty Jude was off at some committee meeting and Uncle Phil had retired to his man cave. My nod to the strange events of the day was to make sure the curtains were firmly drawn.

'For a start,' she said as she leaned over and swiped the biscuit packet off me, 'my professional advice would be to ring Paul, go out on lots of dates and shag him silly, then marry him, make lots of babies and live happily ever after. I think you're on to a good thing there, Sam. Don't ruin it.'

The only reason I didn't throw a cushion at her was because she had a hot drink in her hand. But I resorted to the next adult technique in my arsenal and poked out my tongue.

'Yeah, yeah. If I wanted advice on my love life, I'd ask someone who had one.'

302

'Touché. What was it you wanted to ask me again?'

'Actually, it's about this case. Chuck us another biscuit, please.' One flew obligingly through the air.

'And you think I can help you, how?'

'I need a criminal profile.'

'Oh, okay, no problem, hang on. I think I keep them here in my back pocket along with future lottery numbers and next week's racing results.'

'Sarcastic cow. I'm serious. I know you've only just started this psychology kick, and you're not exactly qualified, but, without wanting it to go to your head or anything, I think you have an instinctual understanding of people, and you might see things in a different way from me.'

'I am good, aren't I?' she said with a smug grin on her face.

'You betcha baby.'

'So why don't you listen to me, then?'

'That's different.'

'What's it worth?'

'You mean besides the satisfaction of helping out the police in putting a dangerous killer behind bars and avenging the deaths of so many unfortunate victims?'

'Yeah, aside from that. Are we talking all-expenses-paid girls' shopping trip to Melbourne, or are we talking ice cream at the corner dairy?'

'Chocolate or hokey-pokey?'

'I suspected as much. You better tell me all about it, then.'

So I did, starting with suspecting the boyfriend, then looking at university colleagues, then discovering the circus link and having the investigation lurch over there, the media, the protesters and the vigilantes. I couldn't help but get teary-eyed when I talked about those who died from the circus, animal and human, and neither could she. I filled her in on the findings of those following up on the animal-rights activists, which were zip, and then Smithy's and my visit back to the university and Rose-Marie's colleagues again. I also told her about my theory on the 'close-your-eyes-and-hold-out-your-hands' thing, which made her reach for the tissues. All in all, I was so repulsed by the end of it we needed a fresh round of Milos and emptied the packet of Toffee Pops.

'Well,' I said. 'What do you think?'

'I think I wished you paid a professional instead of asking me.'

'I'm sure the boss has been asking the professionals, but I don't have access to that information at the moment, and I'd really appreciate your outside opinion. I feel too close to it all. You're a step removed and can bring fresh eyes to it.'

'Okay, then,' Maggie said, reaching forward to deposit her mug on the coffee table before leaning back into the sofa and tapping her fingertips together like some Hollywood shrink. 'No laughing, promise?'

'Promise,' I said and made the Boy Scouts sign.

'Your killer is a very intelligent man, and I

mean very, very intelligent. Look at what he's achieved here. He's got you guys chasing your tails and completely perplexed. At this exact moment in time he's probably laughing. He is extremely arrogant, to go with his intelligence. He has carried out five killings and hasn't been caught, and probably thinks he never will be. That's a weakness to exploit, by the way.'

When I asked for her input, I was expecting a conversational opinion, not a rapid- fire, bullet-point appraisal and I was rather taken aback. Impressed, but taken aback all the same. I closed my gaping mouth and let her continue.

'Part of what is particularly scary about this man, is the strategy. From the outset, he planned this back catalogue of murders to cast suspicion on the circus, on the off chance someone made a connection. Now, you'd think it would have been more sensible to ensure there was absolutely no connection, so each case appeared unrelated. But he thought more globally than that, pulling the circus into his plan because of the misdirected attention it could arouse. And he succeeded with spectacular results. If Rose-Marie Bateman's death hadn't been linked to the circus in Dunedin, then I am certain there would have been another murder, even more violent, in the next circus town, to continue covering up the deception and, more importantly — or scarily, depending on how you see it — because he has a taste for it now. He has found a new skill; he's discovered he's really good at murder, and the police can't catch him. Arrogance again. Of course, all this planning and the other murders took place while he continued to seduce his next victim. This man has no compassion, no empathy, no soul. But you would never know it if you met him because he would blend in perfectly well in the community. A high-functioning psychopath. A genius high-functioning psychopath. You need to look in the university or someone with high tertiary qualifications. You need to look for a Caucasian male, aged between thirty and fifty. Don't look at me like that.'

'Like what?'

'Your mouth's open. Anyway, I got that white-male-age thing straight off the television. But seriously, I think your guy's at the university, and in a position of power — a tutor, lecturer or professor. He had this girl deceiving everyone to hide the relationship. It was probably inappropriate — on many levels, if he was married, and also the whole teacher-student thing is taboo. He's probably very charming and pleasant, but underneath he's a ruthless, cold-blooded killer who thinks that the police are useless and couldn't catch anything right under their nose. Oh, and he must be able to travel easily without being missed or raising the suspicion of his significant other. So perhaps his work or teaching involve going away a bit.'

'Shit, Maggie,' I said, thinking I'd met someone recently who fit that description. 'That was a little more detailed than I was expecting. Have you thought about making a career out of this?'

'Although I have quite enjoyed the papers on what makes the nutters tick, to be honest, I'd

306

find it too distressing and depressing. I like my little rose-tinted view of the world where people are kind to each other and want to be your friend. I think exposing myself to all that would be toxic. Too much for this borderline-hippy chick.'

'You're not wrong. Sometimes it scares me how blasé I've become about murder and death, and I'm far more emotional about it than my colleagues, which means some of them are hardened beyond belief. I don't know how healthy it is.'

'Unfortunately, there are always going to be criminals and there's always going to be a need for police. I think you do a damned good job, Sam, and the world needs people like you. So don't let the turkeys get you down. And for the sake of all the Rose-Marie Bateman's and Gaby Knoweses out there, keep at it.'

'Thanks, Maggs, you're like my one-person cheerleading squad.'

'Actually, there are two of us on that squad, but you won't go out on a date with the other one.'

63

My morning had got off to a slightly better start than the previous day. The shower was hot, for starters, although Mum counteracted that with a touch of the frosty nostril at breakfast and the need to ping me. Apparently, I wasn't visiting Dad enough, but that was a little difficult considering I seemed to be working every waking hour and I'd had a few major distractions in my life. Her presence in the room like Big Chief Thundercloud wasn't any incentive to visit, either. But on the occasions I did, Dad and I had enjoyed the Olympic sport of eyeball rolling and eyebrow lifting behind her back. He knew how it was. They were supposed to be heading home this afternoon, so I'd pop in later.

To avoid any possibility of encountering unwanted windscreen decorations, I'd walked down to work, and hadn't even glanced in the general direction of my car.

The morning briefing was more manic than most, even though depleted in numbers. DI Johns had marched into our office and made the announcement, 'We've got another body' only minutes after I'd arrived. Dunedin was certainly having a bad run. It wasn't doing our image as a safe and sleepy city any favours. A team of SOCOs and detectives had immediately been formed to go to the crime scene, and I, naturally, wasn't a part of it.

Early indications were the deceased was the victim of an assault and robbery. His body had been found this morning down Kaikorai Valley in some trees by the bowling alley car park, his wallet nearby, minus cash and credit cards. He was, according to the wallet, Cameron Ellison — although yet to be formally identified — a young man, early twenties, and although he was another student, at the polytechnic rather than university, his death didn't seem to bear any relation to the Bateman case. A huge relief to all concerned. The last thing we needed in that investigation was another body and the associated government and media attention and demands as to what we were doing. As it was, with yet another student dying, I was sure there would be a number of parents out there having second thoughts about sending their beloved children down this way for their continued education.

The new case did leave the department rather stretched. One murder in Dunedin was rare, let alone two at the same time, let alone the whole circus fiasco, hence the reduced head count at the morning briefing.

For those of us in attendance, verbal reports confirmed what we suspected. The activist angle was a dead end. Rabid though one or two of them were, the overwhelming claim was that human life was sacrosanct, and they were devastated that animals had died as a result of the vigilante actions. In fact, they were more upset by the animal deaths, particularly Cassie's, than the people's. Cassie's upset me more too, but my perspective was a little different. What I did find hard to stomach was the activists' assertions that Cassie need not have been destroyed and the police — i.e. me — had overreacted. What the bloody hell would they know?

To my relief, the focus swiftly moved on from me to the more interesting presence of a flash, out-of-town profiler. His views made for fascinating listening, and a thumbs-up to Maggie because he said pretty much what she had, only with a little more detail as to how Mr Psychopath became Mr Psychopath: that he had a complete distain and disrespect for authority figures, most likely stemming from his relationship with his father, who probably beat, raped or psychologically abused him. Surprise, they always did.

I was quite happy sitting in the back row when a certain voice boomed out, 'Detective Constable Shephard, what have you got to add to Dr Kitchin's assessment?'

All the heads in the room swung around to face me and I was momentarily flummoxed. I was sure the DI wasn't asking because he valued my opinion.

'We need to take a closer look at Professor Simpson at the university,' I said. He fits into a number of those categories and is the age and stature the witness from the Botanic Garden described, although his dress sense is not up to date, but it would be easy enough for someone to dress different for the occasion. He's very intelligent and charming, but he was quite belittling to Detective Smith and I when we talked yesterday.'

'Was there anyone else there who jumped to mind?'

I thought DI Johns slotted nicely into a number of those categories too, except the charming one, but I wasn't going to go there. 'Not specifically, but I'm sure there are a number of men at the university who fit that description. We should cast our net a little wider than her immediate colleagues in pharmacy and biochemistry.'

I thought of another thing Maggie had mentioned which I had been ruminating on and which no one had discussed. Well, not in front of me, anyway. 'One thing. This man has travelled frequently to kill, so either he's single or a loner, but this doesn't fit the furtiveness or secrecy of Rose-Marie's behaviour, acting like she was having an affair with someone, perhaps a married man. Unless he was able to fabricate a reason for frequent travel, so it wouldn't seem amiss to his family. Whether that be for work, research or a hobby; or perhaps even his partner was away a lot, so these activities would have gone unnoticed.' If the DI had thought he'd do some point scoring to my detriment, he'd failed, and I thanked Maggie under my breath.

'Thank you, DC Shephard, that's a good point.' Was I imagining it or did he seem almost disappointed. I could tell from the morning's attitude I was back on his top-ten most-hated list. I wondered what had pissed him off this time. Perhaps the wife didn't iron his shirt right, or he hadn't had enough coffee. Whatever it was, it was in my best interests to give him a wide berth.

'Detective Smith, you and I are going to go and pay a visit to Professor Simpson and invite him back here for an interview. The rest of you know what you need to be doing. Get going, people.'

Smithy turned and gave me a grimace that said he knew too well what was happening, and I, with a sigh, realised my time in the loop was over and I was back to being shark bait.

64

The office was devoid of life. In fact, the whole floor seemed unusually empty. I wondered how Smithy and the DI were getting on convincing the professor he needed to come in for a little chat. Somehow, I could see a warrant in their immediate future.

Seeing as I was effectively grounded, my morning had been spent going over dates of the killings. What Maggie said had got me thinking. All the murders had occurred near enough to a weekend. Friday, Saturday, Sunday and one discovered on Monday, but could have happened earlier. All of which supported the idea that the perpetrator had a day job and his weekends were free. There must have been a bit of flexibility in his job, so he could travel legitimately, or unnoticed. As far as I was aware, most university staff had relatively flexible hours, unless they had a high teaching load.

I checked my watch. It was 10.45 a.m. There was no one here to notice if I popped down to the hospital to see Dad before they discharged him. I thought I'd text Mum and see what she was up to, so reached for my cellphone before realising it was a bit difficult to text someone when they didn't have a mobile. Someone needed to introduce that woman to the twenty-first century. My screen indicated I'd missed a call and there was a message. Must have come through when I was in the meeting this morning. I scrolled down and saw it came from Paul. My belly gave a pleasant little lurch at the sight of the name, but my head overrode it. He was probably trying to arrange lunch or something. I was tempted not to listen to the message and plead ignorance but decided that was a bit too lily-livered. Grown-up girls were supposed to be able to deal with a problem, even if they couldn't figure out why it was such a problem.

Just do it, Shep.

'Sam, it's Paul.' He must have rung from outside the Courthouse, as the wind crackled his voice and the sounds of passing vehicles punctuated the message. 'Hey, I've done a bit of looking into your little . . . ' Another four cars. I wished he'd move. 'Registered to . . . ' A car. 'Ron Ellis . . . ' A truck this time, a double, probably sheep, and two cars. ' . . . near you guys, so I thought I'd pay him a little visit this morning after I get out of court.' The truck must have prompted him to move as it gradually became easier to hear him. 'Do you want to meet for lunch, say, Nova, at noon and I can let you know how I got on? Cheers.'

That was a pretty smooth way of slipping in a lunch invitation. How could I refuse? At least I now knew the name of my mystery stalker. A name made him seem somehow smaller. A flesh-and-blood human being, like the rest of us.

Lunch would be kind of nice, I supposed, and I was dying for a report on Paul's little visit, but how would I fit it in with the parents? I'd have to

314

chance it at the hospital and hope Mum was still up at the house, so I could get some decent time alone with Dad. It must have been driving him spare to have her hovering around like a blowfly, fussing and annoying the crap out of everyone. I grabbed my bag and headed for the stairs. My dad had endless patience, which was fortunate, considering who he chose to marry. He was Mr Steady Eddie, while she blustered her way through life. I didn't know how he put up with her, let alone be so besotted with her, which he was. And it was mutual, even after all these years. Very sweet, but completely baffling as far as I was concerned.

If I got a moment alone, I planned to tell Dad about Cassie. I needed some fatherly reassurance, a pat on the back and a 'you did alright, kid'. I might even mention my little problem with Mister Ron Ellis. The way the name rolled around in my mind, caught my attention; it sounded somehow familiar. I stopped and stood, hands on hips while I ran it through my mental contacts list. Ron Ellis? I was pretty sure that was no one I knew or had been around in recent history. Dad had a hunting buddy Ron Allison, but he'd be at least sixty-five, and last I knew lived in the back blocks of Tapanui, which was a little bit further out than the middle of nowhere. The only things he stalked were deer and beer. A wave of chill washed from my scalp downwards as a name foremost in this mornings briefing played over several times in my mind. Ron Ellis. Cameron Ellis. Cameron Ellison? Had I misheard Paul? Between the wind distortion and traffic noise had he been trying to say 'Cameron Ellison'? Surely not. I turned around and sprinted back up the stairs.

When I rang Paul's number, it went straight to voicemail. Of course, he'd have turned it off for court. Damn it.

I felt the restless itch I got when I knew there was something seriously wrong, something I should think of. Had Paul been trying to say a Cameron Ellison was my stalker? And coincidentally, a Cameron Ellison happened to be identified as this morning's victim of an assault and robbery?

No, that couldn't be right. That was too creepy. The room had taken on a slightly distorted feel as my mind grappled with what was happening here.

'I don't believe in coincidences,' I said out loud to myself, repeatedly, like some mantra, while my brain chugged through this.

The man who had likely been stalking me turns up dead, the day after I finally tell someone about my problem. Make that someones, plural. The only people who knew about the car thing were Paul, Uncle Phil and Maggie, who I finally fessed up to last night. I knew Maggs well enough to know she wouldn't squash a spider, let alone kill a man, and I thought I knew Paul well enough to know his idea of 'checking it out' wouldn't involve permanently checking out the weirdo. Which left Uncle Phil. Which didn't make sense. He was the epitome of the mild-mannered and endearing absent-minded professor. But he was the only other person who knew, and he had offered to do something about it for me, 'have a word', as he'd put it. But this? Surely not.

Coincidence?

It had to be because there was no way in hell I could imagine Uncle Phil being a killer. Uncle Phil was the kind of man who would return a man's wallet if he found it, not mug him for it. And God knew he didn't need the money. But then, if that cold, twitching feeling between my shoulder blades was anything to go by then Cameron Ellison was not mugged and left for dead for the contents of his wallet; it was just made to look that way. A smokescreen to divert attention from the real reason for his death: that he chose the wrong person to stalk?

That cold, twitching feeling spread back up into my scalp and across my cheeks. There had been some other, very complex and spectacular smokescreens happening recently. Could there be a connection?

No, Sam, you're making way too much out of a possible connection, based on a name you can't even verify, from a dodgy-quality cellphone message. Be logical about this.

But that was the scary thing, I *was* being logical about this — farfetched, but logical. What if Cameron Ellison was killed because he was stalking me, and what if the same person who did that, had also covered up some other killings? And by process of elimination, there was only one person left who knew, who fit the profile. Although even entertaining the idea of Uncle Phil as cold-blooded killer gave me the head-spins, the more I considered it, the less unlikely it became. There were some distinct parallels.

I had to think rationally about this, before I leapt to some ludicrous conclusion. I'd run through the checklist, the profile Maggie and the hotshot had come up with for our serial killer.

He would be highly intelligent — check.

White male, thirty to fifty years of age — a little older than the range, but not too far out of that envelope — check.

Someone at the university, in a position of power — check.

Charming — check. I thought he was lovely. In fact, I had a real soft spot for him, which was why this mental exercise seemed so very wrong.

Arrogant — not really, actually, not at all at home. Maybe he showed signs of it in the workplace. Maybe he hid it well. Otherwise, he was no more so than most males I knew.

Disdain for authority figures, bad father relationship? Oh, Jesus. I thought about the box of ashes buried in the laundry cupboard, the box no one would talk about, and that cold feeling fingered my bowels and then clamped around them, hard.

Freedom of movement, not drawing suspicion from loved ones? My mind raced onwards. He could do what he flaming well pleased, because Aunty Jude was never there. She was always off doing coffee or some committee thing or championing the latest cause. She'd said so herself — since the twins had left home, and they no longer had to run around after them, she'd had the time to devote to herself and her other interests. And Uncle Phil had had the time to devote to — what? Affairs with pretty young women? Planning elaborate murder schemes? His wife was never home. In fact, he probably resented the amount of time she spent on everything else but him. Had he found other entertainment? That would be one hell of a hobby.

Knew the victim? Yes, although he said he only knew Rose-Marie in passing. Rose-Marie. My mind played back to some of our conversations. Rosie — he'd called her that, last night, hadn't he? I was sure he'd called her Rosie. I'd only ever called her Rose-Marie when I'd talked about the case, and even then I'd been very careful not to mention particulars or divest any information about it, even when I'd asked his advice about university politics. Rosie — for me, it had seemed disrespectful to call her anything other than Rose-Marie, and he'd called her Rosie. Maybe he'd read that name in the newspaper, although they'd been fairly formal about it too. No, it was the way that he said it. Her name rolled off his tongue with familiarity. It suggested he knew her a little more informally than he made out.

I felt myself break out in a cold sweat.

It was all too unlikely, too circumstantial. Yet, there were enough intersecting points there to raise red flags, and the timing of this morning's grim find couldn't be ignored. I *didn't* believe in coincidences. My body sure as hell was telling me it wholeheartedly believed what my mind was busy trying to counter. Uncle Phil as murderous psychopath?

It was a thought that beggared belief. How the hell was I going to be able to test that theory? And what if I was wrong? I'd look like an utter twat to my work colleagues — yet another wild theory from the interloper. And as for the Kershaws, accusations like that could ruin lives, and these were people I knew and loved.

But what if I was right? The more I thought about it, the more the critical pieces fitted together, and the final scene was becoming clear, like one of those Wasgij puzzles where you looked back at the picture from the opposite viewpoint. Had I been unwittingly living with a killer? A killer whose practices appeared to be escalating and, if the most recent death was anything to go by, was tidying up loose ends? But was it loose ends, or was it something worse? If he had killed Cameron Ellison with the rather extreme and misguided aim of helping my situation, then that was not part of a master plan months in the making; it was less disciplined and more spur of the moment, warped and reactionary. It was more the action of someone losing patience, or self-control, and in a strange land of a way, it was almost brazen. Did he feel he had nothing to lose? Or had it become a sick kind of a sport: he was challenging me to join the dots and uncover him as the clever killer he thought he was? Whether Phil was getting cocky, or losing control, either way it made for one hell of a deadly man.

Involuntarily my body took a sharp intake of

breath. There were others who could get caught up in the crossfire, who could be in immediate danger.

Maggie was home this morning.

Shit.

65

'Come on, come on, pick up, Maggie.' I paced up and down as time warped and elongated the spaces between the rings. Finally, she picked up. I had to play this calm, for everyone's sake.

'Hello?'

'Maggs, it's, me. Don't say my name. Are you home? Is Uncle Phil there with you? Just say yes if he is.'

'No, I'm not at home, I'm down at uni.' Relief flooded through my body and I flopped back into my chair. 'What's this about? What's going on Sam?'

'I can't explain why right now, but I've got this awful feeling that your Uncle Phil is our killer. Too many things point that way, seem to add up. And you know that car guy, the stalker guy I told you about last night? I told Phil yesterday too, and he turned up dead this morning.'

'Fuck.'

'I know it sounds far-fetched, and you'll tell me I'm mad but — '

'No, not that, yes, I mean that too but, I mean fuck, Sam. Your mother was still at home when I left.'

I sat upright, hand clutching at the edge of my desk. I felt a pounding in my temples and a slight greyness smouldered at the periphery of my vision.

'Are you sure? She was supposed to be at the

hospital. She shouldn't be there still. What would keep her there? Was Jude home too?' I was babbling.

'No, just your mum.'

'Shit, shit, shit. Okay, I've got to go, got to sort this. For God's sake, don't go home until I ring you again.' I hung up before she had a chance to reply and then dialled the number for the hospital. Maybe Mum had left after Maggie; I had to check. After what felt like a thousand transfers around half the departments in the building, I finally got through to Dad's ward and was gutted to be informed that no, Mum wasn't there.

Fuck.

I had to warn her.

I took a large breath, steadied myself, and dialled the number for home. After three rings someone picked up.

'Hello?' It was Phil.

Surely he'd hear the hammering of my heart in my chest. I tried to sound casual, but the quaver in my voice felt patently obvious.

'Hi Phil, it's Sam. Hey, is my mum about?'

There was a pause. 'Are you okay? You sound a bit shaky. Are you having problems with that guy again?' he asked. He sounded so genuine, so concerned.

'No, nothing like that. Had a run-in with the boss, that's all.' The moment the lie came out of my mouth, I found myself wondering if Phil would take care of that problem too. 'I need to check out Mum's timetable for the day. Is she there?'

'I think so. I'll see if I can find her.'

I had a few moments to get my head around this. If I told Mum about Uncle Phil, she was just as likely to turn around and have him on about it. How could I get her out of the house without her arguing the point?

'Sam? Is that you?' I never thought I'd be so pleased to hear that voice.

'Hi Mum. Hey, look, one of the doctors at the hospital rang me, trying to get hold of you. They've got some specialist who wants to have a chat to you and Dad, but he's only available for another thirty minutes max, so they were wanting you to get down to the hospital straight away.'

'Oh? Which one was that? I thought we'd seen the specialist?'

She had to question it.

'She didn't give the exact details, only that if you wanted a chance to see him before you left for home, you'd have to get down straight away.'

'Why didn't they ring me here? They've got this as my contact number.' If ever there was a time I wished she'd just shut the fuck up and do as she was told, this was it. It was all I could do not to scream at her down the phone.

'I don't know, Ma. Maybe they dialled the wrong number. It happens.'

'You sound a bit shaky. Is everything alright?'

She chose now to show a smidgeon of concern?

'I'm fine. Work hassles. Look, you'd better hurry. This sounded like a good opportunity for some information.'

'I suppose so.'

'Can you ring me on my cellphone as soon as you get there? And I'll try and get along for the specialist too.'

'Why would you want to be there, Sam? You haven't shown that much interest in your father's medical situation up until now?'

Jesus Christ, Mother.

'Mum, please.'

'Okay, fine. I'll call you. Bye.'

The click echoed through my head, and I sat a moment, paralysed by indecision. Could I trust that she'd get out straight away? Could I trust that he hadn't listened in to our conversation and wasn't convinced by my less-than-stellar performance? It was a big fat negative to both. Should I go home? Make sure Mum was okay and get her the hell out of there? Last time I did something alone like that I got into serious trouble. Team player, Sam, you're a team player now. But what if I was wrong about all this? What if I brought down the full might of the police force upon Uncle Phil and I was wrong? They'd fry me, for sure. But one image replayed in my mind. My mother with a psychopathic killer.

I galvanised into action and sprinted down the hallway to DI Johns' office. Shit, empty. Of course he wasn't there. Where was everyone when you needed them? I grabbed his office phone and hit the Watch House hot key.

Busy signal.

Shit, shit, shit.

Okay, okay, who next? Duty CIB squad? I

looked at the roster on the wall and dialled the number. Straight to voicemail. Bloody hell. Had the whole police force left town for the day?

In case of dire emergency. This categorised as an emergency in my book. Desperation overrode any thoughts of sounding stupid. I rang in.

'111 Emergency, what service do you require?'

'Police.'

'One moment, please.' One agonising moment.

'Police, how can I help?'

'This is DC Samantha Shephard, Dunedin CIB. I require an Armed Offenders squad call-out to number three-forty Highgate. The suspect is Phillip Kershaw, male, fifty-four, one hundred and eighty centimetres tall, short greying brown hair, clean shaven, ah, blue eyes, wearing . . . ' God, what was he in this morning? 'Black trousers, striped shirt and a brown moleskin jacket. He is a murder suspect in Operation Sparrow. There could possibly be an adult female in the house with him, a potential victim.' It killed me to say those words. 'I can't confirm her status as yet.'

'Stand by, DC Shephard.'

I held my cellphone in the other hand, willing it to chirp. I would never whinge about the noises those things made again.

'Dunedin AOS is already in operation on another call-out. I have no estimate of when they'll be done. I can put a call out to all available officers. Is the suspect known to be armed?'

My mind flicked to the contents of his den. There was a safe. He'd used a hunting rifle in the past. All things considered, I would place bets on him having a side arm of some kind. He'd been pretty organised so far. 'I can't confirm that, but consider him armed and dangerous. He's already killed five people.'

'Ah, checking status now. It looks like all units are tied up in the AOS call-out in Mosgiel, and the murder in Kaikorai Valley. It's been a busy morning. I'll get whoever I can who's available and armed.'

Fuck, where was the bloody cavalry when you needed them? I made a snap decision. Actually, circumstance made it for me.

'I'm going armed to the scene now. Please advise I am non-uniform, Caucasian female, one hundred and fifty-three centimetres, blonde tied-back hair, black trousers, white shirt, black jacket. And, please advise,' my voice cracked, 'the potential hostage is my mother.'

'Shit. Okay, understood. We'll have back-up on the way as soon as a possible. Take care, keep us updated.'

I needed a firearm and a vehicle. The latter was sorted by the fact, to my relief, I saw there was a fleet car available. I grabbed the keys and headed down the stairs to the Watch House. I hoped like hell the senior sergeant on duty was cooperative.

'Dan, there's a situation. I need a firearm. Now.'

'If you're referring to the school, you're a bit late. Everyone's gone out there.'

'School? What are you talking about? No. I know who the killer is and he might have a hostage. I have to go now.'

'Slow down, what killer?'

'Operation Sparrow. The killer is Phillip Kershaw, he's . . . '

The telephonist ran in, 'We've got another call-in, hostage situation.'

'That would have been me,' I said. 'This man could have a hostage, he's armed, there's no one else around, I need a firearm, I have to get up there now.'

'Wait a moment. Jesus, what's going on today?' He went to talk to Marg, the telephonist.

'For fuck's sake, just get me a bloody gun,' I yelled. 'The bastard's got my mother.'

Dan swung around. 'What?'

'The bastard has got my mother, so fuck procedure, I need a gun and I need it now.'

'Jesus,' he said. 'Why didn't you say so? Knock yourself out, I'll see what back-up I can scrounge. We're so bloody thin on the ground with the homicides and the AOS call-out to the school.' He opened the gun locker for me.

I grabbed a Glock pistol and ammo, thought better of it and grabbed two. I looked at the Bushmaster, but thought it too obvious. The Glocks I could hide on my person, but not the rifle. Body armour was pointless. Too big for me by far, and I had a feeling charging in guns blazing wasn't going to work here. Mum hadn't rung yet. If we got through this in one piece, I was going to buy that woman a cellphone.

I needed to be clever here, outsmart him, use the element of surprise. It looked like I was in this alone. No, not quite alone. I pulled out my

328

cell and dialled Paul. It went straight to voicemail again.

'Paul, it's Sam. We thought the wrong fucking academic. Our killer is Uncle Phil. I'm armed and going up to the house. He's there with my mum. AOS is tied up and back-up could be slow. Please, if you can get there, get there.'

I hung up the call as I ran for the parking garage.

Come on Paul, check your messages.

66

As usual no bloody place for my car, so I pulled
into a neighbour's driveway. What was the worst
they could do? Ring the police? There had been
no phone call from Mum and her old Rover was
parked twenty metres away from where I sat. I
didn't want to think about what that could mean.
Hopefully, just that she was being belligerent and
not doing as I asked out of some warped principle. She was quite capable of that level of
pig-headedness. The double garage door was closed,
so I didn't know if Phil's or Aunt Jude's car was
in there. I made the assumption that Jude was
still out and Mum was still in with that murdering bastard. There were no audible sirens approaching,
no Charge of the Light Brigade.

I was on my own.

The panic I had felt earlier had been displaced
by anger. I listened to the satisfying click as I
pulled back the slide and chambered a round in
each of the Glocks, and then slid them into the
back of my trousers, butts facing outermost. My
jacket was loose fitting and would hopefully hide
any telltale bulges. I was prepared to risk
shooting my bum off in exchange for the ease of
access and time saved. I had a feeling I might
need it.

I took a deep breath, put on my very best
fifth-form drama-class nonchalance and walked
to the front door.

There were no discernible voices from inside the house. I slid my key into the lock and entered the lion's den. I pushed the door closed, but not fast behind me.

'Hi de hi,' I called out. 'Anybody home? Dopey me forgot my gym clothes.' I was greeted at the door by Fluffy, who smooched around my legs, then by a voice.

'Hi, Sam, we're in the kitchen.' The voice was Phil's. I walked as casually as I could down the hallway and stepped across the threshold.

Two sets of eyes looked at me, but only one person could do the talking. Mum was seated at the table. I took in the details in an instant. She was cable tied by each hand to the chair back. The familiar silver duct tape slashed across her mouth. Terror and desperate pleading screamed out from her eyes. Phil was standing behind her, at the head of the table. His left hand was cupped under her chin, the right held the serrated carver knife to her throat. He held it with enough pressure to create a row of claret dashes, where the tips cut into her skin.

I felt the bitter weight of hatred settle on to the seething in my stomach. I lifted my eyes from my mother's to the killer's.

'Sam, you disappoint me. You'll have to try harder than that. I didn't come down in the last shower.'

My ears detected the crackle of a police radio scanner. Jesus, he knew exactly what I was up to.

'Yes,' he said, leaning his head towards the set on the bench. 'I know you've come armed, and I know you've got no back-up. It's amazing how many officers they'll send off when you ring in and tell them you saw a couple of students with lots of guns heading into a high school, nowadays. One thing we've got to thank the Americans for.' The smile that I had once found charming took on a sinister bent. 'Your guys have taken the bait beautifully. In fact, I've become quite fond of toying with you. It's all too easy. Anyway, enough of this. Time's short. I don't need to mention what's at stake here, do I?'

He gave Mum's head a little shake and I watched her flinch as the serrated tips dug in a little more.

'Now be a good girl and slowly remove your weapon.'

I couldn't move straight away. Instead my eyes kept drawing to the necklace of beaded blood drops growing at Mum's throat.

'Come on, Sam, don't waste my time. I know you're armed. Be a good girl and hand over the gun.'

I carefully reached around with my left hand and pulled a pistol out of my trousers, holding it out to the side for Phil to see.

'Now put it down on the table, and step away.'

I was buggered if I was going to leave him with a weapon to shoot me with, if he didn't already have one of his own. As I leaned over to put it on the table, I slid my finger on to the button by the trigger guard and pressed.

The magazine fell to the tiled floor with a sharp clack that made everyone jump.

'Humph,' he snorted. 'Clever girl. Now why

don't you take a seat down that end, there's room at the table.'

'No thank you, I'd rather stand.'

Phil's eyebrows shot up, but then he laughed and said, 'Suit yourself, you'll get a better view from there, anyway.' For someone who'd obviously been found out, he seemed extraordinarily pleased with himself.

'I was a bit worried you'd make the connection between the little creep that had been pestering you and the extra body. I hope you didn't mind me taking care of that. I get a bit pissed off when people mess with my family and that was quite a pleasant indulgence, actually. Did you like the way I made it look like a robbery?' My fondness for Uncle Phil had evaporated. His previously well-hidden arrogance and condescension were now on display for all to see. 'But it's all worked out for the best anyway, don't you think? I was starting to tire of my little game. Time to move on to other sport, and it looks like this will be a great way to make a parting statement. Although, it's been such fun watching you chase your tails. Thank you for that, Sam, you've been so handy.'

'What do you mean?'

'I've had a front-row seat. It's been quite enlightening, really. I always suspected you police were pretty average, but this has been something else. You should consider a career change. You're not that good at this detecting business. You couldn't even detect what was under your nose, not that it will be an issue any more. I must say though, young Maggie was a surprise. She's got a bit of promise. Great profile by the way, pretty accurate.'

'Have you been listening to us?' I asked, incredulous. Here I'd been so careful not to divulge any confidential information to them, but he'd been listening in all along. He'd heard my talk with Maggie, and shit, with Paul?

'It's a modern age. You can get wireless anything nowadays. Wireless camera and microphones; espionage has been made very accessible and easy. All I needed was the Internet and a credit card and it was delivered to the door. See — wave to the camera,' he said and looked up at the light fitting over the table. I was damned if I could see anything.

'You're very nice naked, by the way,' he said, and gave me a wink. I felt a wave of revulsion shudder through my body.

'Enough of the talking. It's time for business. It won't be long before they find someone spare to throw a gun at and send up here, and by then I will be long gone.'

My options were looking pretty scant. If I drew my gun, Mum's throat would be sliced before I could get a round off. What I needed was to get that knife away from her throat, even for a moment.

A brief flicker of movement caught in my peripheral vision, out of Phil's view. I didn't dare move my eyes to follow it. Instead, I made sure Phil's attention was on me. I knew it wasn't the cat — Fluffy was here in the kitchen, oblivious to the threat, chinny-winnying my leg, so I prayed like hell its source was who I hoped it could be.

Time. I needed to buy some time.

I let my shoulders slump and tried to feign defeat. 'Who is all this in aid of?' I asked. 'What was the point of it?'

He chuckled again, looking so well pleased with himself. 'Me, of course. I had to have some sport. Life had gotten a bit dull since the girls left home, and Jude, who had promised me we'd have time for each other to enjoy once they left the nest, decided to take up every bleeding-heart cause under the sun. I was forced to find other things to do. The student was very sweet, by the way; that kept me quite busy for a while. But she wanted more — they always do. It was almost sad to have to kill her. I got far more attention from her than I ever did from my wife.'

Somehow, I wasn't feeling sympathetic.

'You want to know the huge irony in all this?' His eyes drew heavenwards, as if seeking strength. 'The little diversion I'd set up in Mosgiel, the meticulous planning for today, the down-to-the-minute timing — it was all for her benefit, so I could finally and emphatically let her know exactly how hurt I was by her neglect. She was going to pay, pay for putting everyone and everything ahead of me, and I was going to be free to do as I pleased, the poor widower, rocked by the disappearance and murder of his wife. I was going to get to start afresh without being shackled to her so-called civic-mindedness. I'd finally be seen as Phillip Kershaw, renowned academic and forward thinker, not forever intro- duced to all and sundry as Jude's husband, or the twins' father. And do you know what happened?'

His voice had been pitching higher and higher, as his controlled façade crumbled away. 'She rang earlier and cancelled our lunch date, killed the whole thing, all that I had put in place. And do you know why?' He paused as if expecting a response.

I shook my head.

'I still can't believe this.' He laughed, a scoffing, acidic sound. 'She ditched me to go and 'give comfort',' he said, in an almost perfect imitation of her voice, 'to refugees from your fucking circus.' In his exasperation, he'd moved the knife away from Mum's throat and was using it like a conductor's baton, beating out the time of his words.

My eyes followed the blade away from the throat.

My right hand edged around my back.

In a split second my mind did the calculation. Could I? was there enough time?

Fuck, it was a risk.

A bang, bang, bang on the outside kitchen door shattered the silence.

Phil's head swung around, reflexively drawn to the source of the noise. It was all the distraction I needed. Before he had a chance to turn back I had the other Glock out, raised my arm, sighted and squeezed away two rounds over the top of Mum's head into his right shoulder.

The blasts concussed in the closed space, and in the aftermath, my hearing took on a muted, underwater quality and everything moved in slow motion. Phil's face registered utter surprise as the knife tumbled from his now useless hand.

336

A ruby rose bloomed at his shoulder and he staggered back into the refrigerator before sliding in a big smear of his own blood, down to the ground. I strode around the table, my eyes focused only on that man, that monster. I heard the sound of shattering glass and the scraping of chair legs and Paul's voice yelling out my name. I reached Phil in four quick steps, and straddled him, gun outstretched.

I placed the muzzle flush against the skin of his forehead.

'How dare you, you fucking arsehole.' My words reverberated around the silence of the room. 'How fucking dare you.'

My index finger twitched as I looked into Phil's shocked eyes and by God, it felt like it would be so easy to squeeze that trigger. So easy to destroy this creature, so very much easier than it had been with the last one.

'Sam?' Paul's gentle voice broke my focus. My eyes flicked momentarily to the hand that he now carefully laid on my shoulder.

I breathed out, hard and heavy and my eyes moved back to the creature in front of me. It was pitiful.

I let my arms drop slightly, gun now pointed at Phil's chest, and stepped back, suddenly conscious of the thudding of my heart, the acid in my gut, the tremor of my hands.

'Check him for weapons,' I said to Paul. After a quick pat down Paul held up, then unloaded a Glock 17, retrieved from Phil's jacket. As suspected, he'd been prepared — he'd intended to continue his deadly blood sport.

My gaze flicked behind me to my mother, who had shuffled her chair around and now sat, bound, eyes scrunched shut and shoulders heaving with each sob. I felt devastated she'd been caught up in all this, an unwitting substitute in a sick man's game.

I returned my focus back to the feeble, wimpering creature in front of me. So much heartbreak and devastation had been wreaked by this warped, sick man, and again I battled the wave of searing anger. It would be so easy to . . . but, justice needed to be served. I breathed out, finally relaxed my stance and dropped my arms down to my side. Then with as much venom as I could muster, I spat out the simple truth. 'You're not worth it, you piece of shit.'

Epilogue

'Are you okay?'

'Yeah, I am,' I said, without lie.

'This has all been one hell of a roller coaster ride.'

'You're not wrong there.' Life had seemed so beautifully humdrum up until a month ago. My biggest concern had been an arsehole boss and which café served up the best coffee. Now everything in it had been inverted, shaken, twisted and squeezed.

'Do you wish you'd killed him?'

I risked the honest answer. 'Yes.' I let the weight of my reply hang a few moments, before qualifying it. 'My heart wishes I'd killed him, but my head knows it made the right decision. My head doesn't always win those battles.'

I heard a gentle chuckle.

There was a long, comfortable silence. I replayed some of the scenes in my mind. Although still vivid, they did not feel as raw.

'How's your mum now? How's she taken it all?'

'Grumpily, which means she's fine. If she went all quiet and didn't complain, then I'd be worried. But, she's business as usual, giving me grief.' For once, the old bat giving me a hard time made me very happy.

'What about the hierarchy? Have they got their killer figured out? What do the psych people think?'

'They're rather perplexed, as so much of what he did goes against conventional wisdom. He wasn't your stereotypical psychopathic serial killer. He made a deliberate and almost academic decision to commit these crimes. What kind of person could do that? I think they're looking too hard.'

'Why? What's your theory, given your high-powered background in forensic psychiatry? Enlighten me.'

I smiled, enjoying the ribbing. 'Empty-nest syndrome gone feral. He did it to see if he could.'

'That's an interesting and original idea. Have you mentioned it to your superiors?'

'No, they'd laugh at me. Too simple.'

'You or the idea?'

I gave a strategic squeeze that resulted in a yelp.

'Alright, sorry, I concede, you win.'

'Good to know you appreciate when you're in a vulnerable position'

'Wouldn't want it any other way,' Paul said, and snuggled in closer against my bare skin.

I smiled; a relaxed, reservation-free and contented smile. Many things had changed.

Who'd have thought?

We do hope that you have enjoyed reading this large print book.

Did you know that all of our titles are available for purchase?

We publish a wide range of high quality large print books including:
Romances, Mysteries, Classics
General Fiction
Non Fiction and Westerns

Special interest titles available in large print are:
The Little Oxford Dictionary
Music Book
Song Book
Hymn Book
Service Book

Also available from us courtesy of Oxford University Press:
Young Readers' Dictionary
(large print edition)
Young Readers' Thesaurus
(large print edition)

For further information or a free brochure, please contact us at:
Ulverscroft Large Print Books Ltd.,
The Green, Bradgate Road, Anstey,
Leicester, LE7 7FU, England.
Tel: **(00 44) 0116 236 4325**
Fax: **(00 44) 0116 234 0205**

Other titles published by Ulverscroft:

OVERKILL

Vanda Symon

When the body of a young mother is found washed up on the banks of the Mataura River, a small rural community is rocked by her tragic suicide. But all is not what it seems. Sam Shephard, sole-charge police constable in Mataura, learns the death was no suicide and has to face the realisation that there is a killer in town. To complicate the situation, the murdered woman was the wife of her former lover — and when word gets out, she discovers that small communities can have a mean streak with bigger, nastier nails than a Bengal tiger. When Sam finds herself on the list of suspects and suspended from duty, she must cast aside her personal feelings and take matters into her own hands. To find the murderer . . . and clear her name.